Hook, Line, and Murder

by

GG Calpo

The Sweet TOOTH Murder Mystery Series

Cover Art by *Lea Schizas*

The Wild Rose Press, Inc.
PO Box 708
Adams Basin, NY 14410-0708
Visit us at www.thewildrosepress.com

Publishing History
First Edition, 2026
Trade Paperback Print ISBN 978-1-5092-6406-3
Digital ISBN 978-1-5092-6407-0

The Sweet TOOTH Murder Mystery Series
Published in the United States of America

Dedication

My heartfelt thanks to Nicole Rivera who gave so generously of her time, reading every version of this book and supporting me each step of my way to publication. This book was possible because of you! Thank you to all my other early readers for their cheers and faith in me. Special thanks to my children, Nicholas and Nerissa, and to my husband, Ken, on whose shoulders I have finally learned to lean on.

Chapter One

The divers were still underwater, scouring the bottom of Duck Harbor, searching for the rest of the body.

I was with my friends at Sweet Buns cafe, across from the harbor, our unofficial clubhouse ever since we retired from teaching at Whitman's Port Post Elementary School. Standing right next to the front windows of the café, we had the clearest view of Duck Harbor Park and the blue uniforms swarming there.

We had been on our morning walk, making our way around the edges of the park. Screaming kids played by the playground while teenagers giggled, grouped around benches, or meandered in the aimless way young people do. The day was beautiful, with clear skies and a mild snap in the air. It was cold yet warm with the right amount of heat from the sun, making it the perfect spring day. Motorboats and sailboats dipped in and out of the water, out by Poet's Bay. And at the edge of the harbor were the fishermen, alone or in groups of two or three, a rod in their hands and their tackle boxes opened beside them. We rounded the corner, almost done with our walk, when we saw mothers dragging their children away and fathers covering the eyes of the children in their arms. Pushing against the stream of parents scrambling away were others whose eyes were fixed on the man by the harbor's edge. A man on whose fishing line dangled a catch with, what I thought were, red fins and a red tail swaying lazily around the hook.

Red? In the salt waters of Poet's Bay? As I stood there trying to figure out what I was seeing, Barbara shoved her way into the crowd. I followed, my curiosity getting the better of me. Murmurs of "Good morning" and "Good to see you, Mrs. B" trailed behind me, changing to "You sure you want to see this, Mrs. B?" and "I wouldn't go any further if I were you, Mrs. B." We fetched up to the front and looked down on the ground before us while the fisherman beside us puked his guts out.

It wasn't a fish he had caught.

Instead, on the ground was a hand. Just a hand. Nothing else. Where I thought I had seen red fins and a red tail were fingernails painted blood red. The fingers were tangled in the fishing line with a hook sunk deep into the palm. The hand looked grotesque against the green grass: long, slender fingers and pale skin. My eyes traced the shape of the fingers to the palm and snagged. Glinting and winking back the sun's rays, a signet ring encircled the ring finger, an initial B covered with diamonds. I had seen that very same ring not that long ago.

"Brie? Brianna Townsend?" I whispered in horror, my mind going back to the time when Brie was five, sitting in my kindergarten class, an impish grin on her face. To this past Wednesday, when Brie, now twenty-four and grown-up, had come up to Barbara and me while we were having breakfast at Sweet Buns. Dressed in tight, faded jeans with studded booties on her feet, still with that impish grin on her face, Brie had proudly shoved her right hand in front of us, waggling her fingers rapidly, the diamonds on the ring catching and reflecting the sunlight streaming through the window. The same diamond ring on this hand before us. I thought of how Brie had bragged about how the ring was custom-made for her, and only for her.

Was this hand Brie's? Where was the rest of her?

Well, that was what the divers were down there for.

The café's regulars stood by the window, shoulder-to-shoulder with the staff, except for the half-foot of free space between them and us. All that elbow room was one of the perks of hanging out with Barbara. Crowding the scary principal, the one you got sent to when you messed up in grade school, was out of the question.

Everyone watched the cops milling about at the park, their faces shining with the thrill of watching a real, live crime scene. But not me. And, I noticed as I looked around the café, not Rosita. She was standing alone by the counter with her wallet in hand. She must have been asked by one of the Sands Neck society ladies she cleaned houses for to pick up some of Sweet Buns' famous sticky, soft-baked goods. Why was Rosita standing there, distancing herself from the chaos outside? A crime scene held no glamour for me. Not since last year, when I had stood looking at the broken grass pressed into muddy ground and the tracks made by cops and rescuers when they brought the bodies of my Rich and Jim back ashore. But Rosita?

"Why are we here and not there? Aren't witnesses required to be on the scene? To answer questions, that sort of thing? It's your idiot detective. That's why," Barbara said to me, pulling my attention away from Rosita. Barbara had been harping on this since the cops shooed us away. I could have agreed with the "idiot detective" part if I had known who he was. Except when did I acquire one?

"His man said they had everything he needed, and they'd call if there were anything they'd forgotten to ask. They even told the fish guy to go home to his wife. Why do that?" Barbara huffed.

A murmur went through the crowd by the window, faces who had been watching us swiveling to look outward. The team of divers was back. Three divers approached the group standing around a black official-looking car.

"Looks like they found something." Another friend, Liz, trained binoculars on the men. She gulped once before shoving the binoculars at me.

I opted not to ask where she got the binoculars. One never knew with Liz. She was waiting for us at the café, all flushed and excited after getting a text from a former fifth-grade student that "something" was happening at the park. Knowing Barbara and I would be there, Liz said she hustled her way to us pronto. For support, she said. Yeah, right. I twirled the lenses until my sight cleared. I wish I hadn't.

It was a black bag. And the divers had propped it open. Was that a foot sticking up out of the bag? And was that an elbow?

Covering my mouth against the sudden roiling of my stomach, I handed the binoculars to Barbara. But she refused to take them. Was that fear lacing the whites of her eyes?

"He's moving. I can't see him. Why can't your detective stand there and let others come to him? Wouldn't that make more sense?"

"Barbara, what are you going on about?" I asked,

fed up with her at this point.

"See that? See him?" Barbara said.

"See who?"

Then, I saw him.

The cops by the black car had parted, exposing the man standing aloof from his men in blue. Dressed in a black suit, hands inside his pants pockets, while cops moved around and past him.

Detective Jonathan Storm.

The detective who investigated the drowning of my husband and son last year.

The café faded around me as I faced the man who had let the killer of my husband and son go free. Rich, the man I married forty-odd years ago, and Jim, my only child, the one who owned my heart the moment I felt him in my womb. Once again, I was at the precinct, my heart in my eyes. I had hardly dared blink for fear my tears would overflow. Because once the dam broke, I would be lost. I had begged. I had pleaded. My voice had gone hoarse. My throat had ached. But none of that had equaled the hurt and fury in my heart as Detective Storm turned down each request, each appeal, one after another. I heard, in my mind, the buzzing of his long-ago voice.

****

"No, we didn't find life vests anywhere, not on Nissequogue River or their bodies. If your husband had brought the life vests, they must have shrugged them on and left them open, losing them as they fell in the water. You know how that goes.

"Yes, there was no breeze, but you know how men are on the river. They must have been drinking and fooling around. And if they were drunk, that would explain why the kayak overturned and why they couldn't save themselves. Even in waist-deep water. Have you ever tried swimming while drunk? No, I didn't think so.

"With all due respect, Mrs. Brightbook, focus on the funeral. And count yourself lucky you have your grandson to love and cherish for the remaining years of your life. And your son's widow will take care of you now that your husband and son are dead. And speaking of your daughter-in-law, tell her to call me if she needs anything. I'm always at her disposal."

****

His voice faded back to the past. But not the rage I felt then. That was still very much with me. That man. That heartless, thickheaded, misogynistic man. The man whose head I wanted to smash so badly, I had to march out of the police station before I did anything rash.

Jonathan Storm investigate Brie's murder?

Over my dead body!

Chapter Two

"What is he doing here?"

A cafe regular, coffee mug in hand, startled at hearing the venom in my voice. The woman next to him looked familiar, but I dismissed both of them from my mind after a quick look at them. Binoculars in hand, I took another brief look at the bag.

"Maybe it's time to go sit at our table? Leave the rubbernecking to others?" Liz steered us away from the window, with many covert glances at me.

"Stop that. I'm not falling apart."

Barbara and I settled ourselves at the table. We still had a good view of the park since most of the customers had either gone back to their tables or had left the cafe to go about their day's business. At the counter, the staff was again busy ringing up orders. I saw Rosita was still there, her hand out to take a brown bag of goodies from the cashier. Liz left to join the line. After years of meeting up here at Sweet Buns, we knew what the others wanted to order.

"That detective is not handling this investigation," I said once Liz was back with our food. "No way. I'm not allowing it."

"And how will you stop him?" Barbara asked. "Look out there. I think he's very much in charge."

We all turned to the window. The mugs of coffee and plates of scones and muffins in front of us were ignored for a minute. A diver stood with his hands held out from his body while he was hosed down. The other two divers stood waiting for their turn. And the detective was in the thick of everything, ordering his men around.

"I don't care. He'll mess this up like he did with Rich and Jim." I glared at Barbara. I saw my friends look at each other.

"We can't get him fired from the case, if that's what you're thinking. We don't know anyone," Liz said. "And even if we did, what's our excuse?"

"Is that all you guys can say? A student, a former student of ours, was killed in such a horrible way. And all we can do is…What? Wash our hands of her?"

"We're not washing our hands of Brie," Liz protested. "The girl gave up on us first. We all tried to love her. We knew her mother was never there for her. But did she care? No! She never listened to any advice we gave her or showed any affection to any of her teachers."

"Forget Liz and her sentimental nonsense. The point is, Meg, we're school teachers, not detectives. We're simply saying it's not our job to look for murderers," Barbara said.

Liz gave an indelicate snort. "Why did she have to come back here, anyway? She left town six years ago, right after she finished high school."

"Brie said she came back to work at her Aunt Janet's catering business," I said.

"Work? Brie? Those two words do not go together," Liz said.

"Stop it." I looked at my friends.

Barbara looked skeptical, her head tilting to one side, showing off her buzzed hair. After retiring, Barbara ditched her braided hair in a bun look, exchanging it for hair shaved close to her head, peppered with golden highlights. The buzz cut contrasted nicely with her dark skin and showcased her strong jaw, generous mouth, and arched eyebrows. Unlike Barbara, I had stopped coloring my hair, letting it go gray naturally. After the funeral, getting dolled up had dropped off my to-do list.

Meanwhile, Liz had her eyebrows raised at me, interested but not ready to jump in. Except "interested" was Liz's default setting with anything out of the ordinary. I was reminded of how, when she was much younger, Liz had broken a rib diving off a cliff on a dare. Blonde hair shining with brunette low-lights and manicured nails, both maintained with weekly salon visits, camouflaged the free and daredevil spirit that was Liz.

I felt someone walk past our table. It was Rosita. I smiled at the woman, turned back to my friends, and lowered my voice. "Okay, I get it. Brie was not exactly the most lovable of our kids."

"Forget lovable. I would have settled for ordinary. Unremarkable. Average. Standard. I had her in my class. She was a bully. She had other kids writing her book reports and doing her school projects. That school year was the only year I thought of quitting. It was that bad," Liz said, playing with her Star of David pendant.

I bit my lip. Liz only played with her jewelry when she was stressing out.

"In third grade, Edna caught her ransacking a classmate's bag. Sent her over to me for detention. I suspended Brie for the rest of the week, but the kid kept showing up at the school every morning. The hall monitor didn't know what to do with her," Barbara said.

My friends weren't wrong. The first time I heard an explosive pop in my classroom, it spun me around. Heart thumping, my eyes scoured the room for the source of the sound while I tried to remember the school's active shooter protocols. Only to see Brie convulsed in giggles and laughter. While the children, who had fallen from their chairs when they heard the bang made by the party popper, picked themselves up from the floor. Furious, I sent a letter home with Brie, expecting a call from her mother. Nada. Zip. No callback.

But still…

"She wasn't the best—"

"Far from it," muttered Barbara.

"Are we going to stand by while Brie's killer goes free? Because that's what will happen if we do nothing." I waited for my friends to do the right thing.

Barbara started to fidget.

Liz looked away.

Did anyone want Brie's killer caught? Didn't Brie deserve justice? The justice denied to Rich and Jim? I told my inner voice to shut up. This was not about Detective Storm and his incompetent investigation into the deaths of my husband and son. This was about Brie.

"What do you suggest we do?" Barbara said. "Go up to Detective Storm and tell him we're taking over? That'll go over very well."

Barbara was right. That wouldn't work. I knew that. There must be something we could do.

"We could help…investigate…" I pitched my voice just enough to dare them. "I mean, aren't you tired of sitting around Sweet Buns and having everyone think of us as those poor old, retired ladies? This is our chance to be somebodies again." I knew I was laying it on thick, but I needed a prod for Barbara. A cattle prod would do the trick.

Barbara squirmed. "I might be old, but I'm not a poor anyone," she muttered under her breath, followed by, "Investigate how?" in a louder voice.

"But that's a great idea!" Liz said, her eyes sparkling.

"Meddle in a murder investigation? We'd get arrested!"

"Arrested? For what?"

Barbara stared at Liz, dumbfounded.

"How do you think investigations are done? They go and talk to people. We can do that. We're all Brie's former teachers. Understandably, we would want to talk to Brie's family. Offer our condolences. Make sure they're okay."

"You make it sound easy. But that's not everything. Knowing Brie's family life, I don't think her sister or mother knew much about Brie."

"It doesn't matter if her family knew nothing," Liz retorted. "I am sure…I bet you anything…Brie had her life posted on social media. And not only am I on social media. I know how to find anyone on the Web. No one can hide from me if any part of their life is posted digitally."

My friends were talking themselves into playing detective. Well, why not? Liz had turned into a virtual bloodhound once she retired, aided and abetted by her grandson, who was a year short of finishing his cybersecurity degree.

Barbara leaned forward. "So we go talk to her Aunt Janet, then her sister Selena. Then what?"

"I go on social media and check on Brie. We meet

11

back here and compare what we found. We go on from there."

Yep, Liz was right. Knock on a few doors, ask a few questions. How dangerous could that be? Except, one of those we're questioning might very well be the murderer. I gulped, eyes seeking Liz's and getting nothing but a wink. But wait, I wanted this. Didn't I?

"If we're going to investigate—" Barbara glanced at me, one finger raised in warning. "—then we're going to help, not take over."

I murmured agreement. Help, yes. That sounded good. We were just helping. Helpers got to stay behind, away from the action, the danger.

"Okay, if everyone's agreed. You go on social media," Barbara said to Liz, then turned to me. "And you talk to Janet tomorrow. After, we regroup here at Sweet Buns."

"You coming?" I asked Barbara.

"I can't tomorrow. But I'll go with you when you see Selena." Barbara turned back to her food, muttering to herself, "Who's calling whom a poor old lady?"

Liz and I pretended we didn't hear her. But there was one small thing bothering me. "Barbara, when did Detective Storm become 'my' detective?"

"Don't you know? He's been sniffing around Dora. I saw him at the ER trying to chat her up."

I should have known when that man said he'd be available to Dora any time, any day. That snake. No way, no how. Jonathan Storm was not taking my son's place with Dora and my grandson. Not while I'm around.

Chapter Three

Two white catering vans marked "Black Gloves Gourmet Catering" in black and gold sat in the driveway.

Janet's house backed into an undeveloped wooded lot. From the street, I saw a fenced-in backyard about three times the size of mine. I went up the path to the house's front door, grabbing the box of blueberry muffins I had baked yesterday. I couldn't go empty-handed on a sympathy call, could I? Anyway, indulging someone's sweet tooth always opened doors for me. When I got nearer to the fenced gate, I saw a one-story building at the back of the yard with two sets of windows and double-wide doors. Most likely, the kitchen Janet used for her catering business.

I rang the doorbell and waited.

And waited.

Finger on the doorbell, I fought the urge to turn around and get back in the car. Janet was mourning. What was I doing pressing her doorbell the day after her niece was found dead at Duck Harbor? Detective Storm giving orders to the other cops came back to mind. I stiffened my spine and kept ringing.

"Mrs. B!" A man stood with his hand on the gate, a grin on his face. Dressed in black pants and a plain white shirt, he carried several empty aluminum trays.

"Kyle...Kyle Johnson." That face, the unruly sandy brown hair. I knew him right away. Despite his having shot up from under four feet when he was in my class to over six feet tall now. "Do you work here?"

"Yup," said Kyle. "Waiter, bartender, cook, dishwasher"—he grinned even more—"all-around gopher, that's me. Were you looking for Janet?"

"Yes." Raising the hand holding the box of muffins, I said, "I heard about Brie and wanted to offer my sympathies."

"Right. Brie." The smile wiped away from his face. Kyle looked at my parked car and the woods a few feet behind it, his eyes unfocused. Shaking himself, Kyle forced another smile. He lifted the aluminum trays. "Let me get these over to the van, and I'll take you to the back. She's by the kitchen." Sliding the van doors open, his voice muffled coming from inside the van, Kyle called out, "How did you find out? Janet said the cops were here late last night to tell her. And I found out an hour or so ago when I arrived at work. We're still in shock."

"We were at Sweet Buns yesterday when they found her." I swallowed hard, unable to say Brie's name.

Kyle led me through the gate, stopping mid-stride. Sounds of clanging and banging came from inside the building at the edge of the yard. "Hmmm, now may not be a good time to see her."

I wanted to back out as much as he did. It was incredibly rude of me to hound Janet today. It smacked of an ambush. But people tend to talk more when their emotions are out of control. Squaring my shoulders, I left Kyle behind, who shrugged before following.

"Janet," I called out, watching her slap pots and pans down on the wooden countertops with more force than was needed. "Hi, it's Mrs. B. I was on my way to the library and thought I'd stop by."

Then Janet turned to look at me. She looked like I did a year ago, someone who had lost someone precious. I was touched to my core. I reached out and gave, without hesitation, the comfort others had given me then. Abandoning the box of muffins on a nearby shelf, I went to embrace her.

Only to have Janet push my arms away with a gruff, "Get off me."

I looked back at Kyle, leaning against the door, arms crossed and head shaking, distancing himself.

"And you—" Janet had likewise turned to Kyle. "—The dirt on the van is not coming off by itself, you know."

Snapping Janet a mock salute, Kyle straightened up and ambled back to the driveway.

"Lazy bum. He'd waste the day if you don't keep an eye on him." Turning to me, Janet said, "What do you want?"

Nothing much. We're looking for Brie's killer. Was it you?

Where did those words come from? Why would I think Janet killed her niece? Thanking every deity I knew that I hadn't said them out loud, I said instead, "I heard about Brie—"

"And wanted to what? Make me feel better?"

That was Janet's grief talking. I remembered how angry I was when I first found out about Rich and Jim. Grief and anger were two sides of the same coin, as I knew very well. I followed her eyes as they roved over the one-room kitchen.

The space was impressive. It must be over one thousand square feet; stainless steel everywhere except for the wooden countertops, cabinets, and shelving near the door. A walk-in cold room with a sliding door, open-fire stoves and grills in the middle of the room, double sinks, a commercial refrigerator, and freezer. It all looked shiny and sparkly new…and expensive.

When Janet's husband died years back, she had plowed everything she got from her husband's life insurance into her catering company. I didn't think the money stretched this far.

"Heavily mortgaged, if you're thinking what I think you are."

"Business must be good," I said.

"I manage." Janet flicked the hair out of her eyes. "At least, I used to," she mumbled to herself, but loud enough for me to hear.

"Brie worked here?" I asked, unable to picture the girl I knew working amongst all this shiny equipment, in an apron, sweating over a boiling pot or chopping vegetables.

"Was that what she did?"

I couldn't blame Janet for how she felt. Brie, even in kindergarten, forced others to do her work for her.

"Catering is hard work, and Brie was not a hard worker. I had her serving as wait staff. Look pretty and pass a tray of drinks around. Though she bitched and moaned to me about how people were always asking her to go get them another cocktail instead of taking the one on her tray."

I said nothing. Something didn't sound right here. Brie serving guests? The Brie I knew would have thrown the drink in your face if you had asked her to get one.

"But she was my niece." A pause. "And I needed the money," Janet said so softly I knew I wasn't meant to hear those words.

The silence stretched.

"When did you last see her?"

"Last Friday at lunch. Reminded her of the catering job at Sands Neck the next day, Saturday." Janet moved the pots and pans on top of the countertop, her hands busy with make-work.

"So you were out catering a party this past Saturday? Was there a catering party Friday night, too?"

"No, only Saturday. I was running errands all Friday afternoon, prepping for the party the next day. Why do you ask?" Janet's hands stilled, her eyes narrowing as she turned her head to me.

"Just talking. Was Brie at the party Saturday?" Telling Janet we were out to find Brie's killer was a big no-no. I didn't want Detective Storm to hear about our investigations. He'd shut us down fast.

Janet frowned and rolled her eyes at me. "She didn't show up. I was livid. I thought if she wasn't coming, she should have at least told me that Friday. Had to hire another server last minute at twice the going rate. I called Marion and told her she had better speak to her daughter. Gave her a hard time about it." Shoulders slumping, her voice softer, the anger leaching away, Janet whispered, "And all that time, the girl was in pieces under water in Duck Harbor."

"There was very little to identify her with, you know." Janet's voice was dry, emotions bleached out. "The head. It was a ball of hair and nothing more. The face was all burned and scarred. The detective said they think whoever killed her wanted to delay identification. They did a rapid DNA analysis and got a hit. It was my brother's. The police had his DNA from when he went to prison for defrauding investors. But Christian died last year, and I was listed as next of kin, so they came over to the house last night. Asked me to identify her. It was her hair with those crazy colors and, of course, the custom-made ring she bragged about to everyone she met that I recognized. What a waste. Why go out and ruin such beautiful blonde hair by dyeing it not only red and blue but also purple, green, and orange? I never understood that kid."

Brie's rainbow colored hair was a side issue. I ignored it and asked instead, "Why did you call Marion when Brie didn't show up for work?" Brie's mother had stayed out of her daughters' lives when the girls were in school. Why would the woman involve herself now?

"Marion?" Janet gave a start, her hands got busy again with the pots and pans. She opened a cabinet and moved the bottles and packages inside. "Did I say anything about Marion? Well, why wouldn't I call Marion? She's Brie's mother, after all. Who else should I call when Brie didn't show up for work? Anyway, Marion couldn't help. She's in Europe on vacation right now, with some boy toy she picked up somewhere."

That sounded more like the Marion I knew back when Brie was in my class. "I thought you'd call Selena first," I said.

"Selena? She's back at Sands Neck with Alan, that no-good husband of hers. Marion would be more of a help than Selena. Except Marion moved out long ago and, unlike her girls—believe me, I don't know why those two came back, they were treated like dirt— Marion has no intentions of ever coming back. She never got over how she and the girls were made to feel like pariahs when Christian went to prison and lost all that money, theirs and their neighbors. If it weren't for

Marion's father, she would have had to sell their house at Sands Neck. Her old man paid off the mortgage and gave Marion an allowance to live on and take care of the girls. But still, the party invitations stopped. No afternoon soirees, no coffee and cake, no sleepovers. Marion said her social life died the day the prison door clanged shut on her husband. She sold her house as soon as Brie graduated from high school and moved to a brownstone her father owned in Chelsea Park in New York City."

"I knew Marion had moved. I didn't know Selena's married."

"She's a paralegal for a law firm in the City. Got her GED three years after dropping out of school. She's Selena Reid now. Met Alan at work. He's a lawyer, ten years older. But Selena always did like older men. And it didn't matter if they were married. Anyway, what's with all these questions?"

"Nothing, just catching up. It's been years since Selena left town." I fixed my kindergarten teacher's look on my face. The one that said, "I'm here for you." I hoped that was enough to soothe Janet, get past her defenses.

It must have worked because Janet kept on talking after giving me a hard look.

"Alan was married then, too. However, unlike the other men Selena had dated, Alan had gotten divorced and married Selena about two years ago. Selena went looking at houses in Sands Neck before the wedding. Couldn't wait to show her old neighbors she's in the money again. Even if it's her husband's money. I heard she tried to buy back their old house, but the new owners wouldn't sell. Wouldn't even talk to her."

"But if Selena had a house at Sands Neck, why didn't Brie stay with Selena?"

"Selena let her younger and prettier sister stay with her flirt of a husband? Don't think so."

"So Brie stayed with you." I glanced over at the house across the yard.

"She kept her clothes and stuff here, if that's what you mean. Expensive stuff too," Janet said. "I don't know where she stayed most nights, and I didn't ask. She's"—Janet corrected herself—"she was a grown woman. And I'm not her mother."

"Expensive stuff?"

"You know, handbags costing thousands of dollars, shoes that would put you out several hundred."

I remembered the Gucci strapped across Brie's chest when we saw her at Sweet Buns. It was an itty bitty cross-body, a double G stud embedded on the green quilted chevron velvet and trimmed in leather. I recognized the brand even if I couldn't afford one. A teacher's pension, social security, and the money Rich and I had put away only went so far. "All that and the ring?"

"Plus, the ring," Janet agreed.

There was no way Brie's wages covered all that. "When was the last day Brie worked for you? Whose party was it? Do you remember?"

Janet got up and took down the calendar hanging from the wall. "The Saturday before last. It was at the Whitfield's," she said after checking the date. Janet took out her phone, her fingers dancing. She tilted her phone toward me, showing a woman, elegant in her haltered white knit sheath, hair put up in a hard-to-duplicate messy bun, makeup perfect, smiling at the man beside her, immaculate in a striped, pink shirt and tan linen pants. "Pip's latest wife, Connie. She throws several parties each season. She already had a late winter party some months back. This was an early spring one. Seventy-five guests. Wanted black tie servers. One thing you could say for Brie, she cleaned up very well. She and Kyle."

I looked closely at the photo in Janet's phone. I knew that woman.

"Recognize her? Connie wasn't your student, but she was with Mrs. Feldman's fifth-grade class. She's always at Sweet Buns. Just like you and the rest of those retired teachers from Whitman's Port you hang out with."

So that was where I had seen her, the woman next to the man with the coffee mug.

A commotion at the gate made both of us turn. Shouts filled the air. Followed by the sound of a body slamming the van out in the driveway. Janet eased her way around me and ran out of the building. Left alone, I peeked at the open calendar.

"That's odd." I ran my eyes again over the appointments scrawled on the calendar. Flipping back a few pages, I checked catering appointments for the past months. Janet's calendar looked almost like mine. Practically empty, except for a slot or two. At the busiest time of the year for her catering business. How was Janet making the mortgage payments on all that shiny equipment? Turning the pages back, I followed Janet outside.

Chapter Four

A body rushed into the yard, legs pumping, propelling itself past the kitchen and hurtling toward the back fence. Two others followed, dressed in light blue shirts and dark blue pants. Janet stood still, her eyes tracking the men.

Kyle ran, chased by two cops. He grabbed the dumpster by the fence, vaulted himself out of the yard, and into the woods. With a grunt, the younger and nimbler of the cops followed suit, clearing the fence, as agile as Kyle. Not surprisingly, the two were close in age. The older, less acrobatic one cursed and ran back out of the gate, intent on getting out of the yard and around the house's fence.

"Whoa!" Detective Storm sauntered into the yard, twisting his body and struggling to stay upright as his underling dodged around him.

"Sorry, sir." The cop threw his words into the wind, not waiting for a response as he continued the chase in the woods out back.

I hid my smile as Detective Storm pulled on his shirt and rearranged the fall of his jacket on his shoulders. "Good morning, Mrs. Conner." Jonathan greeted Janet, eyeing me warily as he walked up to us. "Mrs. Brightbook."

"Detective Storm." I returned the man's greetings.

"Ms. Townsend's cellphone. Did you find it?"

Jonathan said to Janet.

"It's not in the house. I called, and I didn't hear the phone ring. What's this fuss with Kyle?"

"I understand Kyle Johnson works for you, Mrs. Conner? And with the deceased?"

"Kyle's been working here for three years now."

"And he's romantically involved with the deceased?"

"I don't keep up with the love lives of my employees. And if he were, why does it matter to you?"

Jonathan pressed his lips closed, visibly holding onto his patience. "A CCTV by Duck Harbor Park showed Mr. Johnson walking by the park, Friday at midnight."

"You think Kyle killed Brie?" My voice rose with each word. That was the most unbelievable piece of nonsense I'd heard today.

"Mrs. Brightbook, this has nothing to do with you. But if you must know, a witness said she saw Ms. Townsend and Mr. Johnson arguing. And the argument got so heated, Mr. Johnson kicked the neighbor's trash can when he walked away. Ms. Townsend was, to quote the witness, smiling like the devil."

"That's it? That's all of your evidence against Kyle?"

Jonathan ignored me. "Mrs. Conner, what do you know of Kyle Johnson?"

"Kyle—" I spluttered to a stop when Jonathan raised his hand at me. I looked at Janet. Arms crossed over her chest, Janet was glaring at the detective.

"Kyle is a good kid. Don't know if he and Brie had something going on. But even if they did, he wouldn't hurt her. It's not in him."

I nodded at Janet's words, glaring as well at the detective.

"Mrs. Conner, I don't need to remind you this is a murder investigation. Of a particularly violent murderer."

"If you think Kyle killed Brie, you're out of your mind. Kyle is not violent." I ignored Jonathan's raised hand.

"Mrs. Brightbook, why are you here? Don't you have someplace else to be?"

Really! Who did Detective Storm think he was? He most certainly had no right to tell me where I could and could not go.

But then the gate banged against the fence, and our heads cranked around in concert.

The two cops walked in, frog-marching Kyle between them. He struggled to break free as they came to a stop in front of us.

"Get off me. What is this all about?" Kyle yelled at Jonathan. "I have rights, you know. You can't just cuff me like this."

"We just wanted to talk. Why did you run?" Jonathan asked.

"Talk? Your guy here"—Kyle's shoulder twitched toward the younger of the cops—"slammed me against the van. You call that talking?"

"I pulled him off you. Again, why run?"

Kyle mumbled something unintelligible.

"Have it your way," Jonathan said. "You just made it easy for me when you ran. Kyle Johnson, you are being held on suspicion of the murder of—"

"No!" Kyle exploded. His body arched, muscles bunching as he tried to get free of the two men hanging onto him.

"—Brianna Townsend. You have the right to remain silent. Anything you say can—"

"You've got this all wrong. I didn't kill Brie. Janet–" Kyle's desperate eyes sought Janet, only to have Janet turn her head away.

I looked on in horror, my eyes wide, hand raised halfway, wanting to stop the words rolling out from Detective Storm. Kyle Johnson was not a killer. Not that sweet boy who smiled his way all through his kindergarten year. Kyle always had his hand up when I asked for a helper, putting crayons back in their boxes and books on their shelves, giving out pencils and paper to the class, and smacking chalk out of blackboard erasers. He brought an apple for me on Teachers' Day, for heaven's sake.

"—and will be used against you in a court of law. You have the right to an attorney." Lips pursed in distaste, Jonathan continued, "If you cannot afford an attorney, one will be appointed for you. Are you coming quietly, or do we have to knock you out?"

Kyle stopped his struggles, pleading instead with the detective. "I ran because I thought you were arresting me for selling pot. Selling pot, not murder. Come on, man. I'm not a killer." Kyle sagged against the two cops by his side.

Jonathan jerked his head at the older cop who had almost plowed into him earlier. "Sergeant, get him in the car."

"Mrs. B…Janet…" Kyle craned his head around. "I didn't kill Brie. I was with my girl this weekend."

"Let's go, men. We're done here." The four men left with Detective Storm leading the way. The younger cop took control of Kyle while the older cop nodded goodbye as he closed the gate.

"Mrs. B, you must believe me. Mrs. B, please!" Kyle kept on shouting until the garage door closed on them.

"Why are you standing there? Do something. You know Kyle didn't kill Brie," I said to Janet.

"Do I? Those two were up to something. They thought I didn't see them whispering and plotting."

"Not Kyle!"

"Kyle is easily led by a pretty woman. Whatever they were up to, it's something Brie cooked up. But, yes, maybe not Kyle. Talk to Connie, she might know something." Janet turned her back on me and walked across the yard to the kitchen.

"Wait—" My cry was cut off by the thud of the kitchen doors closing. I heard the door lock click. Janet was done talking to me. The sound of police cars driving away stopped me from banging uselessly on the door. There was nothing more I could get from Janet.

Chapter Five

"You've come a long way since your first session with me."

Craig watched and critiqued my every move. But that was what trainers did, and Craig was kinder than most. "Move your shoulders like so," he murmured, moving his wrists, arms, shoulders, and body to his words.

The half-smile on my trainer's face and the rare words of praise eased the throbbing in my fists. Changing my stance, I threw more punches, my jabs quick and light, mimicking my trainer.

Through the sides of my eyes, I could see Stefan watching us, his towel slung over his shoulder. "What's got your goat this time?" Stefan asked. Tall and slim, Stefan's figure had survived the seven decades of his life. Not surprisingly, Stefan had never lacked for admirers even before he had divorced his cheating husband.

After the trip to see Janet and watching Detective Storm arrest Kyle, I was all in. Exhausted and stressed, I had called Stefan and asked him to meet me at the gym. The gym was his go-to place since his teens. And it had become mine as well, the place I ran to when my brain froze or ran in circles. And right now, my brain kept freezing, thinking of Brie's killer walking free. I shuddered as my brain jumped to Rich and Jim, and their killer. The fact that their killer was walking free, one year after dirt and grass had covered my loved ones, was a blade of ice in my heart. Kickboxing was the only way I knew how to warm myself up.

"You heard about Brie?" I answered while throwing another punch at the bag.

"Liz called last night."

Figured. What Liz knew, Stefan knew as well, no more than a day behind. Liz and Stefan had met as novice teachers at Post Elementary School. Their friendship cemented when the two discovered Stefan taught band and choir while Liz taught not only fifth grade but also moonlighted with the Whitman's Port Drama Group. It was a friendship blessed by the stars.

"Detective Storm arrested Kyle Johnson for the murder," I said.

"Kyle? That boy faints at the sight of blood," Stefan scoffed.

I raised my eyebrows at Stefan before jabbing at the bag again.

"Okay, I exaggerate. But you know what I mean. Kyle doesn't have a violent bone in him."

Exactly what I told Detective Storm. But would the man listen?

"Now front kicks from your lead leg," Craig called out, motioning Stefan away from us.

I did as I was told. The thud of my foot against the bag vibrating up my leg to my thigh and my back felt good. I did this a few more times while sweat ran down my neck, past the sweat band circling my head.

"Front kicks from your rear leg."

Shifting my weight onto my front leg, I slammed the ball of my foot into the heavy bag.

"So what will we do?" Stefan had moved back in.

"We?" I stopped what I was doing and faced Stefan, ignoring Craig. Our trainer was now shaking his head at both of us.

"You think I would let you, Barbara, and Liz go off on your own on this?"

"We?" I asked again.

"We," Stefan insisted. "You guys are not having all the fun. What do we do next?"

I gave in. "About Kyle? Or about Detective Storm?" Stepping to the side toward the bag, I opened my hips and gave myself the space I needed to rotate and do the roundhouse kicks Craig had asked for. I kicked, varying the height, from low to mid to high while thinking of how to answer Stefan.

What could we do for Kyle? He wasn't giving up the name of his customer.

"Kyle was out selling pot Friday night. You wouldn't know how to go about finding the name of his customer, would you?" I asked Stefan.

"Knee strikes. And the two of you can stop planning whatever it is you're planning. I know Kyle, and I know who he was with last Friday," Craig said.

Stefan and I looked at each other, blinked, and turned to the trainer.

"I'll see what I can do. In the meantime, keep moving." Craig flapped his hand at me.

Smiling, I took a step forward, leaned back, and brought my knee up, hitting the bag, toes tucked in. Imagining Detective Storm's face on the bag made it easy. The bag swayed as my knee connected again and again.

"Time for defensive moves. Let me see you block and parry."

Craig threw shin guards at me. Started throwing kicks and punches at me once I had them on and was back in position. He kept me busy ducking, weaving, and doing some fancy footwork to avoid getting hit. I held both fists in front of my face while my elbows and shins deflected his kicks.

"I think she's ready. You think she's ready?" Stefan asked after Craig called time.

"Yeah, she's ready."

"Ready for what?" I stripped the shin guards off my legs. Thoughts of Detective Storm dropped from my mind. Stefan brought as much trouble in his wake as Liz did. No wonder the two were besties.

"Light contact sparring. What do you say?" Stefan said.

I went still, the hand clearing my forehead of sweat, stopping mid-swipe with the towel in my hand.

"Light contact. Not full. And low power. No one spars at full power except in competitions. Or training for one. No head strikes either," Craig explained. "Your sparring partner will be around your age as well. Don't worry, you'll be safe."

"Stop thinking of Barbara. I can see it in your face," Stefan said, grinning.

He was right. Barbara already thought I was out of my mind, punching and kicking a bag filled with sand. She said it was all good and well for Stefan. He had gotten this crazy idea in his head when he was thirteen and was not planning on stopping anytime soon. I was not Stefan, she said. I was no longer in my twenties, she repeated over and over. My bones had ossified with age, she added. Light or full, contact sparring meant I would get hit. I thought of how red Barbara's face would get when she finds out I had signed up for any form of contact sparring. When? Not if? It seemed I had already made up my mind.

"So, what do you think?" Stefan had his hands on his hips, his stance loose and relaxed. He glanced at the swaying punching bag.

"You don't think I'm too old?" Some days, especially when it's damp and chilly outside, I felt all of my sixty-five years.

"We're not young. And regardless of what Barbara thinks, we're not heading for our graves yet. I was doing light contact sparring most days when I was your age. You've been at this for a year; it's time to move up."

It had been a year since Stefan had hustled me into this gym. The day after the funeral, I woke up to the nonstop shrilling of my doorbell. It was Stefan, dressed for the gym. He had taken one look at my crumpled nightgown, tear-streaked face, and bed-head hair and said, "Honey, this won't do."

Stefan had marched me back to my bedroom, ordered me to the bathroom to clean myself up, and thrown loose pants and a shirt at me, telling me we were going out. Brain fogged with grief, I followed him to the car. Stefan drove us to this gym, where he shoved me at Craig, telling his trainer to teach me how to kickbox.

Three times a week, Stefan picked me up, drove me to the gym, and brought me home. Until the routine had engraved itself in my bones. We traded rides with each other. Whoever said time heals all wounds was half right. Time had eased the pain, but my wound remained open and would remain so until the one responsible for destroying my world was behind bars where he belonged. I sighed at the thought and focused on what

Craig was saying.

"There's a sparring partner I know you'll like working with. I have her training on no contact for the past eighteen months. And until now, there was no one I could partner her with, skill- and age-wise. It'll be good for both of you," Craig said.

"C'mon, Meg, think of the fun I'll have when Barbara finds out," Stefan wheedled.

Barbara's temper bubbled under the surface every time the subject of kickboxing and me came up. She would, no question about it, explode when she heard I had signed up for contact sparring. And Stefan would stand there and enjoy the sight like those storm chasers who should know better than to get in the way of natural disasters. I felt my face stretching out in a smile. "If you put it that way, when do I start?"

Well, why not? I owed Stefan one. And Barbara knew that. She'd go easy on me.

I hoped.

But for now, I'd better get home before my grandson gets off the school bus.

Chapter Six

Behind me, Cannoli was busy chasing down the hard pellets of her kibble while her purple bowl did its best to slow her down. Sable colored with a white ruff and butt, Cannoli had the classic coloring of a Pembroke Welsh Corgi, looking very much like a cannoli, to my and Rich's delight when we first had her in our arms, all of eight weeks old. The clack of her teeth against the bowl and the sporadic slurping sound of her tongue were soothing. I heard how abruptly the sounds of pages being turned and the murmurs of Archer reading homework out loud stopped. Only to restart moments later, starting with the bang of a book slamming closed, followed by a shout of "I'm done." I stood over the boiling pot, trying my best not to curse.

My phone had pinged with a text when the tortellini was boiling. Archer and I knew what it meant. That ping capped the end of a very long Monday for me, and not in a good way.

Dora was working a longer shift at the hospital, covering for another ER doctor. Again. And Archer was not merely eating dinner with me. He was also staying overnight. Again. Dora had given the same excuses; the ones I'd heard so many times before. It was better for Archer to get a good night's sleep instead of getting dragged home at whatever late hour Dora got home. He would have more time to do homework. And time to relax after doing homework. He could wake up later since the school bus picked him up later from my place. Home-cooked dinner with me was healthier than the takeout Dora would have bought on her way home.

Then Dora hadn't been pleased when she found out dinners last week were meatballs and spaghetti, followed by mac-n-cheese the next night, and compounded with takeout pizza and burgers the following nights. Too many carbs, Dora had said. How about some greens? Dora had asked.

I told Dora I had raised Jim to a strapping young man without fighting over how many vegetables he ate. Greens, I said, would be on the menu when Dora started picking Archer up on time. Otherwise, I wasn't wasting my time fighting with Archer on what and how much he ate.

Don't bother telling me I was being petty. I knew I was, and I didn't care. Except, not having a salad with tonight's dinner didn't make up for the hurt I saw on my grandson's face.

Lately, Archer had to bend to kiss me on the cheek. At thirteen, he was on his way to matching his father's height of six feet two. Each time I saw him, I wondered how the baby I had held in my arms had grown to be this sweet, lanky boy with the cheeky grin on his face. Black hair, thick and coarse, like mine and his mother's. His big, rounded eyes were like his father's, with a slight upward tilt, a legacy of his Filipino heritage on his mother's side. His eyes were fringed with lavish eyelashes and framed with heavy brows. His skin was more white than brown. Given the beauty he inherited from his mother, Archer was growing up as handsome as, if not more handsome than, his father.

"How was school?"

Archer had taken Cannoli out for her walk, and my corgi was now resting, facing the dining table. Head on her paws, her back legs thrown out, body splayed like a rug, in a full sploot, she looked completely zonked out. Except for her eyes, big, brown, and full of canine cleverness, tracking both Archer and me.

"Same." Archer took his seat at the dining table and started toying with his food, pushing half of the remaining spinach tortellini back and forth. "All everyone talked about was that girl the cops fished out of the harbor. I asked Rosita about it this morning when she told Mom she was at Sweet Buns Sunday morning."

"What did Rosita say?" I bit into my lower lip to stop myself from saying anything more. Sensing Archer was playing with his food, Cannoli had risen from her sploot, and was now butting her head into him. It was only a matter of time before Archer started feeding my ill-mannered pet.

"Nothing. She said she didn't see anything. How could she not see anything? She was right there! Mama Meg, everyone says the dead girl was in your class. Is it true?" Archer's fork stopped its aimless path, leaving the tortellini pushed up on one side of the bowl.

"Who's everyone? And how did anyone know about Brie?" There was nothing in the papers this morning about the murdered girl. I saw Archer move his body ever so slightly to hide his hand creeping toward his bowl while Cannoli's nose followed. Standing up, I grabbed both glasses on the table and went into the kitchen to get water, where I counted to ten to give the two plenty of time before coming back to the dining table.

"Was Brie the girl who got killed? Were you her

teacher?" Archer must have fed himself as well as Cannoli, since there was less food on his plate. Cannoli was back to splooting, head down and eyes still trained on us.

"Yes, I was." Brie's murder probably wasn't the best subject to discuss with a thirteen-year-old, but needs must. I wanted Archer out of his funk.

"Some of my friends were at the park that day. They saw Principal Roker running, so they biked over to where she was headed. They said there was a hand lying on the ground. I thought they were making things up—"

I shook my head, answering Archer's unasked question.

He continued, "—they saw the divers bring up a bag, but the cops chased them away."

If Archer's friends knew, the entire neighborhood knew. Between the kids and their parents, and the friends of those parents, and the friends of those friends, there was no need for the local news shows and papers to carry the story.

"Do you remember her? The dead girl, I mean."

"I rarely forget a student." It wasn't necessary to tell Archer how memorable Brie was. "I saw her aunt today. Brought her some blueberry muffins," I tossed out, determined to keep my grandson focused on the story.

"What did she say?" Archer asked, his eyes eager for more information, the pain from his mother's neglect gone from his face.

"She was very angry."

Archer straightened up from his slouch. "Was she angry at Brie for dying?"

Whoa! This was the moment I had been waiting for this past year. "I think so. Brie worked for her, you see.

Janet needed her. She was angry Brie wasn't around to help anymore." Keep it light, and maybe Archer would open up some more.

"My mom said it's selfish to be angry when someone dies. It wasn't their fault they died."

Dora, what have you been telling your son?

"Your mom's right, it's selfish." My heart ached when Archer's eyes turned bleak. "But it's perfectly normal. There's nothing wrong with it. I was very angry when your grandpa and dad died. I still am. I love them so much, and I am furious they left me."

"Oh!"

Archer's voice was so soft, I barely heard him. I sat frozen in my chair. I wanted so badly to hug my grandson, whose eyes were blinking as fast as mine, trying hard to stop the brimming tears. But teenagers were prickly about their dignity.

"The anger will go away sometime." I kept my tone buoyant and optimistic. If Archer could see that life goes on, that it was okay to mourn, the boy could move on from his grief instead of bottling it up. "Papa and your dad understand, I'm sure. I'm betting they're as angry as we are that they're not here with us."

With a clatter of a chair being pushed back, Archer rushed to me, burying his face in my chest. I wrapped my arms tightly around him.

"I'm sorry. I'm sorry," Archer mumbled through his tears.

"For what?"

"Mom said I'm too old to cry. I'm sorry."

"Nonsense! I cry, and I'm a lot older than you. See"—I pulled my grandson from my embrace—"look, I'm crying right now."

We must have confused Cannoli—dinner was not usually this muddled—because she barked at us, her eyes locked on what was left of Archer's tortellini. My greedy pet had had her dinner, and she didn't need more. Archer and I looked at Cannoli, then at each other, and smiled. I reached out, took a paper napkin, and wiped Archer's tears before doing the same with my own. We stayed the way we were for a few moments, drawing strength and comfort from each other.

When he was calmer, I whispered, "It's okay to be angry. But it's better to remember them with love. You understand?" I squeezed him tight and nudged him back to his chair.

"Was anyone else there? In Brie's aunt's house?" Archer's voice didn't have tears behind it anymore.

"Kyle Johnson was there. He worked with Brie. He was also one of my kindergarten students." Deciding Archer needed another distraction, I went on with what happened at Janet's. "Archer, you remember Detective Storm?" Seeing Archer nod, I said, "He came with two other cops, and they arrested Kyle."

"They did?" Archer's eyes went wide. "Did Kyle run? Was there a chase? You know, like TV?"

"Yes, it was like TV. Kyle ran and jumped over the back fence. One cop jumped the fence after him, but the other one went back outside."

"Awesome," said Archer. "But how did the cops know to arrest Kyle? They found the body yesterday."

"Detective Storm said they saw Kyle on CCTV walking by Duck Harbor Park on Friday at midnight. I told him that's not enough. I wish I could see that CCTV for myself, see if they missed something."

"You can!" Archer jumped out of his chair, running

over to where he had tossed his school backpack on the sofa. Taking his laptop out, Archer carried it over to the dining room table, stooping to ruffle Cannoli on the head on his way back. Cannoli wriggled her butt and moved her head up and down in a vain attempt to lick his fingers, bringing back a smile to Archer's lips. My pet deserved a special treat before the day ended.

Turning the laptop on, Archer's fingers flew over the keyboard, screens coming to life with images of streets and buildings. "My dad has this app he uses to get into any CCTV. Let's see, Main Street is by Duck Harbor Park. Mama Meg, can you find me an address on Main Street?"

"Waffles and Cones is on Main Street." I gave Archer the name of my favorite ice cream place, my fingers busy with my cellphone. "Their address is 80 Main."

"Okay, that's good. Let's see—"

I moved to stand behind Archer, looking at the town's Main Street blooming on screen. Red dots pulsed in some, but not all, buildings.

"What are those red dots for?"

"That's CCTV. When I click on the dot, it should—" A view of Main Street popped up. At the bottom of the image was a strip with today's date and a time stamp. Archer moved the strip to the right, playing Friday's CCTV surveillance video.

People came and went, some carried bags with a logo I recognized as that of my favorite organic health and beauty shop. I pointed to two figures. It was impossible to miss those purple eyeglasses on Stefan's smiling face and his zebra-striped fitted shirt, making the lady beside him, with her blonde hair and steel-rimmed glasses perched on her prominent nose, Liz. "There's no security? Anyone can view the CCTV?"

"Of course not," Archer said with all the scorn of a thirteen-year-old know-it-all. "Only if the CCTV is in the network Dad managed. Otherwise, you need a password to get in."

The duh left unsaid but ringing clear to me. I forgave him. Seeing him filled with energy was worth more to me than a lesson in manners right now.

"This one must be in the network. Let's try another one." Archer clicked on a different pulsing red dot. "Hah!" He rubbed his hands together when a screen popped up demanding a password. "Dad and I used to play this game. He'd click on a CCTV, then ask me to try to hack into it."

"Archer!" I was horrified. Jim was a cybersecurity specialist, recognized as an expert in his field. The company he started with a friend was respected for its expertise and was hired by many businesses to secure their computer systems. What was Jim doing, encouraging his son to hack CCTVs?

"What?" Archer turned to look at me. "It was for his work. He said teenagers were the best at hacking. And if I can't hack a CCTV, he's done his job. He taught me all the tricks he knew."

Okay, that made some sort of crazy sense. But still! Teaching his son bad habits was not something I could agree with. What was that boy thinking of? I scoffed. Boy? Jim was forty when he died.

"Dad said to erase the program if something happened to him. But I'm not going to." Archer's fingers had stopped flying over the keyboard, and another video of the same street was now on screen. "I'm not going to," he repeated, looking at me with all the defiance his thirteen-year-old eyes could muster.

A responsible adult would insist Archer follow his dad's instructions. But a grandma who felt her grandson's pain, and who suffered along with him, would not. And I was a grandma, first and foremost.

Chapter Seven

"How long do CCTVs record?" Now was not the time to force my grandson to do anything that would make him feel he'd lost his father all over again.

"Dad said it depends on the company. Some only record for a week before writing over the old recording. Others store over a year." Archer blinked his eyes and moved on from the hacked CCTV to another pulsing red dot.

"Wait, I think that's Brie." In a sea of monochromatic hair, Brie easily stood out. "That girl who's about to step into that jewelry store. The one who's waving an envelope in her hand. Can you zoom in closer? And freeze the frame?" Both Archer and I moved nearer to the laptop's screen, our eyes glued as the girl's face zoomed out.

What was that piece of paper in her hand? And the look on her face. Joy mixed with excitement. Glee with a hefty dose of anticipation. Over jewelry?

"What time was this?" I checked the numbers at the bottom of the screen. Three-thirty Friday afternoon. "Can we see when Brie left the store and where she went after?"

"Sure thing." Archer unfroze the screen and let it play.

We watched Brie walk into the store. A few minutes later, we saw an older man, dressed in a black suit, showing people out, one of whom looked very familiar to me. Connie Whitfield. She kept popping up everywhere I turned.

I focused on the store's owner. I knew him. David Katz. Rich had bought most of my jewelry from him. David had taken Jim's nebulous but romantic ideas and designed an elegant and very Victorian engagement ring for Dora. Jim was so proud of that ring. Except I hadn't seen the ring on Dora's hand since the funeral. I quickly threw off the tug on my heart. There were other things, more important things here, for me to think about. I turned back to the scene in front of me. David must have locked the door because it wouldn't open when another person came up to the store and tugged on it. Nothing happened for a while, then Brie came out, followed by the older man. I didn't have to tell Archer to close in on the two. The screen zoomed in on Brie, then the older man. She looked smug. Triumphant, like a Viking would look after a successful raid. The older man, however, was furious, face closed and set, black bushy eyebrows drawn over narrowed eyes.

David as Brie's killer? I remembered Rich telling me of how, one day, he had walked into David's store only to walk right out. David was on the phone, his back to Rich, screaming, ranting, and waving one hand wildly. Rich had said David was entirely out of control, saying he was coming over and when he got there, he'd pull the guts out of the other, hurl it to the ground, and stomp on it. What Rich heard had shocked both of us; it was so unlike David. But the memory made my decision easy. David went on my list of suspects. Right next to Janet.

"Can we follow Brie?" I asked.

Archer fiddled with his keyboard, and I saw a series

of screens go by. The jewelry store's CCTV showed Brie walking away, and the CCTV of the stores on the same block picked her up. It was easy to follow Brie and her varied colored hair. She stopped once to greet a man, lightly patting him on the shoulder. She laughed and moved on as the man jerked back from her touch. And when a woman passed her and joined the man, I saw Brie toss her hair over her shoulders and walk backward, both hands coming up in a thumbs-up gesture to the couple. The man said something to the woman, and the couple stood there glaring at Brie before turning around and walking away. Archer hopped on CCTVs, hacking easily into their security systems, and we watched until we lost Brie when she crossed the street to Duck Harbor Park. By then, it was closer to four in the afternoon.

"If you want, I can go through the rest of the recordings for the night to see what time she comes back from the park," Archer offered.

"No, that's okay. Right now, it's more important we see the CCTV of Kyle the detective was prattling on about." While finding out where Brie was Friday night was tempting, Archer hacking CCTVs without supervision was not.

"Did the detective tell you the street the CCTV was on?"

"No, he just said it was a CCTV by Duck Harbor Park."

"Then it must be one of these CCTVs." Archer moved the screen until it showed the street in front of Duck Harbor Park, pointing at the three pulsing red dots bordering the park.

"Isn't that where the bank is?" I pointed at the red dot closest to the park, offering my cellphone to Archer showing a map of the park and its surroundings, clearly labeling the bank.

"Yeah, let's see if it's part of Dad's network." Archer clicked on the dot.

An image came up. Archer would not be hacking into a bank's security, and police cars would not come screeching up to my driveway, guns out, and shouting for the hacker to come out with his hands up.

"Did the detective say when it happened?" My grandson asked before I could dwell on our good luck.

"He didn't. But Janet said Brie didn't show up for work last Saturday, and we just saw Brie walking down Main Street, at four Friday afternoon."

"That's perfect! We only have to go through the CCTV from Friday afternoon to Sunday morning," said Archer, delighted at narrowing the time frame for the search.

"Start late Friday evening, then. No one is crazy enough to toss a bag into the harbor, whatever is in it, with the park full of people. Someone might notice. Whoever tossed the bag into the harbor did it while it was dark and no one was around."

"Right, right," said Archer, busy swiping at his laptop, images blurring until they steadied and focused, the date stamp showing last Friday at midnight. Underneath the date stamp was a series of side-by-side rectangles. Bars bisected the rectangles, and on top of each rectangle was a time stamp. "Dad called these motion histograms," Archer pointed to the rectangles. "You can go through hours of CCTV faster with these. Each of these rectangles represents a time frame, typically an hour, but sometimes thirty minutes. The bars inside the time frame divide it up into even smaller periods, maybe ten or fifteen minutes. What you do is you look for spikes in the frame. No spikes, no movement."

Archer swiped at the motion histograms, checking for spikes. "Got you!" The time stamp showed midnight on Friday. And there was the spike, right at the first bar of the frame. An image appeared; the video began playing.

A man was walking by the bank, head down, dressed all in black. Tall, like Kyle, and lean, like Kyle.

"Can we see his face?" I asked.

Archer zoomed in on the frozen picture of the man.

"No, it can't be. I refuse to believe Kyle killed Brie."

Kyle, his face drawn and worried, was unmistakably on the screen.

"So that's him. He doesn't look mean to me. This must be why Detective Storm arrested Kyle. But he's not carrying a bag." Archer zoomed out and pointed at the image.

I looked again. Kyle's hands were tucked inside his sweatshirt pockets.

"If Kyle was the killer, this must be after he threw the bag in the bay. But that's weird. There was no movement before this time frame and—" Archer checked the time frames following "–nothing after till early morning at six."

"You think he walked from the other side of the park, threw the bag, and then walked past the bank? That doesn't make sense. Where was he coming from, and where did he go? Is there any other CCTV nearby?"

"You don't think Kyle did this, then?" Archer closed down the video and went back to the map showing the streets by Duck Harbor Park.

"No, definitely not. I told Detective Storm, but he wouldn't listen."

"Nope, that's the nearest CCTV. And it's only pointed at the area in front of the bank." Archer turned to me; his face wide open, willing to believe Kyle was innocent if I did. "What do we do now? Is there something we can do to help Kyle? He shouldn't go to jail for something he didn't do. Anyone could have walked up to the park without being seen by this CCTV."

Archer was right. But I was afraid Detective Storm had already convicted Kyle as the killer, without the benefit of a trial and jury. I hoped Craig could convince whoever was Kyle's customer last Friday to step up and give Kyle an alibi. Otherwise, Kyle's goose was cooked.

Chapter Eight

"Tell me again why I'm getting into this car with you? And not out food shopping like the sensible woman I am?" Barbara had strapped herself into my car, dropping her large, black bag at her feet.

"You've never been sensible. And you're coming with me because you want to catch Brie's killer as much as I do. Anyway, Selena might remember me, but she'll definitely remember you." I eased my car out of Barbara's driveway and headed out.

"Selena should remember me. The number of times that girl was in my office, she might as well have slept there and not gone to her classes for all the good those classes did her. But even if she remembers me, there's no guarantee she won't slam the door in our faces."

"Selena will not slam the door in Principal Roker's face, and you know it. Stop complaining."

"You said Stefan was joining us in this crazy idea of yours?"

I nodded. I had told Barbara about meeting up with Stefan at the gym yesterday, but not about the contact sparring. I was leaving that little tidbit for Stefan to dish out. Barbara was already very unhappy with me when I called for her early this Tuesday morning. My lips twitched up at the memory of the older woman berating me for getting all of us involved in a murder investigation. Foolish was the least of the unflattering terms Barbara had used. Her tirade stopped when I told her Detective Storm had arrested Kyle yesterday for Brie's murder.

"I suppose we need to do this. There's nothing we can do for Brie, but we can help out Kyle. How Detective Storm can even think Kyle killed Brie is beyond me. What was that man thinking?" Agitated, Barbara pulled on her lap belt and fidgeted in her seat. "Who do you think killed Brie?"

"Not a clue. The CCTV Detective Storm went on about showed absolutely nothing. Just Kyle walking past the bank. He wasn't even holding a bag. How can they use it to tie him in with the murder?"

"And that's another thing, why were you aiding and abetting your grandson in breaking the law?"

"Aiding and abetting? Are you a lawyer now?" I slid my eyes over to where Barbara sat next to me, amused at how grumpy Barbara was getting.

"Sure, make fun of me. Anyway, didn't you say Kyle was seen fighting with Brie?

"So what? You don't go around killing every person you fight with, do you? You'd run out of people to talk to if you did."

"Look," said Barbara. "Brie was seen walking down Main Street Friday afternoon, alive and well. Sunday morning, her hand was dangling on a hook. Ergo, she was killed sometime between Friday afternoon and Sunday morning. Kyle walking around Duck Harbor Park, blocks away from where Brie was seen last, on Friday midnight, hours after the last time anyone saw Brie, is pretty suspicious. Don't you agree? And we know Kyle. Detective Storm doesn't. Plus, Kyle ran when the cops came around to ask a few questions. I'm not surprised they hauled him in."

Arguing with Barbara never paid off. I turned our conversation from Kyle and the murder investigation to the one topic guaranteed to keep Barbara talking at length, the indignities brought on by our advancing age. Barbara was still bristling with anger fifteen years after she had traded her four-inch spiked heels for sturdy, no-nonsense flat, black oxfords she hated with a passion but wore in fear of a broken hip. I kept driving while Barbara droned on beside me, while I hummed in companionable agreement.

We made it to Selena's house in good time with both of us in one piece. A stately tree stood guard in front with a mailbox at the end of a long driveway and the number 29 prominently displayed. I parked my car underneath the tree's generous shade. A white SUV and a silver sedan shared the driveway. Both Selena and her husband were home.

"Pretty house," Barbara said, echoing my thoughts. The grass flowing from the house to the street curb was kept mowed to the accepted height. Stucco and stone covered the house's exterior, while evergreen bushes were planted along the perimeter, kept trimmed by suburbia's weekly landscape services. Selena had done very well for herself.

"Come on, we can't stay inside this car forever, neighbors will get suspicious, and next thing you know, there'll be a cop knocking on your window."

"We just parked!" My eyes lit up in amusement.

Box of cookies in hand, I followed Barbara down the paved walkway ending at two marble-like posts stretching from the ground to the house's roof before a double door entrance. Two stories with vaulted ceilings and bay windows flanked both sides of the entry door. Barbara pressed the doorbell, and not even a minute later, the door swung open with Selena at the door, smiling a welcome. She must have seen us parked out front.

"Mrs. B, Principal Roker, hello! Welcome. Come in, come in." Selena stood beside the open door, the tiled floor of her home's foyer ending in the living room's hardwood floors. A man stood there, dressed in jeans with a plain black shirt tucked in neatly. "My husband, Alan." Selena gestured to the man.

Short hair combed and set to perfection, straight, aristocratic nose, eyes sharp and piercing, the easy charm of his smile, lips curved invitingly upward, saved Alan from looking like a snob. It was hard not to smile in return.

Especially since I had seen the man quite recently. Last Friday. At Main Street. When Brie greeted him and he had pulled back in surprise. Except the woman with him was not Selena.

Hanky-panky with someone not his wife, and Brie knew about it? Another suspect for my list?

This one was trouble. Not even counting the mysterious, unidentified woman. But then, Selena always did like trouble, no surprise there. What was surprising was the slight bulge at her waistline. I didn't think Selena had a maternal bone in her body.

"When's the baby due? September? October?" Barbara had no compunctions about asking personal questions.

"October." Selena went to stand beside her husband and cradled her not-quite-visible baby bump tenderly. "We're about four months pregnant."

"Congratulations," I said.

"We're very happy," Selena said.

I saw Alan's smile slip a little.

"Aren't we, honey?" Selena looked up at Alan, a faint question in her eyes, marring the happiness she was trying her best to project.

"Yes, of course." Alan had recaptured his smile and had slung his arm across Selena's shoulders, cuddling her near, his hand resting loosely on top of the sleeveless, striped blue and white sheath midi-dress Selena wore. "Coffee, anyone? We started a pot in case you guys wanted some."

I handed Selena the box of cookies, very glad we picked some up on the way here. Pregnancy and sweet cravings went hand in hand.

"Thank you. How do you take your coffee, Principal Roker?" Selena said over her shoulder, walking through the adjacent dining room and through an opening presumably leading to the kitchen. We heard the clink of cups against the kitchen counter.

"Black's fine."

Urged on by Alan, Barbara, and I had taken seats close to the window. Alan dragged a chair from the dining set nearby and pulled it close to us, sitting on it with his knees splayed out, ankles crossed, and fingers intertwined on his lap with palms out. He was the very picture of confidence. And innocence. I wasn't buying it.

"The cookies are good." Selena savored the bite of a shortbread topped with strawberry jam. "But then, it seems I like anything sweet right now. I have to watch it, or I'll grow too big. Which wouldn't be good, would it?" Selena tipped her head toward Alan.

Still smiling but with a definite strain leaking

through his eyes, Alan shook his head, mock-fondly. "Babe, you're good however you are."

"Good man," Barbara said. "A boy or a girl, do you know?"

"A girl," Selena said. "We found out last week. But I didn't get a chance to tell Brie."

"That's a shame." I didn't know what else to say, but it was a perfect opening for what I wanted to ask. "When was the last time you saw Brie?"

"A month ago, I think," Selena said. "We didn't keep in touch."

I took a sip of my coffee and turned to Alan. "You sure you didn't see her in town? At Main Street, like last Friday afternoon? About four?" I looked over the coffee mug at Barbara. I hadn't told her about Alan and the CCTV.

"Friday?" Selena laughed. "How could he? Alan was away for the weekend with his golf buddies. Left Friday. Didn't you, honey?"

Avoiding my eyes, Alan uncrossed his ankles and planted his feet firmly on the floor. Rearranging the creases on his pants, he nodded to Selena and murmured, "Yeah, sure." His big smile to his wife sealed the lie.

It was official. Alan was definitely on the list.

Selena continued, "I was at work all day, then I stayed over at my mother's place in the City for the weekend. Did some shopping and watched a Broadway show with friends. No, we haven't seen Brie for at least a month. She called from time to time. Mostly to ask if she could drop by for dinner that day."

Startled, I said, "Your mom's back from Europe?" Janet had said Marion was with her boy toy.

"She's flying back tomorrow. For the funeral and

legal stuff."

The poor woman. I hoped Marion would be spared the agony of waking up knowing you would never hear your child's voice again and the struggle to make it through the day. She might have neglected the girls, but I wouldn't wish that pain on anyone. Praying Marion would find peace, I asked Selena, "Did Brie come for dinner?" Brie had said nothing to Barbara and me about having dinner with her sister and her brother-in-law when she stopped by our table at Sweet Buns.

"Unfortunately, we never found time to get together for dinner. Honestly, I don't know if it would have made a difference to Brie knowing the baby is a girl. She wasn't particularly impressed when I told her she'd be an aunt." Selena turned to Alan. "Was she, honey?"

"I have no idea, babe." Alan was squirming in his chair like the worm he was.

Selena's answering smile to Alan glinted like diamonds. The smile of a wife who knew her husband was up to no good.

Chapter Nine

"It makes me…" Selena paused. "I don't know if the right word is sad. Brie and I were too far apart in age for us to be close to each other growing up. Maybe regret? We told the detective who came here yesterday. We must have seen Brie two, maybe three times in the six months she had moved back to Long Island. And it was more like hurried hellos and even more hurried goodbyes. And before that? Not once in maybe six to seven years. She went her way. And I went mine."

"Frankly, I was surprised she showed up at my door. I didn't even know she knew where I lived." A slight frown graced Selena's face, lovelier now than when she was in high school. Blonde highlights expertly done peeked from Selena's rich brown hair. Gone was the garish red lipstick favored by Selena in high school, replaced by soft, muted pinkish-mauve tones, which brought out the shape of her lips. Varying shades of brown eyeshadow made her eyes look deeper and wider while a slight touch of bronzer completed the fresh, free-of-makeup look. Selena blended well into Sands Neck Point society.

"Wasn't she invited to your wedding?" I asked. When Jim and Dora married, all of Dora's family was there as well as numerous aunts, uncles, and cousins. They had two whole baby roasted pigs served at the wedding, complete with an apple in the pigs' mouths.

Dora told me the lechon—meaning the roasted pigs—were there to honor her Filipino culture at her wedding and for her family and guests to enjoy traditional Filipino cuisine. I didn't expect the same extravaganza from Selena, but I still could not imagine why a bride would not invite her sister to something so important as her wedding.

Selena lifted her palms out. "We didn't know where she was. She had moved out of the last address Mother knew. And we weren't holding up our wedding on the off chance we'd find out when she called Mother up for money. Who knew when that would be?" Selena reached for the glass of water, directing a smile to her husband. "Alan couldn't wait to get married, weren't you, honey?"

Alan merely nodded, lifting his coffee mug in a toast before taking a sip.

I likewise took another sip of my coffee. "I'm sorry to hear that. Did the detective say anything else? Or ask anything more?"

"No, that was it." Selena looked at the glass of water in her hands.

"He must have asked you, I'm sure. Who do you think killed Brie?" Barbara was getting ready to go, and I needed Selena to answer this question.

"It could be anyone. My sister was talented at making people hate her. The more she was hated, the happier she got. Though she was very interested in Connie Haddad, now Whitfield, Pip's new wife. Asked me all sorts of questions about her. Wanted to know if we socialized with her. Connie was a few years ahead of me. And we're not exactly neighbors. Connie lived in the even more exclusive parts of Sands Neck." Selena put her glass of water down. "But, I'm a bit confused. Are you helping the detective? He didn't say anything to me about getting help from the outside," she said with a sweet smile on her face.

"Now, why would you think that?" I said, with an even sweeter smile on my face while my mind raced with possibilities. Selena was the second person to tell me about Connie and Brie. "Barbara and I wanted to extend our sympathies. You and Brie, both of you, were our kids once." My face softened on my last words. So did Selena's, though doubt still lurked in her eyes. I didn't blame her. Why were two retired school teachers nosing around her sister's death?

"I think we'd better go. Thank you for having us, but you must have a lot to do." Barbara got up and tugged on the roomy dress shirt she wore over the equally roomy pants with elastic waists.

Right, let's go. Before Selena asked us any more questions we preferred not to answer. I followed suit. "Yes, thank you for having us. Let me know if there is anything you need."

Neither Selena nor Alan demurred. Both stood up without protest and walked us to the door, where everyone said their goodbyes. The door closed right on my heels. It would have clipped me if I had moved any slower.

Outside, a woman, about Barbara's age, stood near my car, a leash held loosely in her hand while her dog sniffed around the tree nearby. "How's Selena?" The woman asked, drawing on the leash to bring the dog closer to her. "I live right there," she said, pointing with her head to the house across from us. It was built along the same lines as Selena's house, including the big bay windows in front.

"She's unsettled," Barbara said.

"She would be." The woman nodded, drawing her dog even closer. "I saw the police cars yesterday, so I went up to ask her what happened. Terrible thing, her sister getting killed. A bit rough, her sister. Not like Selena. But sweet. Always greeted me with a smile. Not like Selena."

"You saw Brie often?" I asked.

"Once a week, at least. She gets here about this time when I'm back from walking Benji." The woman nodded to her dog. "Thursday, most weeks. Sometimes, although not very often, on Tuesdays. She never stayed long. She'd ring the doorbell. Alan would come out. A few words between them, then off she'd go." The woman looked toward Selena's house. "Most days, Alan handed Brie an envelope." The woman looked back at us, quickly lowering her head to fuss over her dog.

"An envelope for Brie? From Alan?" I stared at the woman. "Are you sure Selena wasn't at the house that day?"

"Selena? No, Selena went to work on Tuesday, Wednesday, and Thursday. Anyway, her car was not in the driveway each time Brie came around. Selena drives the white SUV." The woman had turned her back to us, her eyes fixed on her dog.

"What are you trying to say?" I wished the woman would turn around and face us.

"Me? Nothing." The woman shrugged. "Just telling you what I saw. That poor woman has enough to worry about."

"Did you tell the detective?"

"No, why should I? No one came to my door to ask." The woman pulled on the leash. "Come on, Benji, time to go home." Nodding goodbye, the woman left.

"That was interesting," Barbara said.

In more ways than one, I thought. Selena's driveway was twice the length of mine. It wouldn't be easy to catch Alan passing an envelope to Brie. Unless the woman was spying on Alan through those bay windows with high-powered binoculars like the ones Liz carried around with her.

"Back to Sweet Buns, right?" Barbara said as she got into the car. "Liz and Stefan should be there by now."

I started the car, glancing back at the house as I pulled away from the sidewalk. "What do you think Alan was up to, meeting with Brie without telling his wife?"

"Whatever it is, he's certainly not cheating on Selena with Brie. I'm pretty sure about that. Alan might want to, but Brie would not have picked up such a sad sack."

"He is somewhat of a sad sack, isn't he? He didn't act like he wanted the baby, but he's having one anyway. Selena must have slipped it by him."

Barbara chuckled. "No, he didn't want the baby. And Selena knows it, too. But there's something more there. Selena is holding him with claws bared, and he's twitching, with one eye fixed on those wicked tips. The Selena I knew would have tossed him out by now. Unless he's worth more to her than the trouble he's giving her."

"The only thing Selena would cling to like that is money. You think he's worth that much?" I asked in disbelief. "He might not be cheating with Brie, but he's darn well cheating on Selena. I couldn't tell you in front of them, but I saw Alan on CCTV. Brie bumped into him last Friday on Main Street. He met up with a woman. But Selena said Alan went golfing with his friends."

Barbara said nothing. I kept driving. It was possible Selena didn't know of the woman or the weekly meetings between Alan and Brie. Possible but not likely. The lady with the dog was very neighborly. She would have made sure Selena heard about Brie's weekly visits to Alan.

Barbara's phone rang from the depths of her bag. I glanced over at her and saw her eyes narrow at the name coming up on the phone.

"Edna?" She answered the call.

I tensed up, hoping it wasn't bad news. Edna hadn't joined us at Sweet Buns when Brie's body was found. She had a scare last week. Her mother wasn't in her bed when Edna came to help her dress for the day. Luckily, before Edna could panic, her mother's next-door neighbor found Edna's mom walking around the neighborhood in her pajamas and robe, with pink fluffy slippers on her feet. We'd been waiting for Edna to call us with the results of the neurological tests the doctor had done on her mother. We were afraid it might be Alzheimer's.

"What?" Barbara sounded frazzled. "Slow down; you're not making sense. Why are you in the police station?"

This didn't sound good. I looked for somewhere to park, not trusting myself to drive.

"Calm down. We'll be right there. Yes, Meg is with me. And who else should I call? Ferdinand Ocampo? Give me his number." Barbara repeated the phone number out loud. I took it down, having parked by then. "Don't call him Ferdinand, call him Fred. Or Nanding. How do you say that again?" Barbara paused. "Naan…ding? Like the Indian bread and the sound of a doorbell ringing? That's what family and friends call him? Why can't I call him Fred? We're not his family. Or his friend. We don't know the man. A Filipino nickname, you said?" Another pause. "And tell him you didn't call him yourself because they said you can only call one person, and you weren't sure he'd pick up, so you called me? Did I get it right?" Barbara turned to me and shrugged. "Okay, yes, I'll tell him to get there as soon as he can. We're driving there now. As soon as I hang up on you."

Barbara put her phone back in her bag. She met my eyes with hers. "Detective Storm arrested Edna for Brie's murder. She's at the police station and wants us to go there. As fast as we can," she said.

OMG. What an idiot!

Chapter Ten

It didn't take long to reach the Fourth Precinct. On the way there, Barbara called this Ferdinand Ocampo. He didn't ask much when Barbara got him on the phone, only the address of the police station. When I asked her who the guy was, she said, "Must be Edna's attorney. The receptionist answered with a long string of names."

An attorney? With a name like Nanding? My students who had gone on to be attorneys had dropped their childhood names. Robbie was now Robert. Ginny was Eugenia. Something to do with keeping the dignity of the profession, they said. I get their point. It was easier to take advice from a Robert than a Robbie, a Eugenia than a Ginny. How good an attorney was this Nanding? In case he wasn't, I told Barbara to call Dora. Detective Storm might listen to her, which was more than he would do to any of us.

I know, I know. But this was an emergency, and I had to use all available resources, Dora included. And anyway, Dora and Edna were almost relatives. Dora's mother was a cousin of a friend of a friend of Edna's. In Filipino culture, it was enough to make Edna Dora's auntie. Not her aunt. Her auntie. Dora was very specific about that. And she would get mad at me if I didn't tell her Jonathan had arrested her auntie Edna for Brie's murder.

When Barbara got to her, Dora had said, "Jonathan

did what? Is he out of his mind? Never mind, I'm telling him myself."

Dora mad at Jonathan was even better.

Barbara got out of the car as soon as it stopped and walked ahead, not looking back to see if I followed. The police station was crowded. Other than this past Sunday at the park, I had not seen this many cops in one place before. Barbara ignored the crowd and went directly to the desk officer and tapped sharply, drawing his attention away from the phone. "You have Edna Gomez in custody. We want to see her," she said.

The cop pointed a finger at the benches by the wall and, with his eyes, told us to take a seat.

"Young man, get off the phone. Edna Gomez. We're here to speak to Edna Gomez. Where is she?" Barbara persisted.

The cop put the phone to his shoulder, muffling it. "Ma'am, take a seat. I will be with you when I'm done with my call." He turned back to his call, pointing to the benches once more.

I tugged on Barbara and drew her to the seats. It probably wasn't the wisest move to irritate any of these cops now.

Time crawled. The cop stayed on the phone. I checked my watch twice, amazed at how little time had passed. It felt like hours. The cop hung up the phone, and Barbara shot out of her chair. Only to stop short when the cop got up and went inside to the offices beyond the reception area. I worried she'd cause a fuss.

"Hey now, why don't we wait for this Fred Ocampo. If he's an attorney, he'll know how to get the attention of these cops. If not, I'm sure Detective Storm will not keep Dora waiting once she shows up."

Barbara took her seat. Reluctantly, I could tell. I prayed Fred and Dora would get here before Barbara exploded and made things worse for Edna.

Did I say Time crawled? I'm afraid I wasn't clear enough. Time did not crawl. It dropped from all fours, down to its belly, and proceeded to drag itself forward. It felt like an eternity passed us by while we sat on those benches waiting for someone to see us. Two old ladies, completely invisible to all these young, busy cops.

By the time I heard a deep, friendly voice asking for Edna Gomez, I was ready to grab and shake a cop myself or, better yet, let Barbara do the shaking. She was better at it than I was. I turned to see a man, a little older than Rich would have been if he had lived. Abundant salt and pepper hair, unlike Rich, who had lost most of his hair. Light brown skin, not pale like Rich's. Laugh lines around deep-set, hooded, intense, black eyes. I liked laugh lines. Rich had them. About five feet ten inches, he was an inch or two shorter than Rich. I woke up to what I was doing. Why was I comparing this man to Rich?

"Fred Ocampo? Nanding?" Barbara asked, already at the side of the newcomer.

"Barbara Roker?" Fred nodded at Barbara. He turned to me, blinked once, stuck his hand out, and said, "You must be Meg."

I flushed as his twinkling eyes looked me over. Up then down, quickly, discreetly, with a half-smile on his lips. No man had done that for a very long time. Except Rich, of course, when I got dressed up for dinner or parties. I'd forgotten how pleasant it felt to be seen. For the first time in a year, I wished I had taken more care in getting dressed. A bit of color on my lips, maybe?

"In case you two have forgotten, we're here to see Edna," Barbara muttered, giving me a sharp nudge with her elbow at the same time.

My cheeks got warmer, and I tugged on my hand to get it back from his grasp. Pleasant or not, it was too soon for me to enjoy another man's attention.

"Right, have either of you seen Edna?" Fred didn't take his eyes from me, squeezing my hand before letting go.

I tore my eyes away from him. Then snuck a sideways glance at him through my lowered eyelashes. Maybe just a bit of eye candy?

"No! No one wants to speak to us. We've been sitting here waiting all this time for someone to talk to us," Barbara shouted, glaring at everyone within reach.

"Sorry, ma'am. I had something to take care of. Sir, what can we do to help?" The cop who had ignored us all this time had come back and taken his seat again.

"Edna Gomez? You have her?" Fred said, his smile morphing into a polite, somewhat distant, professional one.

I wanted the other smile back, the charming one.

"Let me see," the cop said, pulling his computer monitor closer to him. Behind him, Detective Storm walked into the reception.

"Mrs. Roker, Mrs. Brightbook. I'm afraid you can't see Mrs. Gomez just yet. She's being held for questioning," said Detective Storm.

"About that"—Fred's hand was out, holding a business card—"I'm Mrs. Edna Gomez's attorney. You're not questioning her without counsel present. I expect you know that." Fred was smiling, but not in a nice way.

I was glad to say I was very wrong about this man. His well-tailored suit told me the man made a good living as an attorney. He wasn't a pushover.

Jonathan took the card with the tips of his fingers and passed it over to the cop beside him. "Lawyers," he muttered under his breath.

"Mrs. Gomez is sitting in one of your conference rooms, right? Not in a cell," said Fred with a hard edge to his voice.

Go, man! I cheered him on.

The desk cop looked at Detective Storm and got up when the detective nodded.

Edna, the cavalry is here. But then I remembered…

"Where's Kyle? You arrested Kyle yesterday for Brie's murder," I said.

"We let him go. He had an alibi. Two of his friends came yesterday. One said they were together Friday night till midnight, and the other said Kyle was with her from Friday midnight, all day Saturday, and up to Sunday morning when our divers found Ms. Townsend's body."

Craig came through, and all was good. With Kyle, at least.

"Is Mrs. Gomez the second person you've arrested for the murder? In as many days? Is your evidence any better than it was for the first?" Fred was quick to pounce.

Jonathan shrugged. "I wouldn't have bothered to book him if he hadn't run. And Mrs. Gomez is not under arrest. She agreed to come with us to the station."

"Did she know she had a choice?"

Watching the detective squirm under Fred's questioning, even a little, was most enjoyable, and to make the show even better, right on cue, the door to the station opened to let Dora in.

"Dora, why are you here?" Jonathan left us to walk Dora in personally.

"I heard you arrested Edna. What's happening? You don't believe Edna can do such a monstrous thing as kill Brie. Do you?" Dora said, her beautiful face overwhelmed with distress. Her long, lavish eyelashes swept her face as she looked up at the detective.

Dora, beautiful Dora. Wide, generous, smiling lips, long black hair, and brown, golden skin. But it was Dora's eyes that drew you in. Kind, gentle eyes that made you feel safe, made you feel at home. When Jim had taken her to meet us, I thought I hadn't met anyone so happy and content, so satisfied with her life. Rich had fallen for her as hard as Jim. Neither man would have been happy to see how Dora was now. Gone was the constant smile on her lips. Worry and fear now lurked behind her eyes. Dora had always been slim, burning off calories with the stress of her work. Twelve months after Jim's death, Dora was even slimmer, and the mahogany highlights Jim adored were gone, reduced to stray bits of color at the ends of Dora's black hair. I was livid thinking of Detective Storm replacing Jim in Dora's life.

"Please, there's nothing for you to worry about. We're checking things out. Someone saw something, and we have to pursue it. You know how it goes," said Jonathan, his hand coming up to touch Dora by her waist. She smiled at him briefly and came over to where I was, dislodging his hand as she moved.

"Where is she?" Dora whispered to me as she kissed my cheek. I lifted my shoulders up minutely. Her eyes narrowed. She might have said something more to

Jonathan, but Fred spoke before her.

"Detective Storm, I need to speak with my client. Now would be good."

Jonathan threw Dora a glance. "Excuse me, ladies. This way, Counsel."

"Should we wait?" I called out before the two men disappeared inside.

Fred turned and nodded. Jonathan kept walking.

Chapter Eleven

Liz and Stefan were waiting for us at Sweet Buns when we walked in with Edna. Barbara had called and told them what happened. Veronica, the owner of the café and a neighbor and good friend of Dora's, was standing with them. They took turns hugging Edna. Veronica grabbed Dora's hand and pulled her into the kitchen.

We had caravanned to Sweet Buns from the police station. Barbara and I in my car. Dora in hers. Edna and Fred in his. It didn't take long for Fred to talk Detective Storm out of throwing Edna into jail. At least that was what my watch told me. My heart was convinced a lifetime had passed before I saw Fred come out holding Edna by her elbow. Her steps were hesitant, and her eyes, behind black-rimmed eyeglasses, kept flitting about until she saw us standing in the reception. She broke from Fred and rushed over to us. Barbara, Dora, and I quickly enclosed her in our arms. Edna was so tiny, not even five feet tall. She almost disappeared from view within our embrace. She cried then, with deep, broken sobs. She took her eyeglasses from her face, clutching them in her hands as she tried to stem the tears that kept coming. The desk cop looked away. In shame or discomfort, I couldn't tell.

Barbara and I had driven to Sweet Buns in silence. I had pushed my friends to investigate because I didn't think Detective Storm could solve Brie's murder and catch her killer. Now I was terrified he would stop looking for the real killer, and Edna would pay the price for Brie's murder. We no longer had a choice. We had to find Brie's killer if only to clear Edna.

I led Edna to our usual table. Fred pulled out a chair and got her a bottle of water. Rich was as tender with me. I missed that tenderness, that safety. Would I ever have that again?

We arranged ourselves in our usual seats. Fred dragged a chair over, and we made space for him. He answered questions from Liz and Stefan, except I noticed his eyes didn't stray from Edna for too long. But then, we were all checking on Edna every so often. We were all worried for her. It wasn't every day one got arrested for murder.

We waited for Veronica and Dora to come out of the kitchen with the food Veronica had set aside for Edna and us. You would not have known either woman as one of the Sands Neck society ladies. Both women had black aprons on, the name of the cafe embroidered in green, with their hair bound back with scrunchies, and their faces clear of make-up. Maybe that was why Veronica and Dora were such good friends.

We waited for Veronica to lock the door to the cafe and turn the sign by the door to closed. We waited for everyone to finish their meal. Then we waited some more for Edna to start.

Haltingly, she told her story.

****

"It was about a month ago. Ma had seen the sun shining outside. She turns to me and says, 'Edna, dear. Let's go to Duck Harbor Park. I haven't seen the ducks for some time. Are they still out there waddling around, with the tiny ducklings following after the mother ducks? I miss seeing the children play. I know they can be noisy, but it's good to hear children scream and laugh once in a while. I get to remember how you were all those years ago.'

"I didn't want to go. My stomach bothered me, and I wanted to stay inside, resting. But Ma wouldn't stop. 'Edna, sweetheart,' she tells me, 'See how the sun shines? It's a shame to stay inside today. Who knows how many more sunny days I will have? Let's go, iha.'

"That was that. You know, when your ninety-year-old mother pulls out the 'I don't have many years left' card, you get up and do what she asks.

"We got in the car and I drove to the park. It was sunny. The ducks were waddling around. And the kids were screaming and laughing their heads off. I relaxed after a while. Started enjoying sitting there and watching everyone and everything around me. Especially the smile on Ma's face. She was enjoying herself.

"Then the ice cream man came. You remember the tune he plays? Everyone knows it—even my mother. And you know how much of a sweet tooth she has. She gets up, sees the kids running from the playground to the ice cream truck, and points, 'Iha, look! The ice cream man. Get me an ice cream cone. The one in a waffle cone with nuts on top.'

"I went a little crazy. 'Ma, don't you see the line?' I tell her. By this time, all the kids were out lining up for their ice cream. 'We can go to Sweet Buns and sit and have ice cream. Shorter lines and no screaming kids. And you can even have extra fudge on top of your ice cream, if you want.' I thought that was enough of a bribe for her not to insist on ice cream from the ice cream man.

"Instead, she says to me, 'No, iha. It's not the same. I want the ice cream cone from the ice cream man. The one in a waffle cone with nuts on top. I haven't had it for a long time, and I don't know when I can have it again.'

"There we go again, you see? I give up and tell her, 'Okay, let the kids get theirs and then I'll go over and get you your ice cream.'

"'No, no, iha. He'll leave once he gives the last kid in line his ice cream. And I won't get mine. Go now. Go. The line will go fast, you see. I'll stay here. I won't go anywhere, I promise.' And to show she meant business, my mom pushes me off the bench. She took me by surprise; I almost fell to the ground.

"So I go. I fall in line with the kids. Once in a while, I turn around and check on my mom. Make sure she's still sitting there on the bench. You never know with her. She might take it into her head to follow the ducks. She had always wanted to see where the ducks went when they left the park. I had gotten her to promise me not to follow unless she told me first. But she forgets things now.

"The line was long, and a few of the kids wanted a sundae. The ice cream man took forever making them. Finally, it was my turn. I gave my order and waited for the ice cream man to get it. But one mother came back saying her kid got the wrong ice cream, and could the ice cream man give her the correct one? It took them a few minutes to straighten everything before the mother walked away with the right ice cream cone. The ice cream man handed me my mother's ice cream cone, and I paid him. This took maybe five, ten minutes? I must not have checked on my mom in all that time because I heard a shout, and when I turned around, there was a crowd where my mom was sitting. I hurried over and shoved myself in.

"There, in front of the crowd, was my mother dancing. She was waving her cane around to some beat only she could hear. Some in the crowd were laughing, others were groaning. I dropped her ice cream cone and took her by the shoulder. She had this stupid, lopsided, silly smile on her face. Eyes dilated. High as a kite. I'd seen it before with my nephew, so I knew what it was right away. I ask her, 'What happened?'

"She pointed to a girl standing a few feet away, laughing with her friends. My mom then says, 'That beautiful girl over there with all those beautiful colors in her hair. She gave me her drink. It was red, blue, and white. I said it looked yummy, and she gave me some.'

"'Where's the drink?' I ask.

"My mom pointed to the ground where a plastic cup had fallen, red, blue, and white slush all around it and goes, 'Oops, I must have dropped it.'

"I walk up to the girl. That's when I recognized her. I hadn't seen her in six years. It was Brie. I ask, 'What's in the drink? Why's my mom acting like this?'

"Brie says—as if it was the most ordinary thing in the world—she says, 'It's spiked. But so what? She's having fun, isn't she?'

"I. Got. Mad.

"I got so mad; I slapped her. Hard.

"Then, when she turned to look at me, I say, 'Stay away from my mother. I see you near her again, I'll kill you. I'll kill you and chop you up into tiny bits and pieces. No one will ever find you.'

"Then I left Brie, got my mother into the car, and came home. I haven't seen Brie again since then."

Chapter Twelve

None of us had anything to say after Edna finished her story.

Not for a while, at least.

Then the questions came. Hot and heavy. Fast and furious.

"Why didn't you tell us when it happened?" I was aghast.

"Of all the things you could say, why that?" Barbara demanded.

"You slapped Brie?" Veronica was round-eyed in wonder and, I thought, envy.

"How's your mom?" Dora asked, not caring a twig for Brie.

"And you got mad at me for saying I can see why Brie was murdered?" Stefan ranted at Liz, more upset than I was.

Liz shushed him. "We're focusing on Edna, remember?"

"Oh! Sorry, I got caught up in the story," Stefan said, leaning back in his chair.

Shaking her head at Stefan before beaming at Edna, Liz said, "You go, girl! Give me five! I would have slapped that silly girl three times over if she had done that to my mother."

I checked how Edna's attorney was taking her story. Was it enough to convict Edna? Could he get her off if that was all the cops had on her?

Fred was shaking his head. Not looking sorrowful, but not looking cheerful either. Lawyers. They're hard to read.

"Why did you say that?" He asked.

"I don't know! The words just came out. I wasn't thinking," said Edna.

"Talaga?" Fred asked.

I'd heard Dora say that Filipino word a time or two. It meant...

"Really. Yes," said Edna. "Whatever...the important thing is I didn't do it. I didn't kill Brie. You know me, you must know that."

Edna's eyes begging us to believe her was so wrong; it took me a moment to add my voice to those answering her.

"Mrs. Gomez, how can you say that about us?" Veronica said.

"Of course! Don't be absurd." Dora dismissed the very idea.

"You're out of your mind to even ask." Barbara sounded insulted.

"Edna, we're your friends. We would never think that of you." I put my hand over hers and squeezed it.

"Edna, sweetheart, as much as I love you, you don't have it in you to kill," Stefan said. "You don't even like to cook."

"That's right. Chop Brie up? No way, Edna. Detective Storm is a moron for even thinking of you as a murderer." Liz nodded along with Stefan.

Groans of disgust roiled through the group. Barbara hit Stefan on the shoulder.

"What? Liz and I are saying it's impossible for Edna

to kill Brie. Isn't that a good thing?" He pointed at Edna. "See, she's smiling."

Fred and Edna exchanged a look. It made me uneasy. Somehow, I felt left out. I decided I was being stupid.

"There's more to the story. After I slapped Brie, she stormed out of the park. But not before another girl confronted her. I heard the girl tell Brie to turn around and apologize. At that point, I think Brie had had enough, so she pushed the girl hard. The girl fell on the ground, screaming. I didn't think she fell too badly, but then Brie kicked her in the stomach. I don't know what happened next. I didn't want Ma getting involved in the fight, so I took her back to the car."

"If the police were called, there should be an incident report. I have a contact at the police station. I'll get a copy of the police report if there is one. We could, at least, find out who the girl was and if she's okay," Fred said.

"Yes, let's do that, please. I've been worried sick about the girl, but I didn't know how to find her. I should have stayed and helped her out, but I wanted my mother out of there. The worst part is, I think I know her, but I was too upset to remember who she was. I still can't."

Everyone else made noises about how Edna was not to blame for leaving the girl with Brie, reminding Edna that the girl was stronger than her and younger. I, on the other hand, was thinking this girl might be a suspect. But unless the girl was a certified psychopath, chopping up a body into pieces because she got kicked in the stomach was overkill.

"Nanding, please take me home. Mom is probably frantic by now. I was supposed to stop by and bring her the groceries we forgot to pick up on our way home from the doctor yesterday."

I remembered Gladys's neurologist appointment. No wonder Edna looked so tired and discouraged. It wasn't only being arrested for Brie's murder that was weighing her down.

"How did that go?" I asked.

"The doctor was very nice. He said what my mother was going through was normal and to be expected for her age. I knew that. She has good days. And bad days. Except lately, the bad days are getting longer and worse. She still knows me. Which is good. I think—"

We waited for Edna to continue. Dementia was tough on the family. It was heartbreaking to see yourself erased from your loved one's memory.

"—It's just sometimes it's a younger me she knows." Edna's smile was full of pain. "How much longer can a ninety-year-old brain work perfectly? It's bound to have holes here and there." Edna gave a little laugh. It sounded very like the one I sometimes gave to stop myself from crying in public.

"The doctor made sure I understood there's nothing I could do to make Ma's brain work any better. And he's right. He said it's not like it's a car engine needing oil or whatever else you do to a car to make it run better. My mother's brain will last as long as it can. In the meantime, she'll start forgetting more and more until she no longer knows me. Somehow, I have to make peace with that. And soon, the best place for her might not be at home. But the doctor must be wrong. No one can take care of my mother as well as I do. She knows me. And I know her. Surely, the best place for her is at her home. I might not live with her, but I see her every day. We'll get through this together."

That was Edna, hard-headed as a nut when it came to her mother. Every time we broached the subject with her, Edna refused to discuss care homes or any other solution that would mean moving her mother out of the house she'd lived in since Edna was born. It wasn't done in her culture, Edna had said. Filipinos don't put the Lolas and Lolos in old people's homes. At least not those who grew up in the Philippines. It broke their hearts. They saw it as them being thrown away. If Edna abandoned her mother to a senior home, she wouldn't be able to face her mahjong friends. Abandoned? I suppose assisted living and nursing homes are institutionalized care, but abandoned? That was a bit harsh, and I made the mistake of saying so. Edna blew up at me. Walked out of lunch without finishing her food, something she never did because food was hard to come by when her mother was growing up in the Philippines. We made sure not to push her again on the topic. If this dementia specialist could get through to Edna, I would send a box of premium chocolates to the man.

"Anyway, I want to rest now," Edna said.

"I think you're right." Fred helped Edna stand from her chair, collected her bag, and walked her outside, after saying goodbye to all of us.

Edna merely waved and smiled a sad smile. She patted Veronica and Dora on their shoulders on her way out.

We watched the door close on Fred and Edna.

Barbara rapped her knuckles on the table. "Listen up, we need to get serious here. Edna is not going to jail for Brie's murder. And the only way to make sure she doesn't is for us to find Brie's killer."

I scanned the cafe, my gaze snagged by faces I had seen here before. "Is that Connie Whitfield? Janet said Connie had hosted the last party Brie worked as a server."

Liz looked over from where she sat. "Yeah, that's her. She's cleaned up very well from when she was nine, and she'd come to my class with uncombed hair."

"Who's the guy with her?"

"Lawrence Billings. Larry. He's the husband of her best friend, Eleanor. Sad story." At my puzzled look, Liz continued, "Investment banker. Rich as Croesus. Their house backs up on a cliff. You know how those houses are by Sands Neck? Magnificent views of the bay, with the backyard ending on a sheer cliff. Eleanor fell off the cliff during a backyard party. He tried to save her and ended up almost falling after her. Barely managed to hold on to a root protruding out of the cliff. Happened a few months ago. Rumor has it Larry killed his wife, but the police had to let him go because they couldn't find anything to tie him to the murder."

"If only I were younger," Stefan said, looking at Larry with a wicked gleam in his eye.

"Even then, you didn't stand a chance. Not flush in the pocket enough for Larry," Liz said.

"How plebeian. There are things only I can do that money can't buy. He doesn't know what he's missing."

"Spare us," Barbara said. "Didn't you hear Liz say the man might have killed his wife? You'd sleep with a murderer?"

"If the murderer looked like that, why not? It wouldn't be a bad way to go."

If we wanted Edna cleared of the murder, the four of us had to work together. "Stefan, stop teasing Barbara.

And Barbara, leave Stefan alone. He's winding you up. Forget Larry. Even if he did kill his wife, that's for the police to worry about. Edna is our priority. What do we do next?"

"Fine. You're right. Liz, what have you found so far?" Barbara said.

"I checked Brie. The usual posts. Parties and selfies, all with Brie looking glam."

"Anyone we know with her?" I asked.

"No. Her selfies are almost always just her. Very few with others. And those only show up once. No repeats."

"No partner," Stefan said. "Sexual, romantic, platonic, or otherwise. No one was hanging onto her or glowering at her."

"An obsessed partner would not have let Brie out of their sight. They would have shown up repeatedly in the selfies, even if in the background," Liz agreed.

"How was Selena?" Stefan asked.

"Pregnant," I said.

"Poor child," mumbled Liz.

Whether for Selena or her child, I couldn't tell.

"I found Selena's wedding announcement, so I checked out her husband, too." Liz turned to Barbara. "He's a named partner at Lieberman, Stern, and Reid, out in New York City. The website shows fewer than twenty attorneys. Handles commercial litigation, whatever that is. Divorced with two boys, thirteen and ten."

"Janet told me about the divorce, but not the boys. How did you find out?" I asked.

"His eldest plays soccer, and his law firm sponsors the team." Liz took out a laptop from her bag on the floor. "There's a picture of him and Selena with the soccer team on the law firm's website, with a very short blurb on his family life. Didn't say anything about his divorce, but we would have heard—you know how school gossip is—if Selena had married Alan while in high school, let alone gotten pregnant that young. Ergo, this is Alan's second marriage." She turned the laptop around so the rest could see what was on her screen. "Are we suspicious of Alan?"

"Short answer is yes. He bumped into Brie on Main Street last Friday at four. But Selena said Alan had gone away that Friday on a weekend with his golf buddies," I said. "And there was another woman with him on Friday."

"How do you know Alan was at Main Street last Friday at four? Were you there?" Stefan asked.

"No, I saw him and Brie on CCTV. But let's not tell anyone, especially Fred." I didn't want anyone else to know Archer was hacking into supposedly secure security systems.

"Is Archer hacking into CCTVs? It couldn't be you hacking into CCTVs. You wouldn't know where to start. I would have thought Jim would make sure his son knows not to hack." Liz sounded amused and admiring.

"I would have said so before yesterday. But apparently, Jim was"—I dropped air quotes on the word—"'playing' with Archer on his company's highly secure CCTV network, encouraging Archer to hack into the system. The boy even gave his son hacking tips!"

"We are digressing here, folks. We're talking about why Alan is a suspect." Barbara brought us back to the topic at hand.

"We also met Selena's neighbor as the lady was walking her dog. She said she saw Brie visiting Alan when Selena wasn't around." I gave Barbara a grateful look. Jim teaching Archer how to hack was a subject I did not want to get into. I knew my son was not perfect, but I didn't care to be reminded of it.

Barbara took up the story from me. "And the lady made sure we knew she'd seen them every week. And she also saw Alan hand Brie an envelope every time Brie came calling when Selena wasn't home. An envelope stuffed with money is what I'm getting from her."

"So Alan is paying off Brie. Isn't that wonderful? Brie hasn't changed one bit," Stefan said dryly.

"So that's her game," Liz said, sounding not at all surprised. "Blackmail. That fits. It's not much different from extorting lunch money from classmates scared to fight back. And how old was she then? Nine?"

"It couldn't be anything else, could it?" Thinking of Alan getting blackmailed for cheating on his wife was fine by me. But Brie, as the blackmailer, disturbed me. I still thought of her as my somewhat troubled child, wanting love and not getting it from the people who mattered to her.

"What else could it be? I thought, before you told me about Friday and the woman, that Brie had seduced Alan and threatened to tell Selena. But I didn't think Alan was that stupid. And if Alan was being blackmailed, it had to be over money or sex. I couldn't see Alan paying for anything less. He was either cheating on Selena, who'd strip him of everything he owned when she found out, or he was embezzling client funds. He'd get kicked out of the law firm if that were the case. Losing all that power and prestige can make a man crazy enough to hack somebody into pieces. I would have bet it was the latter. But then, like I said, you told me about the woman," Barbara said.

Liz was busy clicking away on her laptop while Stefan looked over her shoulder. "Do you know you can search the Web for social media posts and news articles using a photo? Will you look at that?" She slid the laptop to the center of the table, swiveling it so we could all see the screen. Barbara leaned over from where she was sitting.

"Is this the same woman you saw?" Liz pointed to the figure beside Alan.

"Yes," I said.

"That is definitely not Selena," Stefan said.

"But this is definitely Alan Reid," Barbara and I said in unison, our eyes on the man whose arm was around the woman who wasn't Selena. And the two were, in the next picture, quite thoroughly and enthusiastically kissing each other while the crowd behind them sprayed them with beer.

Liz took the laptop back, fingers tapping, the screen changing. "Let's see what we find if I crop Alan out and"—a few more screens came and went until Liz stopped and turned her laptop around—"Bingo! I am constantly amazed at how people can find so many ways to screw each other up. Barbara, you weren't that far off in why Alan was being blackmailed."

"Prominent East End residents, Sara and Abe Lieberman, attending the town's annual New England Clam Chowder festival." Stefan read the photo's caption. "She's his partner's wife? The senior partner? He's got balls. Bigger than mine, for sure."

"Wait"—I waved my hands at the group—"We might be looking at this the wrong way. That photo is blatant. That kiss before all those people? With beer pouring over them? Are you sure it wasn't an office party that got out of hand? Bring it back up, Liz. Let's look at it again."

Four heads crowded, eyes scanning the faces behind Alan and Sara.

"I don't see Abe," Stefan said. "Do you?"

Three heads shook "no."

"What makes you think they know these people? The guys spraying them with beer are in their twenties." Stefan peered closer. "And the bar, quite frankly, looks like a dive. Reminds me of the bars I used to hang out in my twenties." A slight smile played on Stefan's lips.

"And this was posted by"—Liz pointed to the tagline—"thedude999."

"If I were Alan, I would pay Brie to bury that photo and keep her mouth shut," Barbara said. "His partner's wife. You're right, Stefan, his are bigger than yours."

For once, Stefan couldn't find the words to answer Barbara. His mouth kept opening and closing. Then he shook his head and looked away. But not before I saw the grin he kept fighting to keep off his face.

As much as I didn't want to, I couldn't help but agree with my friends. Blackmail and Brie. It explained the expensive clothes, shoes, and bags. Come to think of it, it also explained why she was willing to work with Janet. All those society hosts and hostesses with deep pockets, not counting their similarly wealthy, if not wealthier, guests. And almost everyone hiding a secret they're willing to pay money to keep. They might as well have handed Brie the code to their bank accounts.

Chapter Thirteen

"Kyle must have known," I said out loud, startling Barbara.

"About the blackmail? Of course he does."

I was driving Barbara home after a quick stop at my place to let Cannoli out. I had also told my friends about Brie and David Katz, as well as how angry David was with Brie. Liz said she might drop by to see the jeweler on her way home. Stefan said it was a good excuse for Liz to get another pair of earrings. We left the two squabbling good-naturedly with each other while they trolled for information on David.

"Even in high school, Brie always used another to get what she wanted, some sucker who's half in love with her. Or at least, in lust if not in love." Barbara squared her back against the car's seat. "I can't imagine Brie would have changed all that much, six years later on."

"Probably not." I slowly pulled into my driveway. I parked the car and unlocked the seatbelt, grabbing my bag from the back of the car. Pushing the door open, I swung my legs out of the car and stood. Searching for my house keys, I took the few steps needed to get to my front door, inserted my key, and tried to turn the lock. But the door swung open, the key still in the lock. Puzzled, I walked into my house. My bag fell from numb fingers, hitting the carpet with a muffled thud. I staggered forward as Barbara walked into me, unable to stop as suddenly as I had.

"What's wrong with you? You can't stop in the middle of the room—" Barbara's words stopped abruptly.

I stood, bereft of words like her, both hands raised, covering my mouth, silencing my screams as I looked at the wreckage of my home.

Chairs were ripped open, upholstery wires and stuffing flapping free. The brown leather recliner Rich used to sit on was on its side. The large, ornate mirror above the piano was taken off its hooks and was lying face down on the carpet. Family photos joined the mirror on the carpet, broken glass glinting here and there, obscuring the smiling faces of my family. Music sheets that hadn't been touched since Rich died were scattered around the carpet, spilled from the overturned piano bench. A few of the pages fluttered from the breeze coming through the open door. Someone, not me, not Rich, had taken those music sheets out. The baby grand's lid was propped open, piano strings exposed for the first time in twelve months. Someone, not me, not Rich, had opened the piano's lid. I felt violated. Exposed.

Worse, holes dotted the walls everywhere—some massive, others not. Someone had taken a hammer and smashed sheet rock, unearthing electrical wiring and plumbing.

Softly at first, a low humming sound was heard. The sound gained strength as it kept on, building itself up, turning itself into a moan, a keening.

I wondered who it was making all that noise, but then Barbara was there, holding me upright, shaking me hard, making my head snap back. Shocked, I closed my mouth.

The noise stopped.

"Are you okay?" I heard Barbara ask. My friend's voice sounded so far away, almost as if I were hearing it underwater. But that wasn't right. Barbara's nose was nearly touching mine. I opened my mouth to say I was okay, but instead, that uncanny, freaky noise came back. Barbara embraced me hard. I buried my head in my friend's neck, closing my mouth once more, grateful not to hear that god-awful noise.

"Hush, hush. We'll get through this. It'll be okay. C'mon, let's get out of here. Back to the car." Barbara stepped back from the house, guiding me. "Yes, that's it. Let's get back inside the car."

Outside, I stopped. What was I doing outside? My house was a mess. I needed to clean it. Straighten up the chairs, put the photos back on the walls. The walls! I needed to call a handyperson to fill those holes. Holes? I slowly sank to the ground. Brain frozen, I ignored Barbara's pleas to keep standing, to keep moving. The grass looked very inviting, the car was nowhere in sight, no matter what Barbara said, and my legs couldn't hold me up anymore. I collapsed on the grass and folded my head onto my knees. Hands wrapped around my head, I huddled while sense deserted me, and time stood still. For how long, I didn't bother to measure.

It could have been minutes.

Hours.

Years.

I was in a black hole.

Until the feel of a wet nose followed by a flicker of a wet tongue against my fingers brought me out of my stupor.

Cannoli!

Oh, my aching heart. I opened my arms to Cannoli. My pet jumped right in and made herself comfortable. Stroking the wiggling bundle of energy calmed me, and my senses slowly returned, my eyes focusing once more on my surroundings. I unfolded myself and looked around.

A cop car, parked by the sidewalk, had its lights flaring in every direction. Barbara was by the door talking to someone. No ambulance, though. Thank heavens for small mercies.

Standing up, I checked my watch, reminded that Archer would be getting off the school bus soon. I still had an hour to go before he got here. "Barbara?" I called out. Barbara hurried to my side, leaving the man standing by the door. "Where did you find Cannoli?" My hand caressed Cannoli's head.

"She was hiding underneath your bed. She might have made a mess there. Poor dear was shaking when the cops found her."

"One more mess will not matter. Archer will be getting off the school bus in less than an hour. I have to call Dora and tell her I won't be able to have Archer here. I'd have to drive him home. What needs to be done? What did the cops say?" I narrowed my eyes at the man, standing motionless at the side, looking at us talking.

"Are you feeling better, Mrs. Brightbook?" The man had taken the few steps separating us from him. It was Detective Storm. Did I need this headache now? "Can you talk? We have a few questions about the house."

I blinked. "Sure. But my grandson's school bus will be here in an hour, and I need to tell Dora I can't have him here." A movement by the door caught my eye.

Another cop was standing there. "I have to see my house—"

"I'm sorry, but you can't go inside the house right now."

"Not go inside? Why not? It's my house!"

"Yes, but it's being processed. When we're done, you can go back in, but not yet."

"But—" I waved my hands. "How am I—"

"Meg, look at me," Barbara said, touching my cheek and turning my face. "It's okay. It'll be okay."

"Archer—"

"Don't worry about Archer. I called Dora. And the school. His teacher will make sure he gets on the right bus. The one that will drop him off at home. Dora said she'll get Rosita to stay with him until she gets home from work."

"Rosita?" I blinked back the tears threatening to drop and embarrass me. "Yes, of course. Rosita. Dora would call Rosita." I knew Rosita adored Archer. She'd drop everything for him.

"Detective, do you have to question her now? Can't it wait?" Barbara held onto me, kept me standing. "She needs to rest now. Get over the shock. If I bring her to Dora's house, she'll see her grandson, so she can stop worrying about him. And Dora's a doctor, so Meg will get to see a doctor, which is what she needs now. You can come over to Dora's house tomorrow morning to talk to her. Wouldn't that be better, don't you think?"

Jonathan shifted his body, checking on his man waiting for him in front of the house. He glanced back at me, saw how my eyes were going in and out of focus. Saw how my body was convulsing with tremors every few seconds. "Fine. I can see she's very shaky." Turning to me, he said, "Mrs. Brightbook, please tell Dora I'll be over tomorrow. We'll finish this interview then."

"My bag—" My head swiveled, searching the grounds. I had no idea what had happened to my bag.

"I have it." Barbara handed me the bag dangling over her arm. To the detective, she said, "The house key is in the door lock. Make sure you lock up when you're done and bring the key back tomorrow when you see Meg."

Jonathan tipped his head to us and left, waving his man to go ahead of him as he strode inside the house.

Grumbling, Barbara herded me back into the passenger side of my car with Cannoli getting in the back. "Cannoli, behave yourself, girl. No jumping in front and distracting me. Meg, put your seatbelt on. I'll take you both to Dora's house. What a day!" Barbara backed out of the driveway, barely sparing a glance at all the neighbors bunched up on the sidewalk.

I ignored the rest of my friend's complaints, knowing this was Barbara's way of letting off steam. The tears I had held off falling from my eyes, dripping slowly down my cheeks and chin. I made no effort to wipe them off. My heart ached. My home. My beautiful home I had shared with Rich.

Forty-three years we were married. Rich was twenty-four. I was twenty-one. Jim had turned up three years after the wedding. The year Jim turned five, Rich had worked up the numbers and declared there was enough money coming in to upgrade from our poky three-bedroom first home to a four-bedroom, three-bathroom, two-story home in Whitman's Port. Jim could go to the same school I taught in and be with teachers I knew. Jim made friends with kids on the block, all of whom made free of our house, running in and out at all hours during the summer, as Jim did with their houses. Most days, the kids ran out of my house, clutching a cookie grabbed from the cooling cookie sheet on top of my oven. These kids were now grown, as Jim had. Moved away and had families, as Jim did.

Rich would have been livid to see what had been done to the house he had treasured over the years. How could someone treat our home this way? What had I done to make someone walk in and punch holes in our walls? A sob escaped me. My hand came up to stifle the rest, my fingers pinching my mouth hard. I felt Barbara throw me a glance, but I turned my head away. My eyes glazed over, not seeing the houses and streets flying past.

Blinking fast, I struggled to bring myself back under control. Archer would be home by the time Barbara dropped me off. I must not show a tear-streaked face to the boy. He'd panic. I calmed myself down and lowered my hand to my lap. "Thanks, I'll be okay."

"You better be." Barbara's smile took the sting out of her words. "When what happened here goes viral, and you know by this time it has, with all those neighbors watching that show in front of your house. All the cops, whirling lights, and whatnot. I'm sure all the mothers in town have been texting me about you, because my phone hasn't stopped pinging since we drove away." Barbara pressed her mouth into a thin line. "And when I get a chance to answer these texts, I want to say, in all honesty…" Barbara pitched her voice higher, making it syrupy sweet. "She's fine! Nothing to worry about." Her voice changed back to normal. "I probably should make it an auto-answer. Save myself the aggravation of typing it repeatedly."

I laughed shakily. It was good to have friends.

Chapter Fourteen

The doorbell rang, setting off Cannoli, whose docked tail wagged hard as she barked and ran up and down the hallway. The poor dear was having a harder time than I was with our move to Dora's house, however briefly.

Rosita let Detective Storm in while Cannoli followed closely on her heels.

"Is Mrs. Brightbook available? I meant Dora." The man had come early Wednesday morning as he said he would.

"She here." Rosita's light voice floated down the hallway to where Dora and I sat. "Not Mrs. Meg? You supposed to talk to Mrs. Meg about her house. They both in the dining room."

We heard footsteps as Rosita showed the detective to the dining room, taking Cannoli with her when she left. I felt sorry for my pet, whining and yipping as Rosita chivied her away. A nice long walk would have settled her down. And I intended to give her just that as soon as I got rid of the detective.

"Would you like some coffee?" Dora offered as the man came into view.

"Black, please. If you have it." Detective Storm came into the room.

I sipped my coffee, waiting for the detective to begin asking his questions. What happened yesterday still felt unreal to me, and I kept blocking images of my wrecked home from my mind.

Dora had gotten up to pour coffee for the detective. Black, as he had asked, no sugar. After handing it over, she took the chair next to me. Dora had stayed home from work today, on top of leaving work early yesterday for Edna. Archer had been all smiles, getting on the bus with his mother waving goodbye by the curb.

The hospital staff must be in shock, I mused.

"We finished processing the house last night." Jonathan pulled a chair opposite us and sat down. "With no one hurt"—he quickly added when Dora's eyebrows rose—"which is a good thing, not a bad one. No one wants anyone hurt; that would be bad."

I hid a smile as I took another sip of my coffee. The detective was babbling.

"It didn't take long," he continued, bringing his mug to his lips and taking a gulp. I wondered if he had burned himself, as the coffee was freshly made.

"We dusted for fingerprints, but we need yours, your mother-in-law's, and your son's. For elimination purposes." He said wryly, "To be honest, it's a long shot. Perps don't leave fingerprints behind, what with all these crime shows on TV and movies. Gloves, masks, B&E 101. That's Breaking and Entering, in case I wasn't clear." Jonathan's face softened when Dora nodded and smiled at him. The man's arrogance left him when Dora was around. "But we do have some leads."

"Oh?" I perked up.

"Your neighbors—"

"What about them?" I didn't want any of my neighbors messing about with anyone who punched holes in my home with such wild abandonment. Men like that were dangerous.

"Your next-door neighbor came with her son—"

"Nico?" I interrupted, putting my mug down on the table.

"Yes."

The detective's voice sounded clipped, and I could see his temper rising. I clasped my hands tightly and decided I had better let the man finish and not stop him every few words.

"Anyway, your neighbor asked what had happened. I told her you had a home invasion, but you're okay. And your friend took you to your daughter's home."

I kept my mouth shut and didn't correct him.

"She said her son had stayed home from school yesterday. And when he's at home sick, he spends the day looking out the window, watching the street, and the people come and go. About mid-morning, the boy had come clattering down the stairs, shouting that he saw two men go up your driveway and into your house. He said that was not right because he saw you and Principal Roker drive away earlier. And you wouldn't let anyone go inside your home if you're not there."

I unclasped my hands, one hand moving slowly outwards, my fingers looking for something to hold on to. Dora, beside me, reached out, taking my lost hand into her own, patting it between her hands, and squeezing it. I shifted in my chair and clutched Dora's hands. I needed the comfort Dora was giving.

"Your neighbor said she's very sorry she didn't pay much attention to her son, and you would know why."

Like most thirteen-year-olds, Nico made things up for the sheer delight of seeing the shock on his audience's face. He'd start laughing and own up that it was all a big story. He had done the same when he was in my class years back. I didn't blame his mother for not paying attention to every single word he said. I didn't when I was his kindergarten teacher.

Jonathan continued, "She seemed to think she could have done something to stop the home invasion. I said it was better for her and her kids if she had stayed home. If anything, she could have called the police, but she wouldn't have known what they were doing to your house, looking from the safety of her house."

"Did Nico see the men clearly?" Dora asked.

"He thinks he can recognize one, the guy wearing a baseball hat, pulled down. The other one had his hoodie pulled over his head. The guy with the baseball hat looked up, so Nico saw his face, but the other guy must have said something because the first guy pulled his hat down even lower. That's also why the boy was suspicious. He said from then on, both guys kept their heads down, shoulders hunched, and didn't look up or around them."

"Were they carrying something? A hammer?" I said. "They punched holes in my walls."

"No, they had nothing with them. Anyway, they didn't need a hammer. They used one of your solid metal lamps. We found it on the carpet, full of drywall particles and dust."

I released my hand from Dora and pressed my lips closed.

After one look at me, Jonathan hurried on. "We did get the make and model of their car. A gray Honda Accord, four-door. And the license plate."

"You found out who these men were?" Dora demanded, leaning over the table.

Jonathan shifted in his chair, taking another gulp of his by-now cold coffee. "Unfortunately, no. The license plate was for a Ford truck, stolen yesterday evening by the South Shore. And there's a report of a gray Honda Accord stolen early this morning, also by the South Shore. Someone went to a lot of trouble to make sure we couldn't find them. But don't worry, we'll find them. There are CCTV cameras all over those streets."

Dora and I leaned back in our chairs. This was a lot for me to take in, and looking over at my daughter-in-law, for Dora as well.

"What next, then?" Dora asked,

"The way the house was, we think the men were after something. It wasn't a robbery. We found jewelry scattered on the floor and on the bed," Jonathan said. "Mrs. Brightbook, I have to ask. Do you have any enemies?"

"Meg? Enemies?" Dora interjected. "Jonathan, be serious. Everyone I know loves Meg. Enemies? What could she possibly have done to make enemies?"

I kept quiet. Dora was right. There was nothing I did that could have angered someone so much they would send two bullies to my home. And I firmly told myself this had nothing to do with our meddling in Brie's death. All we'd done so far was talk to the girl's aunt and sister. Liz mucking into social media didn't count. Everyone does that nowadays. Anyway, Detective Storm said the home invaders were looking for something. If not my jewelry, which was not worth much, what did I have that anyone wanted?

"And what could they possibly be looking for in her house?" I heard Dora ask Detective Storm, echoing my thoughts.

"We don't know. The boy said the men walked away with nothing."

"They didn't find what they were looking for," I whispered, dread filling my voice. "Will they come back, you think?"

Jonathan said nothing. The silence stretched. Could I go home? Was it safe to go home?

"That settles it. You're staying here. Until they find who did this." Dora got up, her hand on my shoulders. "I'm going to the house to get some clothes and things for you. Cannoli will need her things, too." Turning to Detective Storm, she said, "Can you or one of your guys come with me? I'm not comfortable going alone to the house."

"Of course. Not a problem. I'm free right now, and there are a few things I still need to check in the house." Jonathan also got up, following Dora out of the room, nodding a quick goodbye to me. "I had my guys put back as much as they can..." Jonathan's words trailed off as he followed Dora out of the house.

And that quickly, I was left homeless.

As much as it pained me, Dora was right. I couldn't go home. I wouldn't be able to sleep, thinking how, at any moment, the two bullies could come back, looking for whatever it was they wanted. If they had only left a note for me on what they wanted, I would have happily left it to them. I was glad Jonathan went with Dora to the house in case the two bullies came back. I thought of how Jonathan behaved this morning. He was a very different person around Dora. He had answered my questions and explained where he could.

"That man gone? I put Cannoli in your room. She smart dog. She no like the detective." Rosita came to take the dirty mugs and the coffee pot to the kitchen. "He better off looking for someone else. Mrs. Dora not ready for anyone yet. She busy crying inside."

"Crying inside?"

"Yes, I tell Archer that. He ask one day why his mom not cry. I say, she cry inside. He say, not like me? I cry outside, he say. Poor baby."

"Rosita, I've never thanked you for taking care of Archer this past year. Thank you. I don't know how Dora and Archer could have managed without you."

"Is nothing, Mrs. Meg. Dora and Archer, they part of my family. I been here a long time." Rosita stood still for a moment. "When Mr. Jim died, it broke my heart. It hurt here, bad." She thumped her chest. "Archer, he was not good. Dora was not good. I try to help. Fix them. But hard, you know. Mr. Jim, he a lovely man. You did good there, Mrs. Meg."

I swallowed a sob before it got past my heart.

"I offer to Mrs. Dora I come mornings too. I know Mr. Jim did breakfast for Archer and sent him to school. Mrs. Dora can no do that. I say, I can. I can do that for them. Little help, you know. Easy for me. I get out of the house early. What is that? No one there for me anyway. Jose out to work. All the girls gone. They no need me anymore. Not then, anyway." Rosita gave me a pained smile, her lips stiff and frozen. "But Archer. Archer need me."

Dora had said something about one of Rosita's daughters getting hurt. I hoped it wasn't serious. "Everything okay with you, Rosita?"

"Is life, Mrs. B. What can you do?" With a fatalistic shrug, Rosita carried on with her work. "Sometimes we make mistakes. Some big. Oh yes, some very big,"

Rosita whispered the last words to herself.

What was that about? I resolved to ask Dora about it. Maybe I could help. Rosita's children were all grown now. Two had married in the past three years, but not one had given her and Jose a grandchild. Rosita showered Archer with all of her pent-up grandmotherly love. She had watched him on the few times I couldn't do it, had even slept over when Dora and Jim went away, when Rich and I were also out of town.

Everyone in Sands Neck knew Rosita and her family. Rosita kept their house clean, their pantry stocked, and the fridge full. Sometimes, she even made dinner. The plumbing leaked, and Rosita sent her handyman husband, Jose, over to fix it or anything else broken. Her nephew's landscaping company mowed and fertilized the lawn, hauled the leaves away when they fell, and plowed the snow out of the driveway. Rosita's son-in-law opened the pool, cleaned it weekly, and closed it when the season ended. Rosita or one of her daughters took suits to the cleaners and picked them up. Rosita and her family took over once Rosita was hired, freeing the lady of the house from all her worries.

Eyebrows rising to my forehead, I realized here was someone who knew where the bodies were buried, so to speak.

"Rosita, you've worked at Sands Neck for a long time, haven't you?" I tried to sound casual with my question. Judging from Rosita's puzzled face, I wasn't succeeding.

"Yes, Mrs. Meg. Before Jose and I married. Thirty-five years now."

"The same houses?"

"No. First, I work for Mrs. Connie's mother. When

101

she move to Florida, she said take care of Mrs. Connie. So now I work for Mrs. Connie. Mrs. Veronica's mother died, so she told me I work for her now. The others, they move so I go to another house."

"Where do you go when you're finished here?"

"After Archer get on school bus, I go to Mrs. Connie. I make her breakfast, make her bed, clean up room and make dinner, if she ask. Mrs. Connie, she no like anyone else touching her clothes or cooking for her. She says only I know how to cook her food. I go to Mrs. Eleanor after Mrs. Connie. Clean house and do laundry for Mrs. Eleanor. Afternoons, it's Mrs. Veronica. Wait for kids to get home, drive them to after-school, feed them, and wait for Mrs. Veronica to get home."

"Mrs. Eleanor, is that the woman who fell off a cliff during a house party? Larry Billing's wife?

Rosita nodded.

"Were you there when it happened?"

"Yes." Rosita was backing away from me. "Why you ask?"

"No reason. I saw him with Connie at Sweet Buns yesterday. They're good friends, right?"

"Mrs. B, why you asking me these questions? I not know if he and Connie good friends," Rosita said, taking off her apron and bundling her hands into it. "Anyway, I was at kitchen. Not my job to worry about what they do with themselves."

"You didn't see Mrs. Eleanor fall then?"

Rosita shook her head, her lips pursed and her eyes narrowed, the color in her face draining.

"Were you also at Connie's party the week before?"

"I no remember."

Not remember? Dora always said she only had to tell

Rosita once. The woman never forgot anything. Didn't even bother to make a list. Laughed at Dora for making lists. If I didn't know better, I'd say Rosita was terrified. But of what? I rushed to reassure the woman. "I'm just being nosy, Rosita. Too many sudden deaths lately in town. Larry's wife, then Brie. You heard about Brie?"

"I know nothing. Why you think I know anything? I wash. I clean. I keep my mouth shut. Not my business. Mrs. Meg, don't put nose where it no belong. Let that detective take care of it. His job, not yours." Rosita bustled out of the room and called over her shoulder, "If you need anything, write it on paper hanging on fridge. I buy groceries twice a week."

That was clumsy of me. I spooked Rosita with my questions. Tattling on her employers was the fastest way to get fired, and Rosita needed the money. She wasn't scrubbing toilets for the love of it. I decided it was better to get my information elsewhere. It wasn't fair of me to ask Rosita to risk her job. I went upstairs to fetch Cannoli for her morning walk.

Chapter Fifteen

Noontime. Sweet Buns was busy as usual—noise, lines, crowds. After yesterday, I needed the normalcy of our weekly lunch at Sweet Buns.

Barbara drove up shortly before noon and bundled me into the car, saying the rest of the gang was waiting for us. Stefan and Liz were in line, waiting to place orders. Edna wasn't here yet. Barbara sat with me, looking at me sideways now and then, and not saying a word.

"I won't break, you know. Edna didn't break. Neither will I."

"Maybe we should stop investigating Brie's murder." Barbara finally met my eyes, fear showing deep inside.

"Why would Brie's killer ransack my house? It doesn't make sense. And Detective Storm said the men were looking for something. I don't think destroying my house had anything to do with Brie." My house, not my home. It wasn't my home that was destroyed yesterday. I kept repeating to myself. That had already happened twelve months ago when Rich and Jim were taken from me. I refused to break down over what those two toughs had done to me.

"Why then? Why destroy your house?"

"I don't know. But Nico saw the men and got their license plates. Detective Storm seems to think they've got a good chance of finding whoever did it. Right now, I don't want to think about the house. We can't stop now. How about Edna?"

"Edna has an attorney to protect her. Who do you have against those thugs? You sure you're okay?" Barbara asked.

I looked out the window, seeing the playground, the park, the trees, the bay. Bringing my gaze inside the café, I stared at the line snaking alongside the counter and the tables, the staff taking orders, and the customers giving their orders, shouting so they could be heard over the buzzing noise. Taking the time to ask myself the same question. Was I okay? Was Edna okay?

"So-so," I told Barbara. It was true. I wasn't quite all there, but I won't crumble like a cookie. I was over my hysterics of yesterday. And despite what I said to Barbara, and what I'd been ardently telling myself, a part of me insisted there had to be some connection, some link tying what had happened to my house and Brie's murder to each other. I was even more determined to find Brie's killer. No one was bullying me around.

"I called my niece after I dropped you off at Dora's." Barbara was tapping her fingers on the table.

"Yes?" I remembered Barbara's niece also ran a catering business. One that was also popular with Sands Neck society ladies. Barbara must have decided it was best to change the topic. She knew how stubborn I got when pressed.

"My niece said business has been incredibly busy these past few months. She'd had twice the bookings she usually gets. And wasn't very surprised to hear Janet is struggling because the new business was mostly Janet's old business. Families who used Janet for years were calling and booking the services of Elegant Dining. She felt bad, but business is business. And she hadn't done anything, mind you, to steer them away. Not even a targeted mailing."

"Within the past few months, she said? About the time Brie started working for Janet?" Kyle's arrest had pushed Janet's empty calendar out of my mind.

"I thought you'd find it interesting. I did. But how does that get us anywhere closer to finding out who killed Brie?"

"We need to talk to the ones who hired Janet within the past six months. One of them was being blackmailed by Brie." At last, a clue we could do something with.

"Why kill Brie? Why not call the cops on Brie for the blackmail?"

"And let the whole world in on their dirty secrets? I don't think so."

"So we what? Walk up to these society ladies and say, 'Hi, you don't know us, but were you being blackmailed by Brie? You know, the girl who was fished out from Duck Harbor in pieces last weekend? And by the way, did you kill Brie?' " Barbara's smile was half-amused, half-amazed, and wholly exasperated.

I knew it was a crazy idea. And it would have been better if it came from Liz. She knew how to make anything sound sensible, no matter how crazy. I didn't. The society ladies of Sands Neck moved, as they liked to tell themselves, on a more rarefied level than the rest of us living by Poet's Bay. How could we get to them?

"Veronica," I said. "Veronica is one of them."

"One of whom?" Liz had come back with Stefan, our lunch orders in their hands.

"Meg here thinks one of Sands Neck society ladies

killed Brie," said Barbara, checking the labels of the sandwiches grouped in the center of the table and taking one marked as grilled chicken, lettuce, and tomato, with mustard on rye.

"Because she's twenty-one, fresh and beautiful, and their husband couldn't keep his hands off the girl? Wouldn't it be easier to take said husband to some hot-shot divorce lawyer, clean out his bank account, and shack up with the pool guy? I mean, all that blood and gore? Why bother?" Stefan grabbed a sandwich.

Liz nodded, agreeing with Stefan's every word while taking a bite of her food.

"My niece said her business is booming because Janet's customers have abandoned her." Barbara was slathering more mustard on her grilled chicken. She told Stefan and Liz about my theory, ending with, "So Meg thinks if we can find who was being blackmailed, we'd find Brie's killer."

"You think one of those spoiled, indulged ladies had done something so—I don't even know how to describe it—" Liz shook her head. "What could one of those soft, pampered, manicured ladies do that would make them pick up a carving knife and kill like that? Assuming they even know their way around the kitchen to find the carving knife. Or how to use one."

"Society ladies don't like to get their hands dirty. They might hire someone to do the killing for them. But if they did, the killer wouldn't be this unhinged. This killing of Brie is not by a society lady. Not possible," Stefan said. "And anyway, shouldn't we make sure Brie was indeed blackmailing Alan before we make that leap?"

"Ladies, we don't have much time to argue about

this. Detective Storm has his eyes on Edna. No telling what he'll do next," I said. "We don't have anything else to work with. Do we?"

"Tell you what, here's a society lady who hired Janet this past six months," Liz put her food down, waving a woman coming off the line over to our table. "Let's ask her. Connie!" Liz had gotten up, waving Connie over to where we sat. "I'm sure you know everyone at the table."

"Yes, of course," said Connie, exuding elegance and wealth in every inch, as she had in the photo Janet had shown me. She was dressed in high-end leggings and a cropped top showing a tight, toned midriff. I swallowed a sigh of envy. Not even in my heyday did I look that good. And Connie was in her early thirties. Life was not fair.

"How are you?" Connie included everyone in her greeting, a chorus of "fine" answering her. She turned to me. "How's the investigation?"

"Excuse me?" Startled, I didn't know how to answer.

"Your house," said Connie. "We heard about your house. Did the cops find out who did it? I was telling Larry about it."

A man—presumably, Larry—had come up beside Connie, murmuring his greetings to the group. Larry looked suave and smooth, finished, nothing rough about him. He wore a plain black shirt that rippled when he moved, paired with black jeans tapered to fit his lean, muscled legs. "I'm so sorry to hear about your loss. Whoever did it is a monster."

"Thank you. But not as sorry as I am to hear about your loss," I said, remembering what Liz had said yesterday about Larry, but appalled at myself for bringing it up. I wasn't a gossipy old lady looking for something sensational to pass on to other old gossipy ladies. Like the ones around me right now.

"Poor Eleanor. Larry is so heartbroken. I've been making sure Larry goes out and about, and doesn't molder in his house. That's what friends do, don't they?" Patting Larry's arm once, twice, Connie asked me, "Did you hear back from the police?"

"Detective Storm came by this morning. He said they're following some leads." I was reluctant to give any information. "Did you also hear about Brie? Weren't you two here last Sunday as well?"

"Oh, that girl whose body was dumped in Duck Harbor?" Larry said, shifting the bag of food in his hands. "I haven't seen anything about it in the papers other than the police had found the body and were investigating. Did you, Connie?"

"No, not me. I don't read the papers. Pip might have, but it's not something we'd talk about, you know. I've known Brie and Selena since we were very young. We lived next door to each other. I mean, we didn't exactly play with each other. I was a few years older than them, but we did go to the same birthday parties." Connie hesitated. "Well, for a time at least. They stopped showing up at the birthday parties. Some scandal or other, my mother told me. But I heard Mrs. Gomez was arrested yesterday. Mrs. Gomez? What is that all about? The cops can't possibly think Mrs. Gomez can kill anyone."

"I heard she threatened Brie in public," Larry said. "Something about Brie hurting her mother?"

"We all say things we don't mean when we're

angry," Connie retorted.

"Didn't Janet cater a party for you recently? Did you see Brie?" Liz asked, cutting in and getting the conversation back on track.

"I throw a lot of parties, and I only use Black Gloves, so you'd have to be more specific on the timing. If Brie were working for Janet, she might have been serving. I wouldn't know. I don't pay much attention to the servers as long as they do their jobs. And if they don't, I would have gone to Janet and told her to fix whatever was wrong."

Connie's face tightened up, her eyes hardening and her mouth pursing so minutely it was gone before I was sure of what I saw. She knew something. "Where were you last Friday?" I asked.

"Me? I was in Paris with my husband for the weekend. We flew out late Friday night. He had a business meeting Saturday morning, and I wanted to go shopping," Connie said, surprise showing on her face. "Here's my flight info." Connie took her phone out and, after a few clicks, handed it to me.

Connie's email from her travel agent had the flight number and times from New York to Paris, then back to New York. They were all red-eye flights, with enough time for Connie to have been strolling on Main Street on Friday afternoon, catch a flight to Paris, and return Saturday night to New York and be at Sweet Buns on Sunday morning. Connie might have been dead on her feet, jetlagged, but clearly, there wasn't enough time for her to kill Brie on Friday midnight. But was it true for Larry as well?

"What about you?" I turned to Larry.

"Me?" Larry sounded like a broken record. "I didn't

even know the girl. What does it matter where I was Friday?"

Connie might have been thousands of miles away, across a big body of water. But not Larry. Not the way he avoided answering my question. I waited him out.

"Fine, if you must know, I was out to dinner with a very important investor."

"Where?"

"Some restaurant in the City. I don't remember. You want me to dig out the receipt and get you the name of the restaurant?"

"There's no need to get so upset, Larry. Didn't you say you were meeting Martin at the latest steakhouse by 57th Street?" Connie said. "I don't know how you could forget. The restaurant's name is Fifty Seven. It's very exclusive with a long wait list. Anyway, we have to go. The weather outside is gorgeous, and we're taking our lunch out by the park. Have to run before all the seats are taken." Connie leaned over to Liz, murmuring, "Let's do lunch sometime, why don't we?"

We waited, not speaking, until the door closed on the two, watching Connie and Larry as they crossed the street. Connie waved at us from the street before heading for the park benches by the harbor.

"She's hiding something," Liz said, not a shred of doubt in her voice. "So is Larry. And that something has Brie written all over it." Her voice bleak, Liz continued, "Underneath all that polish, she's still the same Constance Haddad, hiding cigarettes in her backpack. I always knew when she was up to something." Liz was silent for a few moments. "Connie's family owns a meat-packing plant. Out by Brookhaven. Big building. Lots of meat saws."

"You think they killed Brie?" Barbara asked.

Liz looked for Connie amongst the crowd by the harbor. "Connie? I don't think so. At least, I hope not. Larry, on the other hand? I'm not so sure."

"You think he killed Brie?" Stefan said.

"Maybe. But there's nothing to tie him to Brie. His wife used Elegant Dining for catering, not Black Gloves. And everyone says Larry doesn't go for young girls. So, how did Brie find anything to blackmail him over? Even if Brie managed to seduce him and blackmail him, it wouldn't matter. Larry's wife died a month ago. No reason for Larry to pay Brie off, let alone kill her."

Reason or not, I was ready to give Larry up to Detective Storm if it meant getting Edna cleared. More clues. We needed more clues.

Chapter Sixteen

"Where's Edna? She's usually not this late." Stefan checked the street outside. Lunch was almost done, and Edna still hadn't shown up. "I hope Detective Storm didn't come and pick her up again."

"You think he'd do that?" I asked.

Stefan got us so worried, we stared at the door, willing Edna to show up. When it opened, we breathed out in relief. Only to be disappointed when it was Fred we saw. Except it was not the calm, cool, collected, in-charge Fred of yesterday. Today, he looked like a man driven to distraction, out of his wits. His hair stood on end, not combed back, as if he had run his fingers through his hair one too many times. He wasn't wearing his suit jacket, and his shirt sleeves were rolled up and pushed up his arms, showing fine black hair on his forearms. His tie was askew. And his eyes…his eyes had a wild look in them. Like someone desperately looking for something important he had mislaid.

"Good, you're all here," he said, rushing over to their table. "I didn't know any of your numbers, so I took a chance one of you might be here." He faced us squarely and said, "Edna's gone."

"Gone? Gone where?" I said.

"She ran? Why would she do such a stupid thing?" Barbara was as stunned as I was.

"Wait…wait," Liz said. "Is it stupid? If she's not

here, she can't get arrested."

"Gladys?" Stefan asked.

"She's gone too," Fred said.

The four of us looked at each other, our meal forgotten. Fred raked his fingers through his hair again.

He'll lose all his beautiful hair if he's not careful. Maybe I should tell him not to stress his hair so much. Say that again? Maybe I should keep my mind on Edna and Brie's murder. I tore my eyes away from Fred.

"Do you have any idea where she would have run to?" He asked.

We shook our heads mutely.

"And why take Gladys?" Fred groaned.

Of course, Gladys would be gone too. Edna wasn't leaving her mother behind. Who would take care of all the small things Gladys needed? Like getting her dressed? And fed? And cleaned? But how could Edna take care of her ninety-year-old mother away from all the comforts and conveniences of home? And how would Gladys handle it? She was a trooper most of the time, but she liked guilting Edna into things. I didn't want to think of all the different ways things could go wrong.

"Darn it!" Fred gritted his teeth. He dragged a chair over to our table and flopped on it. "I should never have agreed to take Gladys to the hospital."

"What happened?" I said, not liking to see him so upset. And I refused to ask myself why it mattered to me.

"Edna called and asked me to meet her at her mom's house early this morning. She said Gladys had to stay at the hospital for a test, and could I take her? She wasn't feeling up to it because of yesterday. I got there, and she and Gladys were waiting for me in the driveway with two carry-on bags. I helped Gladys into the car and put her suitcases in my trunk. I got back in my car and had turned it on when Edna rapped on the window. She said she had forgotten her mom's toiletries, and could I go inside and bring them out. I thought nothing of it. Edna did say Gladys was staying overnight at the hospital."

"Two carry-ons for an overnight? Man, wasn't that a big enough clue for you?" Stefan said.

"Yes, two bags for one night seemed a lot, but who knows with women?" Fred gave Stefan a dirty look. "I never thought Edna would ever pull a stunt like this on me. It's Edna, for heaven's sake!" Fred threw his hands up.

"And Edna could have been planning on staying at the hospital with Gladys. So two suitcases would have been totally reasonable." I rushed to defend Fred from Stefan, heaven knows why. Only to blush fiery red when the man turned and smiled his thanks at me.

"So I got out of my car as Edna asked. I hadn't turned it off, thinking I'd be just a moment. But when I walked inside the house, I heard my car backing out of the driveway. I ran back outside, but I was too late. Edna had driven away in my car!"

"First, she slaps Brie. Then she drives off with Fred's car. Go, Edna!" Stefan started clapping. "Ouch! Why slap me?" He turned accusing eyes on Liz. "Don't tell me you don't feel the same way."

"Hush, Fred has to finish his story, and he won't if you keep interrupting." Liz mollified her friend, waving her hand for Fred to continue.

"If everyone can wait for me to finish before throwing in their comments?" Fred's voice was very even. Too even.

My friends and I looked at each other and decided

to shut our mouths.

"We're all good now?" When no one said anything more, Fred continued, "I went back inside Edna's house and, after searching her bedroom, the kitchen, the dining room, and the living room, I found her car keys on top of the hallway table. With a note to me." Fred took a slip of paper from his pocket and passed it on to me. "I drove Edna's car to my house, called for a rental car, and waited for it to get dropped off at my house. Then I drove here. Do you have any idea where she'd go? That detective will think he's gotten an early Christmas present when he finds out. If he doesn't outright charge her with the murder, he'll definitely keep her locked up for further questioning."

I looked at the note. It had one word on it, in Edna's handwriting. "Sorry," it read.

"Yes, the note was not very helpful," Fred said when he saw me passing the note to the others. "And yes, running away is a very stupid thing to do."

It struck me he cared for Edna. He wasn't just Edna's lawyer. I wondered who he was to Edna.

"Says you," Liz snapped at Fred. She never could stay silent for long. "You're a lawyer. You're programmed to think that way. This gives us a chance to prove she's innocent without worrying about her getting arrested again."

"You're wrong. This makes it more likely it will happen," Fred snapped right back.

"Liz is right. Detective Storm has to find her first if he wants to arrest her," Barbara said. "And our job is to make sure that doesn't happen. Not until we've solved Brie's murder."

"Sounds like a plan to me." Liz turned to me. "We

need Dora for this. You think she'd help distract Detective Storm?"

Remembering how Dora had helped spring Edna out of jail, I was sure she would and nodded at Liz.

Fred looked thoughtful. He was there when Dora pulled her act on Detective Storm. "Wait, are you ladies seriously thinking of solving the murder? And covering up for Edna?" It wasn't logical, but Fred's face started to brighten up. He was now fighting to keep a smile off his lips.

"Why not? So far, we've found Brie was blackmailing her brother-in-law and possibly some of those pampered dolls in Sands Neck."

I could see Barbara was getting tetchy. I needed to move everyone along. "We need to get going on that. We can't distract Detective Storm for too long. How do we get to the Sands Neck society ladies?"

"That's easy. Get Veronica to throw a party, and we'll go undercover as servers." Liz looked around for Veronica.

"That sounds fun. If you're going undercover, I'm coming with you," Fred said, unable to keep the smile off his face this time.

"As what? You can't be a server. I'm sure most of the guests will recognize you right away," Liz said distractedly while waving for Veronica to come over to us.

"Not if he's undercover. Doesn't that mean he gets to wear a disguise?" Stefan said, earning an even bigger smile from Fred.

"I'm sure I can do something to change how I look." Fred was almost begging now.

Barbara and I exchanged looks. The man wanted to

do this. Why was he no longer worried about Edna?

"What happened to you? One minute you're worrying over Edna, the next you're begging to get into costume," Liz echoed my thoughts.

"It's a party. With lots of people about. Most of whom I know. How dangerous can it get?" Fred said with a laugh. "I'm sure Edna will call one of you before the day ends. When she does, tell her to call me."

"Whatever. Do what you want." Liz had gotten Veronica's attention. "Veronica, darling. We need to mingle with your Sands Neck high society friends. Find out who among them killed Brie. Can you throw a party, and we go undercover as servers?"

Veronica laughed. "You and who else?" Nodding when she saw Liz throw her hand out to us, she said, "When? This Saturday? That's three days away. Oh well, I'll call Janet now. I heard she's not busy. She should be able to fit me in. But you'll have to tell her your shirt sizes. You do have black pants, right?"

See what I meant about Liz?

Chapter Seventeen

Veronica had left us to tend to other customers. She had no problem buying into Liz's undercover idea, calling and making the arrangements then and there, her grin spread ear to ear.

Meanwhile, Barbara kept muttering, "Am I the only sensible one in this group?" No one paid her any attention, including Fred.

"Don't forget to call me when Edna calls you," was Fred's parting shot to me.

"Sure, sure," was mine. I'd leave it up to Edna to decide if Fred needed to know where she went.

"Do you want to hear what we found out about David Katz? We ended up not going to his store." Liz had opened her laptop and was looking at me while she waited for it to boot up.

David Katz, the jeweler who custom-made Brie's ring. Brie had been so proud of her ring. Why did Brie see him Friday? And why was he so angry at Brie?

"David must have a very smart attorney on retainer, or he must be very stupid to make the same ring as Brie's," Stefan said.

"Why wouldn't he?" Barbara defended the man. "If he gets paid enough money, he'd make the same ring. Anyone would."

"You told me Brie made him sign something. I'm not a lawyer, but I think he's asking to be sued if he doesn't do what he signed up for."

Stefan was right. Brie did say that. Brie also said she promised the jeweler she'd make his life a pure torment and misery if he broke his word. Knowing Brie, she was quite capable of doing so.

"I don't think David could make enough money on one piece of jewelry to pay for his legal fees if Brie decided to sue," Stefan continued. "But then, maybe he didn't think Brie was serious about suing him. Girls her age do not go out and hire an attorney for stupid stuff like this. If anything, they ask for their money back, but they keep the ring."

"Do you guys want to know what I found?" The screen on Liz's laptop was up and running, showing a party in full swing. After making sure everyone was listening to her, Liz continued, "David's a very boring person. His social media feed is all about family, featuring his wife, ten children, and two grandchildren. One of his daughters—he has seven of them—just got engaged. It's his brother who's interesting. His younger brother, who used to design all the jewelry the shop was famous for."

"Used to," I murmured. I could see where this was going.

"Yes." Liz grinned at me. "The brother left and set up his shop over a year ago." Liz showed us a social media feed of a jewelry store in the next town over. The owner stood proudly at the counter, a big, welcoming smile on his face. A face so closely resembling David Katz, anyone looking at the picture would have been forgiven if they thought it was David from a few years back. "And if you scroll through the posts, you'll see a lot of the brother's customers used to be customers of

David. Worse, the posts go on to say how the jewelry in David's store is now stale and dated without David's brother there to do the design."

"And David's brother was the tech-savvy guy. His store's website and social media are very much on trend. He even has influencers puffing off his products online. Meanwhile, David's website and social media have been frozen for a year. Look, no posts for the last fourteen months." Liz turned her laptop toward us.

"Rich must have heard David screaming at his brother," Stefan said.

I gave voice to what I knew we were all thinking: "We need to talk to David. Barbara and I might as well stop by his store on our way to Janet's."

"Stefan and I are staying behind. There's something funny going on with Connie. I want to see what I can dig up about her and Larry," Liz said.

Stefan agreed with Liz, saying work made him hungry and thirsty, and he had nothing in his fridge except wine and cheese. Why was I not surprised?

It didn't take us long to get to David's store. The last time I was there, Rich and I were looking for a baptismal present for one of his grandnieces. The girl must be nearing two years old by now. The family had moved to Arizona, and except for holiday greetings and the shared photo album showing the girl's first tooth, first walk, and first jiggle of her hips, we'd lost touch. Another relationship I had neglected since Rich and Jim died. Maybe it was time I started mending fences.

The store hadn't changed. Display cases of rings, earrings, and necklaces abounded, the glittering merchandise separated by the color and grade of the gemstones. I noticed there␣was no one else helping

David, unlike before, when there were two other salespersons behind the counters and a jeweler busy with fixing watches and broken jewelry in the semi-enclosed booth up front.

"I'll be with you in a moment," David called out as we walked into his store. Then he saw me. "Meagan," he crooned, hands spread wide as if to hug me.

I didn't move. David wasn't one to get physical. He'd stop a few feet from me, clasp those hands together, and give me a perfect, gentlemanly bow—a short one, of course. Barbara, on the other hand, took one look at the approaching man and slipped behind my back. Only to slowly slide out when David did just that.

"And who is this with you?"

"This is my friend, Barbara," I said.

"Welcome, Barbara, browse as much as you want. Let me know when you see something you like." David greeted Barbara and turned to me. "Meagan, it's been years! I'm sorry for your loss. They were good men, your Rich and Jim."

"Thank you, David. That's kind of you." I blinked back the sudden tears. Words of sympathy were scarce after twelve months, but they still had the power to unnerve me.

"What can I do to help?" David asked.

Then and there, I had to decide. David and Rich weren't exactly friends. But Rich had trusted David through several decades of giving David his custom. Do I betray that trust? Or do I build on that trust?

I decided Rich was an excellent judge of character. Furthermore, my husband had never let me down.

"David, you remember Brie? Brianna Townsend?" I asked as gently as I could.

"Why do you ask?"

I could see the hardness creeping into David's face. Barbara hadn't said one word, nor had she moved from my side.

"We saw her last Wednesday at Sweet Buns, and she told us you made her ring. I was hoping you might know something that would help catch her killer." There, that was blunt enough. David would know exactly what we were about.

And he did. His face softened; his stance relaxed.

"You don't trust the detective to do his job, do you?" David narrowed his eyes at me. "Well, I don't blame you. Accidental death." David made as if to spit, but caught himself in time. "Forgive me, but anyone who knew Rich and Jim knew their deaths were no accident. They were both healthy, strong swimmers. The Nissequogue River is spring-fed, a freshwater stream. How could two strong men drown in it? On a calm day? With barely a breeze? It is absurd, I tell you."

I tried very hard not to cry, as hearing my thoughts spoken out loud was painful.

"My dear, I've distressed you. I am so sorry." David reached out his hands but stopped short of touching me, instead clasping his hands tight once more.

"No, no. I'm fine," I said, wiping the few tears leaking from the corners of my eyes.

"All right, you asked about Ms. Townsend. Wait here. Better if we are not disturbed." David checked to make sure no one had walked in while he was talking to us. He went and locked the door.

"Ms. Townsend is a right little madam, I tell you. You know she made me sign a document saying I was not to make another ring like hers?" He waited for me to nod. "My attorney says it's a bunch of nonsense. The design was not unusual enough. My attorney had several examples of designs very close to that ring. He also said no one can own the letter B, or any other letters of the alphabet. But do I want to pay his fees to fight the girl? And my attorney, he's smart, but he's honest. He said he could bring his family for a week's vacation to Hawaii if I decide to sign that document and then be stupid enough to do another B ring."

"I will be honest. Times are hard. My brother left me last year. Opened up another store. This was the first custom-made ring someone had asked me to do since my brother left. So I decided, why not? There are twenty-five more letters in the alphabet I can do, and I know Brie would brag about her ring all over town. It would do my store a great deal of good for a young girl like her to wear something I've made. She looked very put together. That influencer look, my daughter told me. Influencers, my daughter said, meant more business for me."

The poor man didn't know a thing about Brie. I didn't have the heart to correct him.

"When she came to my store Friday, late afternoon," David said. "Your friend looks shocked. Yes, she came to my store. I admit it. The cops haven't been around to question me. Maybe they will, maybe they won't. I heard they arrested an old lady for the murder. An old lady, do you believe that? How could an old lady cut up a body? My cousin—he's a butcher—he tells me, 'No way an old lady cut that body up.' But I digress."

"Ms. Townsend came Friday, waving a piece of paper, saying she was suing me. She says she has proof I made another 'B' ring. I was shocked, I tell you. I may not be very smart, but I am not stupid. I had not made any 'B' ring. So she shows me a picture of a girl with her hand up, wearing a 'B' ring, and besides the girl was a man who looks like me but is not me."

"Your brother made the ring," Barbara said.

"Exactly." David smiled at us. "I told Ms. Townsend she was mistaken. It was very easy to compare the photo of my brother to me as I stood in front of her. Any fool can see how much younger he is. Well, this little madam says, 'that might be so, but if you don't want me filing this lawsuit, you better give me my money back, and I'm keeping this ring.' "

Stefan would split his sides laughing at how right he was.

"My attorney did tell me it could come down to this one day. So I took out the cash she paid me from the drawer where I had kept it, waiting for this day to come. And I gave it back to her. But my attorney also gave me a piece of paper he said she must sign before I hand the money over. That she did. And I have it to prove to anyone who thinks I had anything to do with her murder. Ms. Townsend and I parted on good terms. She had no hold over me."

"One thing, though, after Ms. Townsend signed the paper, she kept asking me about Mrs. Whitfield. You see, Mrs. Whitfield was at the store Friday, too. I had to ask her to leave when Ms. Townsend came waving a paper in the air. I wasn't telling the little madam anything about Mrs. Whitfield. She and her husband are one of my best customers. Do you know why she's asking after Mrs. Whitfield?"

Connie.

Again.

Chapter Eighteen

The ride to Janet's house didn't take long.

Barbara slid her car by the curb, parked, and turned to me. "This is Liz's craziest idea yet. What do we know about working at a party? Do you know how to balance a tray in your hands? I don't."

"Well, Liz and Stefan volunteer in the soup kitchens. I know, I know," I said. "It's not the same, but it's what we have."

The two white vans parked in Janet's driveway didn't look like they had moved at all from the last time I was here. That was Monday, and today is Wednesday. So much had happened to us since then. But, apparently, not for Janet.

"Do you think this will work? This undercover stuff?"

I saw the fear in Barbara's eyes. It probably mirrored the one in mine whenever I thought of Edna. "It has to. We can't let Edna down." So far, we had nothing to show for all our work. Time was running out for Edna and Gladys.

Barbara nodded and got out of the car.

"Mrs. B!" Once again, Kyle was standing by the gate, no aluminum trays in his hands this time. Instead, he held a bucket with washcloths stuffed inside. Delight turned to chagrin as he took in the person behind me. "Oh…Principal Roker." Followed by confusion: "Why are you here?"

"I'm glad you're out," I said. "Is Janet inside?"

"Yes. But she's busy prepping for a last-minute party for this Saturday. I'm supposed to clean the vans in time for the party." Kyle held up the bucket for us to see. "Wait…are you the servers who would be helping at the party? Janet said Veronica Adams insisted she bring four people to help." Kyle put the bucket down on the ground and crossed his arms. "You are, aren't you? Are you guys going rogue?"

"Going rogue?"

"Come on, Mrs. B. Everyone knows you're investigating Brie's murder. You're going undercover, aren't you? Can I join you? What are you going as?" Kyle was beaming.

What was wrong with this picture? I understood Liz. She'd always been crazy. But Fred couldn't wait to go in disguise. And Kyle looked just as eager.

"We'll be servers. And you're already a server," Barbara said.

Kyle must have heard the silent "you fool" Barbara did not say because the smile left his face, and his shoulders slumped.

"And what do you mean by 'everyone knows'? What does everyone know?"

Kyle shrugged.

I gave Barbara a look to make sure she didn't spook Kyle any further. We needed to know what Kyle knew about the blackmail. "Kyle, I don't know if you've heard about Mrs. Gomez?" At his nod, I continued, "This investigating you're talking about, that's us trying to help her. Please be honest with us; this is important. Were you and Brie blackmailing Janet's customers?"

Barbara and I heard a deep-throated rumble. Kyle had thrown his head back and was clutching the back of his neck, groaning as he did so. We were shamelessly exploiting Kyle's fondness for Edna, knowing Edna was the boy's third-grade teacher.

"Stop that." Barbara slapped Kyle on his arm. "Who thought of the blackmail? You or Brie?"

"I don't know how you found out. Are you telling the detective?"

"No, we only want Mrs. Gomez cleared. And the killer arrested. That's not you, right?" Barbara said.

"No, gods, no. I wouldn't hurt Brie." Kyle swayed in place for a moment, hand still gripping his neck. "It was Brie. She thought of everything. I looked for the dirt. It was easy enough. You won't believe what happens at those parties."

"What did she have on you?"

When Kyle muttered something unintelligible, I knew we were on to something.

"Well?" Barbara prodded.

"Okay, okay," Kyle said. "It was about a week or two when Brie started working, back in November last year. I was in the kitchen, straightening things. Brie walks in and puts her phone down in front of me. She's taken a picture of me." Kyle stopped; lips pressed closed, upper teeth working his lower lip.

When a few minutes had passed, Barbara prompted, "A picture of you taking something that's not yours, maybe? Something of Janet's? Money, perhaps?"

"It was a big misunderstanding. I was not stealing."

"You were what? Merely borrowing?"

"See, you understand. I was going to pay Janet back the next day as soon as my client had paid me. And I did pay Janet back, honest. It's just I needed to pay my supplier first. They're very sensitive, my suppliers. They like getting their money up front."

"But Brie—" Barbara left the rest of the sentence for Kyle to finish.

"Brie didn't see it the same way I did. Said she'll show it to Janet. And Janet, for sure, won't see it the same way I did. She'd let me go. And I've been with Janet for years! It's become my second home. I stood there like a lump. Didn't know what to say. When Brie said she'd give me another chance to make things right, I jumped on it," Kyle scoffed, his voice bitter and hard. "Jumped out of a frying pan, right into the fire, I did. No one ever said I was smart. Isn't that right, Mrs. B?"

I decided it was better not to say anything at this point.

"She asked me what I knew about Sands Neck society ladies. Any secrets, the ones people paid money to keep. I hated the idea of blackmail, but I hated not having a job more. The society ladies could afford the blackmail much more than I could afford to be unemployed. And after all, it's not like they're innocent. Can't blackmail an innocent."

"Who were the victims?" I asked.

"Back then, I didn't know any secret worth anyone's money, so it took a while before I could pay for Brie's silence. Until the late winter party at the Whitfield's back in February of this year," Kyle said. "You see, I was at this bar out East with friends, maybe a week before the party? Everyone was in their twenties, getting crazy. Then a man walks in with this woman. Much older than everyone else. They both looked so out of place; they got stuck in my head. So when I saw him at the party, I recognized him right away. It was Brie's brother-in-law."

"You're thedude999?" Barbara asked, horrified.

"You've been following me on social media? That's so cool, Principal Roker."

"I am not on social media," Barbara snapped back.

"How about Larry Billings? Did you find anything about Larry?" I said.

"Eleanor's husband?" Kyle sounded unsure. "No, Eleanor was Connie's best friend. The Billings were always invited to Connie's parties. Connie and Larry began spending more time together after Eleanor's death. I think Connie felt Larry was some sort of hero. The way the man tried to rescue his wife was so sick."

"He meant awesome," I muttered to Barbara, catching how her face wrinkled up in a frown at Kyle's words.

"Awesome, yes, awesome"—Kyle nodded at Barbara before hurriedly moving on—"speaking of Connie, Brie was obsessed with Connie. It was Connie this, and Connie that, most days. It got to be"—Kyle slowed down—"I mean, it was petty of Brie. It was such small stuff. I don't think we even got a hundred dollars out of it. I don't understand why Brie went after Rosita—"

The sound of the gate banging shut and a gruff voice barking "Kyle" made all three of us jump. We turned to see Janet standing by the gate.

Kyle picked up his bucket and went to clean the vans. But not before he whispered, "Janet and Brie had the most godawful fight last Friday. They were screaming at each other. I heard Janet say, 'I'd see you in hell first.' But I'll deny everything if you tell her what

I told you." He winked and left.

I twisted to look at Janet.

"Listen, I don't care what you and your friends do. Why a bunch of comfortably off, retired school teachers all of a sudden decided to work as catering staff, which is more work than any of you have done lately, is beyond me. You're all supposed to be taking it easy in your retirement, not going ape-crazy like this," Janet said, hands on hips and eyes narrowed. "I don't care what your brainless scheme is, but if Veronica is willing to foot the bill, I can use the money as long as you don't go off accusing me of killing Brie. Don't pay attention to whatever crap Kyle is saying about me and Brie. I might not have been the best aunt to those two girls, but they're still my nieces. So you better stop whatever it is you're thinking of right now." She turned back inside. "I have your shirts set aside. Don't worry about returning them. I'm adding the cost to Veronica's bill."

Janet led us to the one-room building where she had her kitchen. She opened a cabinet stacked with black polo shirts, arranged in different sizes, and took out four in the sizes we told her, handing them over to us. She turned her back on us, dismissing us. Barbara and I looked at each other and shrugged. We left without saying goodbye or thanks.

Neither of us thought anything more about what Kyle said about Brie and Rosita. What was a hundred dollars after all? It wasn't worth killing over.

Chapter Nineteen

"Hello?" The static from the phone was awful.
"Hello, who's this?" We were on our way to my house
to pick up the black pants I needed to wear for Veronica's
party when my phone rang.

"Meg? Is this Meg?"

"Edna? Is that you? Where are you? I can barely
hear you?" I clutched at the door handle as the car
swerved, then righted itself. Barbara threw me a glance
and headed for the parking lot of the shopping center
coming up on our right. I put Edna on speaker phone.

"Meg, oh good! I was hoping I'd catch you," Edna
said.

"Where are you?" Barbara nearly screamed.

I hadn't realized how wound-up Barbara was over
Edna's disappearance until I heard the controlled panic
in her voice.

"I'm okay. Don't worry. I'm in a camping resort
somewhere in New Jersey. My nephew owns a seasonal
camper here. Really posh. Full kitchen, it even has a
fridge and a microwave. There's a bathroom with a
stand-up shower. Mom has the bedroom, and I'm
sleeping in one of the bunk beds. There's a sofa, a TV
over the dining table, and lots of windows all around. I
told my nephew I was taking my mom over for a few
days. We're good, don't worry."

"We tried calling you, but it kept going to voicemail.

Why am I getting a different phone number for you? Whose phone are you using?" I said.

"I turned off my phone. The cops can find me by my phone if I use it, don't you know? It's the GPS in my phone. That's what they say in those crime shows."

"Edna—" Barbara groaned.

"What? You watch the same crime shows I watch. They all say the same thing about cell phones and GPS. Anyway, I got a burner phone." Edna gave a little chuckle. "I went up to this store clerk and asked for a burner phone. He laughed and gave me this phone. Showed me how to set it up after I'd paid for it. I asked him if I should throw it away when I'm done with it. He said I don't have to, but if I do, make sure I send it to an electronics recycling company. Such a nice boy."

"Never mind the phone. Why did you run away?"

"What do you mean? I didn't want to go to jail! That's why. Who's going to take care of Mom if I'm in jail? I don't trust Detective Storm. He's not very smart." Edna paused. "Is Nanding very upset with me? I left him a note. Tell him I'm sorry I took his car. But I wanted to make it harder for the cops to find me. The cops trace the license plates, and that's how they find the killer. Oh, what am I saying! I'm not a killer!"

"You're not a killer. And you're not going to jail," I said firmly. "But yes, stay away for now. No need to tempt Detective Storm into arresting you. We will find Brie's killer. We already found out Brie was blackmailing people. Once we find out who, it'll be all over, and you can come home."

Edna didn't need to know we had no idea what we were doing. We heard Edna gulp and sniff. She sounded so scared; I wanted to scream.

"How's Gladys?" I asked, hoping this would give Edna a chance to get herself under control.

"Fine, she's fine. She thinks we're on vacation. She goes for a walk and talks to everyone. She's having fun."

"Well, go for a walk and meet your neighbors, too," I said. "But stay put. Don't go anywhere. I'll call you at this number."

"Yes. Okay. The boy at the store said the phone is good for thirty days. I'll be home by then, right? Please tell Nanding I'm sorry, will you?"

"Yes, of course. But don't worry. He showed us your note. He's read it, so he knows you're sorry. Should I tell him where you are? He's worried." It wasn't any of my business who Fred was to Edna.

Edna didn't answer.

"Edna?"

"Maybe not? I don't want him coming over and bringing us back. Once you tell him we went camping in my nephew's seasonal unit, he'll know where we are. He's been here before."

That was pretty clear. No wiggle room there. Sorry Fred. Edna said no.

"I think I'd better go now. That's Mom screaming in the background." Edna disconnected as we heard faint screams coming through the phone.

Barbara pulled out of the parking lot, and we went back on the road. Both of us were quiet with our thoughts.

I didn't tell Edna about the party this Saturday. If Edna knew Liz had set up a…what was it Kyle said we were doing? Going rogue? Edna would freak. And we couldn't have Edna freaking out more than she already was. She sounded so cheery; I was afraid she'd break down crying soon. Who would take care of Gladys if Edna fell apart? I spent the rest of the ride looking out the window. Barbara must have felt the same; she didn't say one word to me.

Arriving at my house, Barbara parked her car in the driveway but made no move to get out. She did ask if I wanted her to come in with me, but I didn't want anyone else seeing my house the way it was now.

After one quick look around my living room, I tried to keep my face pointed toward my bedroom. The sofa and armchairs were back upright, with their seat cushions in the correct position. The piano bench was pushed into its place by the piano. The mirror and family photos had been stacked against a wall, and the broken glass had been tidied up. But the recliner caught my gaze and held it. Rich had sat there while Jim sat on the sofa, both men enjoying their beer while binge-watching their favorite crime shows. Gathering up the empties and dumping them in the recycling bin Friday morning was my chore, the only morning Rich stayed a few more hours in bed, paying the price for his Thursday nights with Jim. Every Thursday, Jim would walk through my door just as he used to when he was younger. He'd shout, "I'm home. Dinner smells good!" and he'd give his father and me a hug. Dinner was almost always pot roast, Jim's favorite. I no longer cook pot roast on Thursdays. The first Thursday after the funeral, I took one look at Jim's favorite dish and threw it in the trash.

I tore my eyes from the recliner and walked unsteadily to my room. I didn't think Dora had packed my black pants this morning when she came over to get some of my stuff. Not that she would have known I would need them. I hadn't known it myself. The last time

I wore the pants was to a funeral: Rich's and Jim's. I had hoped never to wear them again. But needs must. I grabbed the black pants and walked out.

Back outside, I saw a school bus stop across the street. When it pulled away, Archer and Nico were standing on the sidewalk. The two kids saw us and ran over, backpacks bouncing at their backs.

"Aren't you supposed to be home with Rosita?" I asked Archer after giving each kid a hug and a kiss on their cheek.

"Hi, Principal Roker." Archer waved to Barbara, who had gotten out of the car when she saw the kids cross the street to us.

"Rosita couldn't make it today. She had to go home early. I think her daughter needed her or something," said Archer. "I asked Mom if I could go home with Nico instead. His mom said she'll take me home after."

I eyed Archer's backpack and the laptop I knew was inside. "Archer, can you check some CCTVs for me again?"

"Meg—"

I waved Barbara off. Edna and Gladys were out in a cramped trailer in some woods in New Jersey. Edna was probably not sleeping or eating because she's terrified she'd go to jail for something she didn't do. All while taking care of Gladys and making sure Gladys knew nothing of what was happening. We needed to do this.

"Sure," said Archer, swinging his backpack free from his shoulder. Balancing his laptop in his hands, he tilted his head toward the house.

I shook my head. I didn't want him inside the house until the walls were fixed. "House still has to be fixed. Let's do it out here."

Archer put the laptop on top of Barbara's car and brought up the program he used a couple of days ago. "What are we looking for?"

I gave him Edna's address. Barbara leaned over. She understood right away what I was looking for. If we could prove Edna's car was in her driveway all Friday night, maybe Detective Storm would get off her case.

"Mama Meg, are there any banks or businesses on that street?" Archer said, glancing at me and seeing my confusion. "CCTVs are not set up on streets where there are only houses. It cost too much, Dad said."

"Can you look anyway?"

"I am, but I'm not finding any," he said, moving the laptop so I could see the map showing Edna's street.

I saw some blue dots scattered over the map, but not pulsing red dots. "What are those?" I pointed them out to Archer.

"Those are Ring cameras. I can't get to those. Dad didn't show me how." Archer brought up another screen and zoomed in on the street. "That's a satellite view of the street, maybe about a month or two ago. Here's the driveway of the house you wanted."

Edna's car was in the driveway. A month or two ago. Not helpful. "Try this address." Hoping there were CCTVs by Gladys's house, I gave Archer her address. Normally, I would be very proud of how Jim made sure Archer knew his limits. Sadly, my priorities were out of whack right now. I needed to clear my friend of a murder charge.

"Nothing here, too. See…" Archer had stepped back from his laptop. Nico stood watching and listening to us, fingering the straps of his backpack.

I had hoped, for a minuscule second, we could give

Edna an alibi. Easy peasy. But no, we were doing it the hard way.

Then I thought of something else. Liz had mentioned Connie's family owned a meat processing plant, one with meat saws, machines to cut up animal carcasses. Why not a dead body, too? And there should be CCTVs around these buildings. A quick search on my phone yielded addresses for two such buildings in Suffolk County.

"Archer, can you put this address in and see if anyone was lurking around late Friday night?"

My grandson went through the motion histograms and found nothing. No spikes. No movement. I noticed he didn't need a password to get in.

"How about this one?" I gave Archer the second address, out by Yaphank, miles away from Whitman's Port and Duck Harbor Park. But not far for anyone with a car.

Archer hummed. "Mama Meg, there's nothing here."

"Nothing? Like the other place?" Again, no password was needed.

"No, I meant there's no history here. Someone removed the videos for Friday of last week. See—" Archer pushed his screen to us. Below the motion histograms, we saw last week's dates. Archer swiped at the screen, showing us the dates moving forward, ending on Thursday of last week and restarting on Saturday at three in the morning.

All of a sudden, the mild spring day felt like the coldest day of winter. The killer took Brie to this place. Cut her up and packed her in a bag like some animal. We needed to find out who owned this plant. A car passed by, lighting up the sign on the building's front. But all I saw was the letter H.

H for Haddad? Was this the meat-packing plant Liz said Connie's family owned?

If Connie didn't kill Brie—not when she was on a plane flying to Paris—then why were security videos from Friday night missing? Who deleted the footage, and did Connie know?

Chapter Twenty

Thursday morning, and here I was trading kicks and jabs with my sparring partner.

Before I left for the gym, Detective Storm had passed by the house looking for Edna and Gladys. Lying didn't come easily to me, so I panicked. Blabbed about non-existent doctor appointments Edna and Gladys were supposedly at, and Edna being so law-abiding she wouldn't answer phones while driving, and would not cross the streets except at designated crosswalks. It took all of my willpower not to collapse in relief when the detective left without taking me into custody for obstruction of justice or as an accessory to murder. But I didn't escape unscathed. I, somehow, inadvertently, foolishly, made Jonathan think Dora was going to call him and, possibly, go out to dinner with him. Probably why the man left happy, having forgotten what he came for in the first place. Which was Edna, not Dora. I called Fred for help, but he didn't pick up his phone. By the time I got here, I was ready to hit and kick that bag.

Thirty minutes of kickboxing and punching left me primed for light contact sparring. Anger gone, stress levels bearable.

Craig had laid down the ground rules. For our first session: pull our punches and kicks, don't land any blows, keep the hits below the shoulders, only body punches and kicks to the shins, and definitely no head strikes. Two rounds of two-minute sessions, with a minute for breaks. Not too strenuous. He moved around us, calling out instructions from time to time. Stefan stood to the side, watching.

My eyes lit up when Craig introduced Tara to me. She was the woman I had seen the day Stefan had dragged me to the gym. About my age, hair in a ponytail, wrinkles lightly gracing her face, I had seen her put boxing gloves on her hands, then hit and kick a punching bag. Looking at her, I saw myself doing the same; the force of each punch exploding in my brain and shattering the tendrils of despair and regret before they burrowed any deeper into my brain. There was my way out of grief. Should I tell Tara how much she meant to me that long-ago day? Better not, I didn't want to embarrass the woman.

"Good first session," Craig said as he called time for Tara and me. "By the way, did Kyle get off?"

"Yes, thanks for talking his customer into giving him an alibi." I stripped the gloves off my hands.

"It was the right thing to do." Craig busied himself attending to another student.

"Are you talking about that girl's murder? Brianna Townsend?" Tara stood to our left, listening to us. "Who's Kyle? Didn't someone say the cops arrested a retired Post Elementary school teacher for the girl's murder?"

Great. Edna was the hot topic even outside of town. Tara lived in the next town over, and even she knew about Edna's arrest. Edna would hate it if she knew.

"I heard the teacher had slapped the girl and threatened to kill her. Over a spiked drink the girl gave to the teacher's mother?"

"She wasn't arrested, only questioned," Stefan said. "And Kyle is someone Brie worked with. The detective arrested him first, but had to let him go the next day."

"So the teacher was released as well?" Tara asked. At Stefan's nod, she continued, "Good, I thought that story was bonkers. Who would kill over a spiked drink? Plus the way the girl was killed…" Tara shuddered. "I can't see a retired school teacher doing that. Too gruesome for words. Unless she's insane?"

"Edna's not insane. And she most certainly did not kill Brie," I said, my admiration for Tara waning with each word.

"My granddaughter was at the park that day with her friend. She said the teacher was her third-grade teacher at Post Elementary School, and Mrs. Gomez—do I have her name right? You two seem to know her—my granddaughter said Mrs. Gomez would never hurt anyone. The worst part, my granddaughter told me, was when her friend confronted Brie. Her friend thought it was cruel of Brie to make fun of a ninety-year-old woman."

I wondered if Tara's granddaughter was in my class.

"My granddaughter agreed, but she told her friend to stay out of it, especially after Mrs. Gomez slapped Brie. By then, my granddaughter thought Brie had gotten what she deserved. But her friend thought differently. Her friend insisted Mrs. Gomez deserved an apology, so the girl stopped Brie on her way out of the park and told her so. Why do the young think they're invincible?"

I agreed with Tara but wondered what the point of this was.

"Anyway, Brie pushed my granddaughter's friend to the ground. Her friend was hurt badly, hitting the ground hard and doubling up in pain. But the girl refused to go to the hospital even as she doubled up in pain, clutching her stomach. My granddaughter was so upset. She tried texting her friend to check up on her, but so far her friend hadn't texted my granddaughter back."

"Why don't you tell your granddaughter to go visit her friend instead?" I said.

"That's what I said to her. Texting is great when you want a quick answer, but when you're worried about a sick friend, it's better to visit. That's not how it's done anymore."

"What's the name of your granddaughter's friend?" Stefan asked.

"Leni," Tara said. "They were schoolmates together. I'm happy Mrs. Gomez is not in jail. My granddaughter will be delighted to hear the news." Tara picked up her gym bag and, with a wave, left the gym.

"At least we know the name of the girl Edna is looking for," Stefan said. "We should have also gotten the name of Tara's granddaughter. It might have made it easier to track Leni down."

Leni was a pretty name. I'd heard the name before, but I couldn't figure out when and from whom. If it were important enough, it'd come back to me.

"Do you need a ride home?" It was Stefan's turn for gym pickup and drop-off.

"No, Barbara is picking me up. We're going to see Alan and Selena again, remember?"

"Now?"

"No, in an hour. I have to shower and change."

"Perfect. I have time to get some training in. I can meet you out front. Barbara will want to know how well you did with your first session of contact sparring."

Stefan's smile was part imp and all devil.

I hope Barbara remembered to take her high blood pressure meds.

Chapter Twenty-One

"Remind me why we're going to see Alan? We've proved the blackmail. What do we need to see Alan for?" Barbara said, a lot calmer now, keeping her eyes on the road, refusing to look at her rear-view mirror where she could see Stefan standing by the sidewalk, waving goodbye to us.

"Alan lied when we asked where he was Friday. Why would he lie?" I tried to sound meek in case Barbara was still fuming over my sparring. It didn't help that Stefan had so obviously enjoyed himself at Barbara's expense.

"Simple, he's cheating on Selena, and he doesn't want her to know. He didn't lie because he had anything to do with Brie's murder."

"You don't think Alan killed Brie?"

"That snowflake? No. He might be a very good attorney, but I doubt if he had it in him to kill, let alone cut the body up into pieces. Two different skills, I'd say."

I had to agree with Barbara. "Maybe he'll tell us something we don't know? We're not getting any answers; instead, we have more questions. It didn't look this hard on TV."

"TV? You believe what you see on TV?"

I shared a laugh with my friend. Then, a sigh. "I hate the idea of Dora going out with that detective. I left a message for Fred. Told him to call or meet us later at

Sweet Buns. He hasn't called back. Maybe he'll meet us at Sweet Buns. I hope so anyway."

Barbara parked in front of Selena's house. Pointing to the driveway, Barbara said, "Do we ring the doorbell? The white SUV is not here, only the silver sedan. Only Alan is home. Exactly as we want."

"Let's go then."

We walked up the driveway and rang the bell.

"You're back? How'd you know I'd be home?" Alan was not pleased to see us.

"Your neighbor," Barbara said.

"Nosy old b—" Alan cut himself off, lips thinning. "What do you want?"

He was done being nice to us, was he? "We know about Sara," I said.

"Sara"—Alan took a step back, shook himself, and stepped out of the house, closing the door behind him— "What about Sara?"

"Knock it off," Barbara said. "Going macho is not scaring us. Sara Lieberman, your partner's wife. The one you're sleeping with? Besides your wife?"

"We also know about the blackmail," I put in.

"You have no proof."

If looks could kill, Barbara and I would be clutching at our hearts now.

"We're not cops. We don't need proof. But if we were, the way you're acting now is proof enough," Barbara said.

"Tell us about the blackmail," I added.

Alan glanced away. After a minute or two, Alan started talking. "Brie came to me, two…two and a half months ago. She had downloaded a video from social media. Of Sara and me. In some bar. Kissing. We thought we had gone far enough away, and no one we knew would be at that bar. Blame it on social media. You can't hide from it." He uncrossed his arms, twined his fingers together, and hit his forehead gently.

Letting his hands fall to his side, Alan said, "She wanted money, of course. I paid. Of course. But that supposedly one-time payment became more. She came again, a few more times. I gave her what I could."

"Honestly, I don't think she cared about the money. Never counted it. Took the envelope, got back in her car, and drove away. It was more about the hold she had over you. The fear you have of her. That's how she got her high." He closed his eyes.

I agreed with Alan. That sounded very like Brie. "And Friday? We saw Brie bump into you on Main Street. Sara was with you then."

A white SUV screeched into the driveway, the door opening and closing with a thud. Selena was home. Unexpectedly, judging by the way Alan jumped.

"Sara? Sara Lieberman? A golfing weekend with the guys? You bastard!" Selena threw her bag at Alan, shouting curses at him nonstop. Her keys, wallet, and the rest of the contents of the bag spilled out into the yard. The three of us cringed back, trying our best not to get hit by the stuff shooting out of Selena's bag. I saw the neighbor across the street, watching from the sidewalk, her dog sitting by her side.

"How'd you know?" Alan asked for the second time.

"Our video doorbell! You dumbass! I heard everything you said," Selena said. "And you two—" She rounded on Barbara and me. "—you vultures. Did you come to gloat? To see how Selena got it wrong again?"

"You know better than that," Barbara said, eyes thick with rage, every inch the Principal Roker students of Post Elementary School knew from long ago. "You know me better than that."

That shut Selena up. She looked to where I was looking and screamed at her neighbor, "You don't have anything better to do?"

The neighbor shook her head and tugged on her dog. She continued her walk down the street, not looking back.

Measuring Barbara and me with her eyes, Selena said, a statement, not a question. "You can't possibly think Alan had anything to do with Brie's death." Turning to her husband, dismissing him with a few words, she said, "He's not man enough for that."

"No, we don't," Barbara said, and with a look at Alan as dismissive as Selena's words were, continued, "No, he's not."

Alan moved forward in protest. "Hey! I was with Sara that weekend. No way—" subsiding when he realized he was getting himself in more trouble.

"What are you here for? If not that, then what? What do you want?"

I got tired of the drama. I asked what we wanted an answer to. "Why did your Aunt Janet take Brie in? After all the years she spent ignoring the two of you, why now?"

"And why marry Alan here?" Barbara added.

"You mean that gossip is not making the rounds in Whitman's Port? You're not keeping up with the news." Selena rolled her eyes at us. "My grandfather died close to a year ago. Maybe eight months ago?"

"We heard about that," murmured Barbara.

"Did you know the old man was worth millions?"

Barbara and I nodded.

"Well, Brie and I didn't," Selena said. "We thought he'd leave us something when he died. Not a lot, but some. We weren't close. Grandfather disapproved of Father. Didn't want Mother marrying him. But you know, Mother, she does what she wants; there's no stopping her. Brie and I thought, growing up, that Grandfather was stingy with us. Mother never said how Grandfather had paid off the house, and gave her money for the house and for us after Father went to jail. We thought the money came from Father. That's why we didn't have as much as we used to. After the funeral, Grandfather's will was read, and it turns out he left us…would you believe it? Millions."

Alan twitched. "You didn't say anything about that to me!"

"Hush, it's got nothing to do with you. But like the old bastard he was, he tied up his millions with a condition. Mother had to prove she had raised us right, and we were both productive citizens, not slackers. She had three years after his death. If she succeeds, we all get our money. If she doesn't, Grandfather's favorite charity gets the money."

"The lawyer was nice, though. He said since Brie and I had finished high school, Mother could get half of her money. But she would have to wait for the other half until Brie and I showed we were productive citizens. And for Brie, that meant getting a job and keeping the job for a year. But for me, because I was five years older, that meant marriage and children." Selena scowled. "Brie burst out laughing at that point. She thought it was hilarious that I, who had a job and was already married, needed to have a child before I could get my inheritance."

"Mother didn't think it was all that funny. She also knew how Brie was. There was no way Brie could keep working nonstop for one year. She'd get fired, and the year would have to start all over again. And Mother didn't want to give up the rest of her millions. Neither did we. Because we only got our money when Mother got hers. Mother approached Janet—I refuse to call her Aunt Janet. That woman was never an aunt to us—anyway, Mother made her an offer."

"What did your mother offer Janet?" I asked, caught up in the story by now.

"If Janet kept Brie employed for one whole year, Mother would pay all of Janet's debts. All of it," Selena said. "Janet thought it was a sweet deal. Until her business started to suffer. But by then, she became even more desperate for the money Mother was hanging over her head. Six more months of Brie, and all debts were paid off. Janet thought she could limp along with Brie for six more months. Then she'd cut Brie and rebuild her business."

"And you? Why do you stay with Alan?" Barbara asked. "The Selena I knew would not have put up with this. You're no fool, you must have known he would cheat."

Selena shrugged. "To get my money, I needed to be married and have children. It was hard enough switching out my birth control pills with a placebo, so Alan had no idea I was trying to get pregnant. But if Brie managed to screw it up, and you never know with Brie, I'd be stuck as a single mother with very little money if I left Alan."

"And with Brie dead? What happens to the money?"

I asked, noting how avidly Alan's eyes gleamed. He must be counting his share of the millions.

"I swear, that lawyer is super nice to us. Mother must be keeping him sweet, as ancient as he is." Selena laughed at how Barbara and I cringed.

"Anyway"—Selena stifled her laughter so she could continue—"Mother and I met with the lawyer this morning. I was a few blocks away, on my way home from the meeting, when I got this ping from the Ring camera. The one you put in on Monday, Alan? I should have asked you to put one in earlier. I would have seen Brie coming around."

Alan winced.

Selena turned back to us. "The lawyer said since Brie died while holding a job, she's pretty much fulfilled the one-year work requirement. And as long as she's not wanted by the police for anything before she died— knowing how Brie died, I made sure to ask—then, technically, the lawyer said, she can inherit. But since she's dead, the money she would have inherited would go to the person named as her heir under my grandfather's will. Which happens to be any children I have." Selena smiled all around, patting her bump. "This baby will be worth millions when she's born. She's not going through what I did growing up. And"—turning to Alan—"don't think you're getting your hands on her money. My uncle, my mother's brother, is the trustee, and he's not a pushover. He has his own money, and he's a miserable scrooge. I expect he'll be as penny-pinching with the baby's money as he is with his own."

"Does the baby have to be born alive for you to inherit?" Barbara asked, curious.

"No. The lawyer said I had to have children, which

I would have, technically, whether it was a live birth or not. Except if I got an abortion, but it's long past the time I could have one. And even if it weren't, I have no plans to get one. But I have to remain married unless"— Selena's eyes opened wide—"unless my husband cheats on me. I can get divorced without losing my inheritance then. The lawyer said he had to fight my grandfather for that. It didn't make any sense to him to force me to stay married if my husband was cheating on me." Selena laughed out loud. A gleeful grin had taken over her face, her mouth stretching wider with each word, and her eyes sparkling with her mirth.

"You're right, Alan. Brie wasn't after you for the money. That witch knew what she was doing to me." Shaking her head, Selena muttered under her breath, "Good thing she's dead."

Turning to Alan, Selena said, "But you…I can get rid of you now. Come on, Alan, time to pack your bags."

"Pack my bags? I paid for this house," Alan said.

"Yes, but did you forget we put this house under my name? Before we got married? You didn't want your soon-to-be ex to get the money, remember?" Selena said sweetly. "This is my house. Not yours. Hurry along now. I want you out before night comes. Excuse me, ladies, I have a cheating husband to throw out of the house." Selena shut the door on us, cutting off the sound of Alan spluttering his protests.

I stood, speechless. I looked over to Barbara, whose face was as shocked as mine. The door opened again. It was Selena, poking her head out the door.

"By the way, if you don't know by now with all your poking around, the lawyer told me Brie came to see him two weeks ago. She wanted to sue the jeweler who made that gaudy, tasteless ring she was so proud of. She picked up the complaint from his office that Friday. Said she would serve the papers on the man herself so she could enjoy watching him read it."

"And when you do find out who killed Brie, let me know, would you? I'd like to start an online fundraising campaign for the legal bills. My sister must have done something horrible to whoever it was. The least I can do is help." Selena pulled her head back and closed the door.

Chapter Twenty-Two

"Veronica must be sick and tired of us by now." My heart gave a little jump when I saw Fred sitting with Liz and Stefan at Sweet Buns when we got back from Selena's. What? I was relieved he was here for Dora's sake. And Edna's.

Not mine. No, not mine.

Maybe if I kept repeating that to myself, my heart would settle down to the business of beating regularly and keeping my blood flowing smooth and even, and not have all of it rushing to my face.

"What are you going on about? Veronica loves us. Okay, who am I kidding? She's enjoying the intrigues right now more than our company." Barbara made a beeline for the table where Fred, Liz, and Stefan sat. "Good morning. What do we have, Liz?"

Liz was shaking her head mock-mournfully. "I have moved my things to Sweet Buns. Certainly, my laptop has found a new home. Veronica tells me I can sleep comfortably if I pull a few chairs together. That is, if I don't mind my feet hanging off at the edge of a chair and my body molding itself on a rock-hard wooden surface. Alas, I am grown old, and this will not do."

Barbara and I laughed. Liz kept her acting skills fresh with her work at the Whitman's Port Drama Group.

"Before we get to that"—I took the chair beside Liz—"Fred, did you get my message?" My face, which had stopped flaming, went red again. Of course, he got my message. Why else was he here with us? I covered as best as I could. "About Detective Storm and Dora?"

That was real smooth.

Not.

Blast, I needed to get myself together.

"Dora can't go out to dinner with the man. That's like throwing yourself on a grenade." Liz made us laugh and saved me from myself. "Kaboom, no Dora."

I stopped laughing. No sacrificial offerings allowed. Certainly, not Dora.

"You said Jonathan had questions for Edna? He can't question Edna without her attorney present. That's me. It's not like he doesn't know that. I've reminded him at least twice. I don't know what that man is doing showing up at your front door asking for Edna. He knows the number to my office. All he had to do was call me."

Competence was such an attractive trait. I relaxed.

"Dora thought it was an excuse to ask her out to dinner again."

"That's even worse. Using his office to get sexual favors."

I wished Fred had put that another way.

"I tell you what—" Liz cut in "—I'll call Detective Storm and make believe I'm Edna. He's spoken to Edna how many times? Once? Twice? He won't know it's me. Anyway, I bet you I can mimic Edna's voice." She cleared her throat. Paused for effect. Then, "Good morning, Detective Storm. I heard you were looking for me?" An impish grin took over Liz's face as she checked for our reactions. Liz hadn't forgotten any of her training. She sounded exactly like Edna, complete with a slight Filipino accent.

Fred had his head buried in his hands. Stefan was clapping. And Barbara was somewhat…smiling. It wasn't a total scowl, so I'm calling it a half-smile.

"Where's my phone? I'm calling the detective right now." Liz got her bag and started pulling stuff out. Phone in hand, she said, "Fourth Precinct? Can I please speak to Detective Storm?"

"No!" Fred lifted his head, his hand snaking out to grab Liz's phone.

Liz made a face at him, batted his hand away, got up, and moved closer to the window. "I heard you were looking for me?" Liz widened her eyes at us and smirked. "I was out with my mother. At the doctor's."

A pause while we all stopped breathing.

"Was I supposed to check in with you every time I left my house? My attorney said I was free to go as I wanted. Should he call you? I'm sure he said I wasn't under house arrest? Was I under house arrest?" Liz was shaking her head at us while holding up her cell so we could all hear the detective stammering and stuttering.

We remembered to breathe.

"What's that you said? You wanted to talk to me? Oh, wait"—Liz covered her cellphone with her hand and counted slowly up to five—"the nurse just called us. Have to go. Next time, call my attorney. Didn't he give you his number?" Liz hung up.

Fred glared at all of us. "You guys are—"

I saw him swallow what he wanted to say and change it to "—not thinking this through completely."

Insane was the word he wanted to use. Out of our minds. Completely batshit crazy. He was talking about Liz after all.

"You lied to a police officer. Even if we get Edna

cleared, he can still arrest you for obstruction of justice."
Fred had both hands clasped firmly around his coffee
mug. Was he trying to stop himself from strangling us?
Make that Liz, not us. Maybe...

"So? You'd defend me, no doubt. Anyway, I don't
think Dora would let Jonathan Storm arrest me for such
a piddling excuse. Not when he made such a huge
mistake on Edna." Liz came back to the table, not
worried at all.

Fred closed his eyes and rapped on the table with his
mug. "That's not the way to go about this."

I wondered if he wanted a gavel. Something to
remind us how serious this was.

"This is what will happen. I'll call Jonathan and
remind him Edna's my client, and he needs to go through
me for any meetings or conversations with her. And he
can't go around asking my client's friends to get my
client to call him. If he wants a meeting, I am not free for
the rest of the week, but I can meet him with my client
on Monday. That gives us this weekend to get Edna to
come back, and maybe find something to clear Edna or,
at the very least, point Jonathan in another direction."

"And if we don't find anything at Veronica's
party?" Stefan said.

"Don't think that way," Barbara said. "We'll find
something. It doesn't have to be the killer. Like Fred
said, anything we can use to make the detective start
looking at someone else. That shouldn't be too hard to
do. We watch everyone closely and listen hard."

"We picked up the shirts from Janet on the way here.
Remind me to give them to you," I told Liz and Stefan.

Fred didn't need a shirt. He was coming as a guest.
Veronica refused to have him serve, saying he was well-

known in the community. Some of his clients were Veronica's neighbors. Fred said Veronica could hire a clown to entertain the guests. Between the make-up, the costume, and the balls he'd be juggling, Fred didn't think any of his clients would recognize him. Veronica just laughed and said no.

I looked over to where Fred was and tried to picture him in a clown suit and make-up. Could he really juggle? The thought of him as a clown juggling balls made me smile.

Fred saw me smiling and smiled back at me.

That unsettled me. Should I tell him why I was smiling? That I was picturing him as a clown? Or maybe I should say nothing? I mean, how do I explain why I was even thinking of him dressed as a clown? Why was I thinking of him? This was absurd. The man smiled at me. So what? I felt an elbow hit me on my side. "What?" I said to Barbara.

"Liz wanted to know if we could talk about Larry now," she said.

"That's my cue to leave," Fred said, getting up. "I'll see you ladies. And if you speak to Edna again—I know she called yesterday, there's no way you haven't spoken to her—please tell her to call me. I can't help her if she's not talking to me."

When Fred turned to me, I almost broke my promise to Edna. Those eyes looking straight at me were deadly.

Was it bad that I only just remembered Rich? What was wrong with me?

Chapter Twenty-Three

"He's gone. You can breathe again." Barbara nudged me with her elbow.

She looked at me. I looked right back at her. Only to give up a few moments later. I'd never won a staring contest with Barbara.

Ignoring her, I turned to Liz. "What do you have?"

"You asked for Lawrence Billings. We have"—Liz turned her laptop for us to see—"Lawrence Billings!"

I started to read what Liz had brought up, then remembered we hadn't told them about yesterday's meeting with David. "Oh, you can cross David Katz off the list."

Barbara filled them in about David, as well as Alan and Janet. "We're losing suspects faster than a tree sheds its leaves in a hurricane," Barbara said when she finished going over what happened yesterday.

"You'll like what we found then," Stefan said with a smirk at Barbara.

"Investment banker," I murmured, ignoring Barbara and Stefan. "Graduated from a state university, not a private one? Wait, I thought you said he was as rich as Croesus? He's not old money?"

"I was wrong." Liz refused to get drawn into any more discussion.

I decided I'd better finish reading before saying anything more.

"Founding partner. Worked hard to get to the top. Preeminent in his field. Tons of satisfied investors. Unparalleled double-digit investment yields. Give him your money and he'll make you a millionaire?" I paraphrased Larry's bio on his investment firm's website.

"That's if you're not one already," Liz said, her face bland and noncommittal.

"Lawsuits from little people like us?" Barbara hazarded a guess.

"Little people like us don't have the money to sue men in suits like Larry. The cost of one of his suits is enough to feed me for a month," Stefan said. "And I'm talking fine wine and caviar."

We all took another look at Larry's suit. Stefan was right. Tailored and bespoke, that suit would have cost us more than a month's pension. Actually, maybe two.

Liz took back the laptop from me, fingers clicking, waiting for another screen to come up, then turning the laptop around.

"What's this?" I had no idea what this website was for.

"It's a regulatory website. It reports on investment broker-dealers like Larry. If you want to do a background check on your stockbroker, check if there are complaints or investigations, things like that." Liz took the laptop again and typed in Larry's name and the name of his investment firm. Clicked on a few tabs when the page for Larry came up and slid the laptop so I could see the search results.

Several lines of complaints and disciplinary actions showed in Larry's profile. I clicked on one, scanned it, and leaned back in my chair. Barbara grabbed the laptop and scrolled through the list.

"He played fast and loose with other people's money," I said.

"They all do," Barbara said. "That's how they make those double-digit gains. You don't think you could make that much money without gambling, do you?"

"So Larry's a gambler. A high-roller gambler, not afraid to break a few rules. Except he's only gotten a few slaps on the wrist so far, nothing major. What else did you find out?" I asked Liz.

Liz took back the laptop and typed a different name. A wedding photo came up, a society wedding. Black ties and gowns. The bride wore a wedding gown all in lace, and the couple posed against the backdrop of green, lush lawns and extravagant flower arrangements. In her early twenties, the bride was radiant in her youth and at the height of her beauty.

"Eleanor Hawthorne, 24, only daughter of real-estate tycoon George and Rachel Hawthorne of Kansas, was given in marriage by her parents to Lawrence Billings, 35, of New York." I read the photo's caption. "The money was all his wife's?"

Liz nodded in agreement.

"He made his money the old-fashioned way. He married it." Barbara was amused. "Then, his moneyed wife dies in an accident."

"Ten years later," Stefan said.

"Yes, but did you read the latest disciplinary action against him?" Barbara retorted.

"You're the best," Liz chuckled. "I knew Barbara would see it right away." Liz took back the laptop and clicked on the keys some more.

I bent sideways to watch Liz's progress, letting me

see the news captions before Barbara. Articles discussing the possible failure of the investment house led by Larry because of the regulatory investigation, some declaring that more capital was desperately needed to prop up the business. Photos of Larry with other men dressed in black suits, bodyguards by the look of them, warding off reporters and photographers. Liz pointed at the dateline of the articles. And when both Barbara and I had noted the date, Liz leaned over and brought up a different screen. One with Eleanor's photo and, beneath her photo, an obituary. I felt the hairs on my arms rise, felt my heart constrict in fear, and my throat tighten. I knew what was coming next.

The news articles now dominating the laptop's screen were dated a week after Eleanor's death. Larry's investment firm was saved. Monies had poured in and rescued the ailing company. Larry was smiling at the photographers again, though the men in black still kept them at a discreet distance away.

"You think Larry killed his wife?" I was shocked. And Connie was constantly by the man's side. Kyle said Connie and Eleanor were best friends. It didn't make sense.

"The police didn't think so." Liz brought up Eleanor's death certificate, the words "accidental death" listed as the cause of death. She brought up another screen, a news article about the accident. "The paramedics had to wait for a helicopter to bring Eleanor up from where she fell on the beach. But Larry had been rescued by his guests. They had heard him screaming for help, holding on to the roots of a tree growing out of the cliff. He was in shock when the paramedics came. They had to sedate him before they could get him strapped to a stretcher and an IV put on his arm for the shock. He kept trying to get to Eleanor, who had gone over the edge and was clearly dead to everyone who saw her lying broken on the beach. The police ruled out murder quickly, and Eleanor's death was pronounced accidental within a few days." Liz slowed down and met my eyes, square on. "Detective Storm led the investigation."

"Him again," I said.

"Well, it's not crazy to say it was an accident. The man was found hanging over a cliff, holding on for dear life on tree roots, screaming his head off for help. If he had planned to kill his wife by pushing her over, wouldn't he make sure he didn't follow her over the edge? Killing yourself as well sounds very counter-productive," Barbara said.

"As not crazy to say Rich and Jim drowned by accident? Eleanor lived in that house for years. She knew her backyard. How could she fall by accident?" I wasn't convinced.

"They were having a party," Stefan said. "She might have had too much to drink."

"Could he have staged his fall?" I wondered.

"How? Push his wife over, slide into place by the tree, and hold on to the roots? That's cold-blooded," Stefan said.

"Larry's a hedge fund manager. He's a gambler. Doesn't ice run through a gambler's veins?" I said. "How else could they take risks without falling apart?"

"She's got a point," Barbara said wryly.

"You all ready for the last piece? My pièce de résistance?" Liz asked everyone brightly.

"The both of you!" I scolded. "Why do you have to piece it out like this?"

"And spoil our fun? No, thank you." Liz was now scrolling through social media photos. She turned the laptop back to us and sat back, hands on her lap, waiting with a faint smile playing on her lips.

Stefan had the same self-satisfied smile on his lips. That man, he just had to play the devil's advocate.

I scrolled through, Barbara peering over my shoulder.

The screen showed photos of a lawn party. Guests mingling with drinks in their hands. Servers in white ties could be seen mingling with the guests, offering plates of hors d'oeuvres and glasses of champagne, wine, or cocktails garnished with flowers. Eleanor and Larry could be seen in some photos, clearly the hostess and host of the party. And by the date stamped in them, the photos were of the party where Eleanor had fallen to her death. I glanced sharply at Liz, who nodded at me to keep on looking.

It was Barbara who first saw it.

A gasp and sharply indrawn breath warned me. Barbara's finger pointed shakily at a photo.

Dressed in a white suit, her blonde hair stylishly done in an updo, diamond studs in her ears, Brie was in one of the photos, handing Eleanor a cocktail. Brie worked for Elegant Dining? Since when? Why didn't Janet tell me? I reordered my chaotic thoughts. Did Janet know Brie worked for the competition? She scanned the faces of the other servers, not finding Kyle. Only Brie. Was this the connection between Larry and Brie we were looking for? The rest of the group had fallen silent. They were waiting for me. I looked around and saw the conviction in their eyes.

Larry had killed his wife for her money. And Brie

for the blackmail.

I took my gaze away from Brie's photo. All that life gone in an instant.

"I'm calling Edna. This might be enough to get her cleared." I reached for my phone. Knowing there was a better suspect than her would make Edna feel better.

"Why didn't you tell Fred you have Edna's number?" Liz said.

Barbara raised her eyebrows at me.

"Edna said not to tell Fred where she was. If Edna didn't want Fred to have her number, I wasn't about to give it to him either. She can call him as easily as she called us." I hated how my voice sounded defensive and felt the flush creeping upward to my cheeks. "Edna? Hi, it's us."

"Meg, hi! I was waiting for your call. How's everyone?"

"Everyone's good. They're all here with me at Sweet Buns." I put the phone on the table and Edna on the speaker.

"Hi, hi," she said. "Ma, the gang is on the phone. You want to say hello to them?" We heard a faint hello from Gladys. "She's not feeling well today." Edna was back on the phone. "It's all the chocolate she's been eating. Her sweet tooth is giving her indigestion. Then there's the hot dogs, potato chips, and popcorn. Not good for her blood pressure or heart, but there's not much else in the camp stores. I was in a hurry and couldn't go food shopping. We only have what we can buy from the store here."

"You won't believe how much she loves the popcorn," Edna continued. "She insists it is better than any other popcorn I've given her. I tell her it's because of that obscene amount of butter the boy at the counter puts in her popcorn. He gives her whatever she asks for, with the biggest smile on his face. He won't listen to me when I tell him no butter. And when I tell her the popcorn is bad for her diverticulitis and the butter will spike her blood pressure, you know what she tells me? 'Iha,' she says, 'I have to go sometime, don't I?' And that boy chimes in with 'You go, grandma!' I'll lose my mind here, I tell you."

We didn't know what to tell Edna. And this was only the second day since they ran away.

"Not that I blame the boy. I swear she's bewitched the boy. You know how she is. Ma had always gotten what she wanted. My father spoiled her. Her friends spoiled her. And now Papa and her friends are gone, I spoil her. At the rate she's going, everyone in camp will adopt her and make her their honorary grandmother. She'll be impossible to deal with if that happens. I'll be the big, bad wolf. And all I want to do is make sure she's okay. I know you guys think I'm crazy keeping her with me, but I'm greedy. I want whatever time she has left. I don't want to miss any of it. Is that so wrong?"

Stefan pushed back from his chair, eyes blinking rapidly. His parents had died in his early teens, and the aunt and uncle who had opened their hearts to a grieving boy and raised him as their own had moved back to Greece when they retired. Nowadays, Stefan saw them only through FaceTime. Liz kept biting her lips and scratching at her eyebrows. Her parents were in California, living near her sister. Barbara crossed her arms and looked daggers at everyone. I took the phone back from the table and walked away from the group. Both Barbara and I had lost our parents years back, mine after a long battle with failing kidneys and all the complications it brought.

Standing by the window, I looked out at Duck Harbor Park. "I'm sorry, Edna."

"It's not your fault. If anyone is to blame, it's me. I shouldn't have slapped Brie. Or if I had to slap her, I shouldn't have said those words. I was just so angry." Edna sounded so tired and defeated.

I had to keep her spirits up. "Listen, Edna, I called to tell you we are looking into someone Brie blackmailed. Once Detective Storm hears about him, he'll forget all about you. Sit tight there. We're working hard for you."

"Do you think I could go home soon?"

"Yes, of course you can. You can come home right now. Fred wants you to call him. He wants you back. Here at your house and not out there in the wild."

"You didn't tell him where we are, did you?"

"No, no, of course not. You told me not to." When I agreed with Edna that she should stay away, I hadn't counted on Gladys getting sick. Maybe I should have given Fred her number. He might convince her to come home.

"I don't know. Am I doing the right thing? What do you think? He's an attorney. He once told me that means he's an officer of the court. He can't lie when he's asked if he knows where I am. No, don't give it to him. If I need him, I'll call him."

I hate it when I'm right for the wrong reasons.

I felt for Edna. I understood her pain and the constant on-call care demanded of her. The doctor appointments, the tests, and the medicines she needed to make sure were taken on time. And like her, I'd take on all that again for a few more days with my parents.

I made the mistake, once, of worrying about Edna and Gladys out loud in front of Jim and Dora. Jim had turned to Dora and asked if she could see herself putting her folks in assisted living. Dora, not missing a beat, said, "Not on your life. I'd get expelled from the family as an ungrateful, worthless child. None of my uncles and aunts would talk to me. Or if they did, they'd ask why I didn't ship my parents to the Philippines, where other, better-raised children could take care of them. No thanks, they're staying with us when they get old." Jim had laughed and hugged his wife, telling me to lay off worrying about Edna and Gladys. Instead of making me feel better, Dora's words scared me. I wondered if that was her not-so-subtle way of saying her folks get priority if it comes to a choice between us and them. Jim was my one and only. Dora had a brother and a sister. These past twelve months, I'd worried if Dora's choice had gotten even simpler. Without Jim around, would Dora still feel the need to take me in? Would anyone care for me as well as Edna cared for Gladys?

Chapter Twenty-Four

We got up to leave without our usual cheerful goodbyes. Edna and Gladys weighed heavily on our minds. Barbara gripped the table's edge before levering herself upright. Liz picked up her bag from the floor and slung it over her shoulders. Stefan kept breathing in and out, steadying himself.

Wiping my lips with a napkin before tossing it into a garbage can with the remnants of my lunch, I glanced back to make sure the table was clean and ready for the next customers before following Barbara out the door. Liz and Stefan were ahead of us. Stepping up to the curb, I waited for a car to pass by.

Barbara's car was parked across from Sweet Buns. The weather was gorgeous. Warm with a bit of a breeze, not enough for me to need a heavy coat. The sky was clear with the sun shining through.

And then...

I felt something slam into my shoulder. My bag went flying. My body followed. The shoulder straps of my bag tangled with my arms and hands. I heard Barbara scream and the screech of an oncoming car.

I saw the road coming up to meet me. In a fog, unable to believe what was happening, I realized I was falling. My reflexes took over. I felt muscles bunching. My body fought to lean away from the car, trying to get back to the safety of the sidewalk. Despairing, I flailed my hands, expecting to grab nothing but air. I didn't want to break my hip. Not my hip, I prayed. My fingers flexed and reached out. Was this the end? There had been so many times when I wanted nothing more but to join Rich and Jim, to no longer be alone in my empty house. Why was I fighting for life when what I thought was my dearest wish was within my grasp? I almost laughed at the absurdity of my thoughts. It was a very inconvenient time to find out how much living I still wanted to do. I stretched my arms and reached for life, for more years with my friends…with Archer…Dora.

Then…

Magically, the road stayed far away. The car didn't get any nearer. I was caught mid-air.

Shoulders held firmly, my waist leaned against a trunk of a body, and strong, solid thighs and knees supported the rest of me. Voices, some shrill, some throaty, spilled all over me. I closed my eyes, brought my hands to my chest, and huddled deep inside someone's embrace.

Saved. The thought exploded in my mind. I burst into tears.

"What happened? Are you okay?" I heard Barbara's frantic demands through my tears. "What happened?"

"Someone pushed her," Liz wheezed her words out, as if she had just come back from a run. "Stefan is still out there, screaming at everyone to catch the man who shoved Meg. But the jerk's gone by now."

Others had come to aid the man holding me. I was helped to my feet, shivering with shock.

"Here, have her sit here." Veronica was there, motioning everyone to the chairs set by the patio in front of her cafe. "What happened?" She asked Barbara, who had fought her way to my side.

"Someone pushed her," Liz answered instead, repeating herself.

"He's gone." Stefan was back. "A car pulled alongside the rat. Guy jumped into the car and off they went, too fast for anyone to get the license plate." Stefan pushed his hair back from his face. "Is she okay?"

Veronica's arms were around my shoulders. My heart twinged with the irony of how former kindergarten students of mine, like Veronica, whose tears I wiped and whose faces I coaxed smiles out of when they were five, with their teeth either falling out or coming in, were now giving me the comfort I used to give them.

"I'm fine." The solidity of the chair and the distance between me and the street had calmed me down. I had been so afraid I would find myself hurled across the street. I dreaded planting my face on the gravel road and the bruises that would scar my face for days. But I didn't want to think about what my chances were if I had gotten hit by the car that was heading toward me as I fell. My breathing slowed, no longer coming in ragged gasps punctuated with sobs.

The man who saved me stood in front of me, his face crinkled in a fierce frown. "I saw his face clearly. Can someone please call the cops? I can describe the guy."

Veronica held her phone up, showing she'd dialed nine-one-one, turning away when the call was picked up.

Turning to me, the man said, "You sure you're okay? That was nasty. If I had laid my hands on him, I'd have broken his face for what he did." He ran his fingers through his hair. I saw thick, strong hands. I didn't doubt he could break anyone's face with a punch from one of those hands. "Why push a total stranger?" The man was saying, glaring at everyone who stood near. But my friends were made of sterner stuff and not one of them backed down from his glare.

Veronica handed the man her phone. I heard him give a description. I hoped an alert was issued for the man and that he was captured and put behind bars.

Two days ago, my house was ransacked. Today, I was shoved into oncoming traffic. After one quick look at my friends, I avoided their eyes. I could see the doubt behind their worried faces. I fancied I could smell their fear because it smelled exactly like mine. Was this because of our meddling in Brie's murder? The threats started with me. Will it end with them? Were any of us safe?

My savior stood nearby, craning his neck up and down the street. The dispatcher had told him someone was coming to take his statement. I heard him muttering over and over how lucky I was he had parked right beside the café and was getting out of his car when the man shoved me. That he had seen the man lift his arms, and knew right away what he would do. I would have been dead, according to the man, if he had not caught me.

I kept thanking him over and over. But he kept answering I should always check who was beside me. Situational awareness, he called it. Couldn't he see I was old? Old people were situationally aware. Of potholes, steps, uneven ground, running children, and a long list of maybe disasters. Murderers were not on the list. Not until today. How long was it until the cops got here? And my rescuer could go and leave me alone with my aches and pain. How was that for being thankful? I felt ashamed of myself for a moment until the man started on his tirade again on the need for being alert and mindful.

Then I saw the man striding up the steps to where I sat. Detective Storm. Why him? Wasn't there anyone else in the police force they could send?

The crowd around us parted to let the detective in. Raising my eyes to the skies, I stretched my neck and shoulders as far back as they could go, working out the kinks in my body from that nearly disastrous fall I'd barely avoided.

"Mrs. Brightbook, I should have known," Jonathan said. "What are you up to now?"

The man beside me, the one who had saved me, twitched, his eyes opening wide. He took a step back, putting distance between himself and me.

Trust Detective Storm to blame the wrong person. This wasn't my fault. Any fool would know this, but not Detective Storm, of course.

"Detective, you're not blaming Meg for getting shoved into traffic." Barbara's voice was so acidic, it would have sizzled a hole in the man's polyester pants. Liz and Stefan stood ranged beside her; all three pairs of eyes focused on the detective.

Jonathan wilted under all that attention. "No, no. I meant, her house was ransacked the other day. Then someone tries to kill her? This is highly suspicious, don't you think?"

The man beside me took another step back. "Ah…ransacked? This isn't some organized crime nonsense, is it?" His gaze hop-skipped around our faces, stopping at the detective.

"Organized crime? No, there's no organized crime here. Get a grip, man, we're in Western Suffolk County, not New York City. It's more likely a prank, a bunch of kids back home from college, working off a high, acting on a dare. That's all this is. Organized crime." Jonathan's voice could have soured a freshly picked tomato from my garden. He motioned to the cop standing behind him. "You, take this man's statement. He told nine-one-one he saw the perp."

"You know what? I didn't really see who pushed this old lady here. He had a hoodie on, and I was busy rushing to catch her. Come to think of it, I didn't get a good look," the man said, all while backing up even farther from where I sat. Facing me, he said, "I hope you're good now, but I have to go. And don't forget, situational awareness. You're too young to die yet." The man turned and quick-stepped down the sidewalk, taking his car keys out of his pocket. A car parked right beside the cafe's curb flashed its lights on, then off.

I heard the man mutter to himself as he hurried away. But his words made no sense to me. Something about the cops holding on to his expensive fishing rod?

Jonathan put his arm out to stop his man from following. "Let him go. No use forcing him to give a statement. It'll be riddled with 'I don't know' and won't stand up in court even if we catch the perp."

My now reluctant savior got in his car and drove off. Leaving me in the care of Detective Storm.

Chapter Twenty-Five

"If you hadn't scared him with your inane 'highly suspicious,' you could have had his statement," Barbara said.

"We have his name. We can find him anytime," Jonathan said, looking around at the crowd still lingering around. "This is not the best place to talk. Better we continue this at the station."

"I'll bring her," Barbara said, inserting herself between the detective and me. "You're not putting her in a police car. She hasn't done anything wrong."

Liz, Stefan, and Veronica closed in, shielding me. Jonathan rolled his eyes and walked away, his man following.

Barbara gave her arm for me to lean on. Liz handed my bag over to me, leather scuffed and scarred in places. Stefan offered my left shoe, the one I hadn't been aware I was missing. And Veronica dusted me off, making sure no dust or street dirt clung to my clothes and tweaking my shirt over my shoulders.

"Let's go," Barbara said. "I don't imagine Detective Storm would have many questions for you. His mind seemed pretty made up as to what happened and who was responsible."

Waving goodbye to everyone, I gave Veronica a quick hug and limped my way to Barbara's car. The Fourth Precinct was not far from Duck Harbor Park.

"By the way, that man who rescued you? That was the fisherman who fished…well, you know what," Barbara said as she turned into a parking lot.

I'd been so busy thinking, I hadn't realized we were already at the police station. "So that's what he was grumbling about," I said, the mumbled words of the man now making sense to me. "You think that's why he thought organized crime was involved?"

Barbara got out and went around the car to help me. "No, blame that on Detective Storm. Don't try getting out of the car till I get there."

My body still ached, and I wasn't sure if I could stand unassisted, so I waited, watching cars come and go from the parking lot. And that's why I was the first to see Dora's dark blue SUV drive by. Still in her emergency room scrubs, hair in a ponytail, her eyes scanned the area for a spot to park.

"Just what we needed," Barbara mumbled.

I didn't bother answering. Walking slowly to the building, we let Dora go ahead, my rescuer receding from my thoughts.

"You're straining Dora's patience this week, you know. That's twice she had to leave work early."

"It's not like I mean to. Things happen. And, anyway, it's not like I asked her to handle it. I'm quite capable of cleaning up after my mess." I was being unfair to Dora, I knew that. But my foot felt swollen, my shoulder hurt, and my heart was beating fast. I wasn't feeling charitable toward anyone. What I needed was a cool drink of water. Maybe then I'd get myself under control.

"There you are!" Dora rushed to my side, displacing Barbara. "You should not be here. You should have gone to the hospital and got yourself checked out. Who's the moron who dragged you here?"

"Ahem." Someone to our right cleared his throat. "Dora, please." Detective Storm had come out to meet us. "She didn't look all that bad a few minutes ago. I would have put her in the ambulance if she did."

"How did you find out?" I asked Dora. "I'm fine. The drive here made things worse. I think I stiffened up. Maybe a chair and a drink of water?"

"Veronica called me. Let's get you inside," Dora said.

"Oh sure, come this way." Jonathan led the way in, opening the door to a room with a table and four plastic chairs. He left us briefly to speak to one of the cops in the room. I eased myself down on a chair. Barbara sat on my right while Dora hovered on my left.

"We should go home. You need to be in bed." Taking the glass of water from the cop, Dora placed the glass in my hands. "Here, drink this. It'll ease you. How's your heart?"

Jonathan twitched. Didn't he think I'd be in shock and my heart affected? Silly man.

"It's fine. I need to rest a bit. Really, I'm fine." I put the glass down, having drunk it half empty. Dora nodded to the waiting cop, silently asking for another glass of water. He went to get another, leaving the door open. When the cop came back, he handed the glass to Dora and went over to Jonathan, whispering something to him.

"Who?" Jonathan said.

"Detective," said Fred, walking in after the cop.

"Oh, good, you're here," Dora said. "I couldn't understand why Meg had to go to the police station, so I called Fred. Just in case."

"Why was Mrs. Meagan Brightbook asked to go to the police station? Wasn't she the victim? Shouldn't she be in the hospital, considering the condition she's in?" Fred's voice was clipped and quietly furious.

"Two days ago, someone put holes in her walls and ripped her stuff apart. Today, someone tried to kill her. And I don't bring her in?" Jonathan said.

I saw how angry it made him to have Fred question his judgment in front of Dora.

"Someone went through your house?" Fred asked me, then turned back to Jonathan. "No, you don't bring her in. She's the victim. You bring in the one responsible for the crime. The criminal, remember? The one you're supposed to arrest. Not the one you're supposed to be protecting. And speaking of protection, did you assign one to my client? It's clear someone is out to get her." Turning his head back to me, he asked, "Meg, how are you feeling?"

"The water helped, but my heart is still racing. I think I need a few more moments." I wasn't sure why Fred was so furious, but I was willing to play sick if he needed me to. "And I don't need protection. I really don't." Did Fred forget we were supposed to go undercover at Veronica's party in two days?

"Protection?" Barbara exclaimed. "What for? We don't need someone following Meg around everywhere."

"Dora, dear, am I clammy? I feel a bit faint," I added, hoping to distract Fred from any more talk of setting guards on me. In case he hadn't picked up on what Barbara meant. Except I wasn't sure if I was only playing sick. My heart was racing and my hands were trembling.

"Is she okay?" Jonathan asked, panic coloring his voice at last.

Good, maybe next time he'll do his job the way it should be done and not drag innocent old ladies like Edna and me to the police station.

"She needs to rest," snapped Dora, her eyes hot, eyebrows furrowed.

"Can I take my client home now?"

When did I become Fred's client? I don't remember getting myself a lawyer. Let alone needing one.

Jonathan shifted from foot to foot. Then he stilled. I saw his face change, becoming surer of himself. "Client? Yes, where is Mrs. Gomez? I passed by her house, and she wasn't there."

"You passed by her house? To do what? It's not so you can question her without her attorney present? Because you know you can't do that, right?" Fred wasn't at all disturbed by Jonathan's dodge. He just tightened the screws more.

I started to raise my hands to clap and opened my mouth to call out "Bravo." Except I remembered I was supposed to be sick, so I put my hands down and closed my mouth.

"Of course not," Jonathan said. "I wanted to check in. Make sure she hasn't skipped town."

"My client is not under arrest. She's not out on bail. Why can't she go wherever she wants to go? Am I missing something here?"

"You know what I mean. Mrs. Gomez is to make herself available to us in case we have questions for her."

"Questions you will not be asking unless I am present. Let's be very clear on that, Detective," Fred retorted. "I will not have my client harassed. Or any of her friends. You have questions for my client, you want to see my client, you call me. No one else. Are we clear, Detective Storm?"

Jonathan's face was red, from anger or embarrassment over the dressing down he was getting in front of Dora, I couldn't tell. I loved how Fred took him down. But pushing him against the wall might make the detective reckless.

"Fine. Take this as a demand to bring your client to my office tomorrow morning for an interview. Ten o'clock in the morning, sharp," Jonathan growled.

I stifled a groan. I need not have bothered; no one heard me. Barbara and Dora were busy watching the two men face off.

"Not possible. I'm busy until Monday. We'll be there Monday morning, ten o'clock," Fred shot back.

"No, no, no." Jonathan smiled, and it wasn't a pretty sight. "You're bringing Mrs. Gomez to my office tomorrow morning, Friday, at ten o'clock, or I'm issuing a warrant for her arrest."

"On what charge? You don't have enough to charge her with murder."

"I might not have enough to charge her with murder, but if she doesn't show up tomorrow at ten o'clock sharp, I can get her for obstruction of justice," Jonathan said, smug and sneering.

I hated it when men started crowing like roosters.

Chapter Twenty-Six

It was noon Friday, two hours past Detective Storm's ten o'clock deadline for Edna.

We were all gathered at Sweet Buns again. Except it was Fred having lunch with us, not Edna. Knowing there was an APB out for Edna gave me a headache. But that was nothing compared to the roiling of my stomach and the pounding of my heart when I thought of how I almost died yesterday. It made eating difficult. I dropped the fork in disgust. "Why? Why ransack my house? Why try to kill me?" I braced myself, facing up to the thought I couldn't avoid anymore, the one that had kept me awake all last night. "Is this because we're looking into Brie's murder? You don't think it's Larry, do you?"

Eyes flitted here and there except where I was looking. No one wanted to meet my gaze.

"Barbara?"

"What else can it be?"

I saw how worried Barbara was.

"We could—" Stefan cut in "—you know, backtrack. It might be the killer. Or it might not. It most probably is, but in case something else is happening here? I don't think we should just assume what's happening to Meg is because we're looking for Brie's killer."

"Because of what, then?" Liz asked, taken aback. "No...you don't think?"

"Why not? No one knew how they died."

Stefan meant Rich and Jim. Was it possible? Did I do something to flush out their killer?

"Let's see. My house was ransacked on Tuesday. Barbara and I were coming back from Selena and Alan. We were going to Sweet Buns, but Edna called and said Detective Storm had arrested her. We went to the police station. Waited for Fred to come and get Edna free. Then we all went to Sweet Buns. From Sweet Buns, I decided to stop by my house to let Cannoli out before taking Barbara home. That's when we saw the house—"

"You know the time they ransacked the house?" Liz asked.

"My neighbor said about mid-morning?" I started to shiver. I knew I was inside a warm café, packed with warm bodies. But my body insisted I was standing at the front door of my home, looking at the wreckage it had become.

"Then it had to be something you did before then," Stefan insisted.

"We were at Selena and Alan." I shook myself back to the present.

"Not Alan," Barbara said. "Or Selena. The timing is not right. We were at their house when it happened."

"Okay, let's try Monday. What did you do Monday?" Stefan asked after a moment.

"Monday." I racked my brain; it seemed so long ago. "I went to see Janet. Detective Storm came over while I was there and arrested Kyle. After that, I went to the gym, then home because Archer was coming over. Had dinner with him and…" I felt the hairs on my arm standing up. "The CCTV"—I turned to Stefan— "Dora texted me asking if Archer could sleep over. She was working another early shift the next morning. Archer was sulking. I wanted to distract him, so I talked about CCTV and Detective Storm. Archer said he could hack into a CCTV. Said his dad showed him how." I remembered something else. I slowed down. "And yesterday, when I was shoved into traffic? The day before, on Wednesday, Archer and I went looking for CCTVs near the streets where Edna and Gladys live. But there were no businesses near them, so no CCTVs, only Ring cameras. I got this bright idea to ask Archer to check on the two meat processing plants nearest to Whitman's Port. Maybe the killer used one of those places to cut the body up. I was in my driveway, and Archer had the laptop on top of Barbara's car. We were using the program Jim had installed in Archer's laptop both days."

"The program Jim told Archer to get rid of if something happened to him?" Stefan said, his voice sharpening.

My bewildered eyes met worried ones.

"Did you see anything?" Fred said.

"The first place was clear. No one in and out all Friday night. Or Saturday night. The second one…there was a gap in the CCTV footage from about Thursday night to Saturday early morning. Parts of the video were cut."

"Why didn't you tell us!" Stefan was almost shouting, clearly infuriated with me.

"I forgot. Yesterday got so busy. So many things happened."

"Which meat-packing plant? The one by Yaphank?" Liz asked me. Seeing me nod, Liz turned to Stefan. "Connie's family owns that meat-packing plant."

Quiet descended.

"The cops are waiting for the warrant to get those security videos," Fred said, breaking the silence.

"What?" I squeaked out, turning to him.

"I got fed up with Jonathan and his fixation with Edna, so I pressed him the other day. Turns out, they already have the CCTV recordings from both warehouses, and they know about the deleted videos. Police forensics wants to recover the deleted videos. But Connie's family is refusing to surrender all deleted files without a warrant. The hearing is today."

"That's good, then. We don't have to say anything to the police about Archer's hacking. Anyway, it can't be Connie. Both Connie and her husband were in London this past weekend." Barbara kept the conversation moving. "What I want to know is why Meg was almost killed yesterday. Is it because we're getting ourselves involved with Brie's murder? Or is it because of Rich and Jim? Is there anything else out there that makes Meg a target?"

"Let's not get ahead of ourselves. The cops are busy looking for the man who did it. When he's caught, and he will be, we'll know why Meg's house was ransacked and why she was pushed into the street. Let's stop this guessing around. It doesn't do anybody any good." Fred met each of our eyes while he spoke.

To my surprise, the others calmed down. Even Barbara. Me? I pushed all thoughts of the past few days out of my mind.

"Will Detective Storm actually put out an alert on Edna?" I poked at the lettuce, tomatoes, and cucumbers on my plate.

"How will they find her? She's not driving her car.

And Detective Storm doesn't know she's using Fred's car." Liz tried to cheer the group up. "Edna could stay free if she stayed inside the campgrounds."

"They give out a description of Edna. Possibly also of Gladys. If Detective Storm was smart enough to figure out wherever Edna goes, her mother goes with her," Barbara pointed out, playing with the salt and pepper shaker.

Stefan took them away from her and placed them in the middle of the table.

"So, the cops are looking for two old ladies together? How many old ladies go out in twos?" Liz said. "That's not much to go on."

"No, it's not. And Edna's car is parked in my garage. Out of sight. I've been using a rental car," Fred pointed out. "I haven't asked before. But I need to, now. What else have you guys found out about this murder? If they do catch Edna, I'll have to give the District Attorney's office something to keep her out of prison."

Barbara, Liz, and Stefan looked at me. It was time to come clean. "We think Brie was blackmailing Larry Billings. She worked as a server at the party where Larry's wife, Eleanor, fell to her death."

"I heard about that case. I thought the cops ruled it an accidental death."

I had nothing to say to that.

"Excuse me, I have to shake the precinct up. Get them looking into Eleanor's death again. Those guys are going to hate me when we're done with this." Fred got up to leave. "It's okay if you don't want to tell me Edna has been calling you. But make sure she knows about the alert. She needs to keep her head down a few more days."

We waited for the door to close on Fred. I took out

my phone. "I'm calling Edna first. She needs to hear what Fred said."

"Hey, it's you. I've been waiting for your call. Are you with everyone?" Edna sounded very cheerful. Too cheerful. I put her on speaker phone.

"How's Gladys?" Barbara said.

"Still eating hot dogs?" Liz asked, getting a smack from Barbara.

"No, no more hot dogs. We got mac-n-cheese from the store. I'm afraid it's not much better. Ma stopped being regular. It's a good thing the store also had prunes. That helped."

We all groaned.

"How far away are you? Maybe I can drive over and bring some groceries?"

"Thanks, Stefan, but we're at least six hours away if you don't stop. Ma wanted to stop every two hours. I had to make her wait for three, or we would have gotten here too late. I had to change her as soon as we checked in."

We all gave another groan. Stefan looked pale.

"But don't worry about the food. When I was at the store buying prunes for Mom, I met the store manager. I must have been babbling to myself. She asked me what I needed, and when she heard how I had nothing to feed Mom except hot dogs and mac-n-cheese, she showed me how to order online and get groceries delivered. We should have real food in about an hour."

"So we're good here. Except..." The cheeriness left Edna's voice. She spoke so softly we could barely hear her.

"Except what?" I asked when we heard nothing more from Edna.

"Well, you haven't said anything about it. And Fred

said he'll look into it. I don't want to make more work for you guys. You're already doing so much."

"Edna, what is it?" Barbara said. "So much has happened since you left. If Fred forgot to do something, tell us and we'll remind him."

"I wouldn't ask, but I'm worried about her."

"Is it the girl? The one Brie pushed?" Stefan leaned closer to the phone.

"Yes! Stefan, do you know who she is? Is she okay?"

"We know her name is Leni. But other than that, no, sorry. As Barbara said, we've been so busy."

Stefan looked as unhappy as the rest of us did. Edna had asked us to find the girl, and we forgot all about it.

"But Liz and I will be on it today, I promise. We'll find out where she is and if she's okay." Stefan waved at Liz and pointed to her laptop.

"Edna, listen. Fred was just here," I said.

"Oh?" Edna didn't know it yet, but she had bigger worries than this girl.

"Detective Storm insisted he meet with you and Fred this morning. When you didn't show up, they put out an alert on you." I hated being the one to break the news to her.

"This morning? You didn't tell me I was supposed to meet with the detective this morning!" Edna sounded upset. And scared.

"We didn't tell you because we didn't want you here in case Detective Storm decides to arrest you." When Edna didn't say anything, I plowed on. "Fred said to stay put. Your car is parked inside his garage. The cops won't find it. And they don't know you have his car." When Edna still didn't say anything, I decided to tell her more.

"Fred is shaking things up at the precinct. And he's making them look at other suspects. He's there now. If the cops find evidence of the blackmail"—I crossed my fingers—"Fred thinks that might be enough to get you cleared."

"What if they can't find any evidence?" Edna sounded very close to crying.

"Don't worry," Liz spoke over me. "Veronica is throwing a party tomorrow. And we're going undercover as servers. We'll find something. You'll be home by Sunday."

"Edna, Sunday is two days away. Stay where you are." I followed up after Liz. "Don't go anywhere near a cop. Barbara said they might have a description of you and Gladys. It's only a few more days. Keep your head down."

"I could do that. Easy. But what do I do about my mother? If she goes off on her own when I'm not looking, I need help finding her." Edna sounded frantic. "I can't lock her in. I did that yesterday when I went to the store, and she banged on the door nonstop, asking to be let out. I came back to our neighbor, shouting to her from outside, while her husband went to their camper to look for something to open the door. Imagine if they let her out? I wouldn't know where to start looking! Now they know not to let her out, but I can't lock her in anymore. Someone else might decide to call the cops on us."

We all looked at each other. We didn't know how much longer Edna could stay away. Gladys was becoming a big problem.

The call ended shortly after. We didn't move from the table. Despite Stefan's repeated urgings, bordering on begging, Liz refused to take out her laptop and start looking for the girl. Barbara added her voice to Stefan's, but that didn't work either. Liz kept tapping her finger on the table while her eyes roved around the room.

"Do you have to do that?" Barbara sniped at Liz.

I stayed quiet. Liz was planning something. She was only this difficult when she had something on her mind. Something mad. Deranged.

"If the hearing is today, the search warrant would go out today. Tomorrow, at the latest. If the one who erased the video didn't know what they were doing, I could probably recover whatever was erased," Liz said. "And there's nothing in Larry's background that makes me believe he's a tech wizard; he probably just used the software's general functions to erase part of the recording. The video must have him breaking into the building. Otherwise, why delete it?"

Stefan and Barbara gaped at Liz, their mouths hanging wide open.

"Don't you want to see what's on the video? Why should the cops have all the fun?"

Stefan's face morphed into joy with a smile spread from ear to ear, while Barbara's turned red in anger, clamping her mouth closed, lips pressed tightly together.

"Awesome! You can do that?" Stefan crowed.

"Are you out of your mind?" Barbara snarled.

I heard both speak at the same time. It was a measure of my desperation I took Liz seriously. Madness was acceptable at this point. No one, not even me, objected to Liz casting Larry as the murderer. He was the only suspect we had left.

"How do you propose we do this?" I asked.

"Simple. We break into the warehouse." Liz smiled.

"Tonight. At midnight."

Great, now we're on the other side of the law. Breaking and entering. At least, Rich wasn't around anymore to bail me out if things went wrong.

But Fred was, the voice in my head piped up.

Shut up, I piped back.

Chapter Twenty-Seven

"One more house, Cannoli, then we're turning back," I consoled the tired corgi by my side. The everyday chore of walking Cannoli made the past days feel distant and unreal, and tonight, much farther away than the few hours it was. And I needed that distance. So much so, I walked farther than I usually did.

Tongue out and panting, Cannoli had been trotting by my side for a few minutes now, no longer interested in burrowing her nose in the manicured lawns we'd passed by. Except Cannoli had decided enough was enough; she wasn't moving another foot. My attention focused on my pet; I wasn't aware of the house we had stopped at or the car coming up from its driveway. Not until it was right on top of me.

"Good afternoon," a familiar voice rang out. Larry Billings was leaning out of the car window, sunglasses perched on his dark hair.

"Oh, hi." I didn't pay much attention to Larry. I had Cannoli to worry about. "Cannoli, sweetheart, I promise, we're turning back, and we'll be at Dora's soon. So come on, let's get moving. I can't carry you back, you know." My jaw tightened at hearing Larry laugh. I knew we looked comical right now, but I wasn't amused.

"Do you need a ride home?" Larry asked, his voice slightly raised to be heard over the purr of his car.

That got me swiveling to face him, hope lighting up

my face. "Would you mind? Cannoli sheds terribly, though. You'll have dog hair all over your chairs." I warned in case Larry wasn't familiar with how much corgis shed. Cannoli was blowing her fur as she got rid of her winter coat for the coming summer. Larry would regret giving us a ride when he finds out how impossible it was to get dog hair out of his car. Sleek with sporty lines, Larry's car reminded me of a wild animal, a very expensive one at that.

"Don't worry, I'm on my way out to work anyway. I'll swing by Dora's. You're only a few houses down. Cannoli, is it? She'll only be a few minutes in the car. Someone at work can bring the car to get it vacuumed."

Poor deluded man. He'll know better next time. I wasn't turning his offer down. Cannoli wasn't giving me any other choice.

"Hop on." Larry leaned over and opened the passenger door to his car.

And of course, Cannoli knew the sound of a car door unlocking. Up went her butt, her docked tail wagging. She trotted over to the car, barking in short bursts, eager to get in.

Settling beside Larry, I was glad for the ride. Then I froze for a millisecond before pushing the seatbelt lock in. This wasn't the wisest move I'd ever made, getting into the car of a man who we thought was a double murderer. I felt the blood drain from my face.

The car surged forward, like a wild animal given its head. Larry turned onto the road and pointed the car toward Dora's house. Too late for me to get out now. And I wasn't leaving Cannoli in the car with him anyway.

I relaxed in degrees as I realized it was a straight

shot to Dora's house. No turns. Not until he was past the house. We were a house away from Dora when I started worrying again. Would he stop? Or would he keep going? I was clasping my hands so tightly it hurt. Cannoli had no such concerns. Her nose was propped on the console between the two front seats, saliva dribbling onto the black leather. The car slid to a stop in front of Dora's house, and Larry turned to face me.

"Brie worked for Elegant Dining." I heard myself say. "During the party, when Eleanor fell." What was I thinking? I was inside the man's car. My hand crept onto the door handle.

"You found that out, did you?" Larry's eyes turned cold and hard in an instant. "Not that it was hard to find. I certainly wasn't hiding it. And before you go blundering about where you don't belong, you might as well know Brie was there when my wife slipped and fell to her death. She saw everything, including how I almost killed myself trying to save Eleanor."

I felt pinned to the seat of the car. But no, that was the seatbelt. I took my hand off the door, unlocked the seatbelt, and flung it off.

Larry smiled, sensing my unease. "My wife and I left all the party planning to our personal assistants. That's what they're hired for. I can arrange for them to talk to you. Let me know when and where."

"No, no, that's fine. Forget what I said," I stuttered, hands grasping once more for the door handle and stumbling out when the door opened. Cannoli hurled herself over the front seat into my arms. Staggering a bit, I slammed the car door closed and moved back, not letting Cannoli go, afraid she might get run over when Larry drove off.

Instead, the tinted window slid down. Larry leaned over the passenger seat. "Mrs. B, whoever killed Brie, it wasn't me. She's worth more to me alive than dead. And it's not one of the Sands Neck society ladies. You see, they like to keep their hands clean." Nodding at Cannoli clutched to my chest, he said, "She's very cute. You don't want anything to happen to her." The windows went back up, and the car came to life. Larry drove off, gliding back onto the road.

Was that a threat? Against Cannoli? Did Larry just warn me off?

I was shaking so bad I had to let Cannoli down.

Larry was right, however. If Brie were Larry's alibi for his wife's death, killing her would make him the prime suspect for both deaths. He was too intelligent to let that happen. And Stefan had said the same thing as Larry did about revenge and society ladies.

But what if Larry thought he could double-bluff the cops? He was smart and cunning, and so arrogant I wouldn't be surprised if he thought he could get away with it.

I was so confused, I didn't know what to think anymore. When we got inside the house, Cannoli headed straight for her water bowl; her noisy slurping made me feel guiltier by the second. I had worked her hard this morning. Thirst satisfied, Cannoli sought her bed. Soon, I heard her rhythmic snoring. Cannoli didn't even twitch when the doorbell rang. Heading down the hallway, I saw a fuzzy figure of a man through the glass panels of the door.

"Good afternoon." The man before me was the older cop with Detective Storm, the day they arrested Kyle.

For a second, I was brought back to that awful day

one year ago when another cop had rung the doorbell at my front door. It was Saturday, about noon. An accident, he had said, his eyes showing the sorrow his words did not. The kayak had overturned. The bodies found a mile down. CPR was performed, but life had fled and refused to come back. The poetry of his words was impossible to reconcile with the tragedy it expressed.

The sergeant must have seen something in my eyes because he started waving his hands. "Hey, hey, hey. It's nothing bad. I wanted to update you on our investigations into the ransacking of your house."

I pulled myself from my past.

"We arrested a suspect, and he's being held at the station," said the sergeant. "Someone recognized him from the APB and called it in. Lucky for us, there was a patrol car nearby to pick him up before he could get away again. Your neighbor is coming with her son later this afternoon to pick him out from a lineup. Could you stop by, and if the boy does pick the suspect out, see if you know the man? Or recognize him, at least."

"My grandson is coming home, and I can't leave him alone. What time do you need me there?" I wondered how I would do this with Archer coming home in less than an hour from now.

"Right now is good. I'll drive you to the station to make it easier for you and bring you back home once you're done."

"Come inside. I'll be right with you." I went to the kitchen, picked up my phone, and called Rosita. After a few rings, she answered the phone.

"Mrs. Meg?"

"Yes. I'm so sorry to call on short notice. But there's a cop at my front door. He's saying they caught the man responsible for ransacking my house. And they want me to go to the police station to see if I recognize the man. Can you come and stay with Archer?"

"Sure, Mrs. Meg. I be there for Archer. Also, Jose said he start work tonight. You go home next week, then. You miss your bed?"

"My bed, my kitchen, my plants," I said with a laugh. "Dora is very good to me, but, you know, home is home."

"Si, si. Mrs. Meg, I tell my kids, you go anywhere in this world, but where I am is home to you. I take care of you, no matter what." Rosita was silent for a few moments.

I remembered how Archer had to stay with Nico the other day because Rosita's daughter was still sick. "Is everything okay, Rosita? Archer said your daughter needed you home this past Wednesday?" I heard Rosita swallow hard. Was Rosita crying?

"No mind me. I not change what happened. Done is done."

I heard a sigh, another sniff.

Then Rosita said, "I tell Jose to start tonight. He call you for how much. Bye, Mrs. Meg."

I stood there, looking at my phone. Were Rosita and Jose not getting their daughter the medical help she needed? Maybe Dora could help them. In the meantime, the cop was waiting to take me to the station.

Chapter Twenty-Eight

"Tell me again why I'm driving the getaway car?" Barbara said.

We were parked across from H Meat Processing. It was close to midnight, and Barbara was at the wheel, looking nervously out at the darkness surrounding us.

Hours earlier, I had felt exposed and vulnerable at the police station, thinking how a total stranger could come in and destroy everything I held dear. Nico had identified the man as the one he saw go into my house, but I, on the other hand, had never seen the man before in my life. Even when the sergeant said there was a good chance it was the same man who tried to kill me. All I kept thinking was Nico had seen two men, and only one was behind bars. Sitting now in Barbara's car, getting involved in Liz's insane warehouse break-in, somehow eased the helplessness gripping me. I watched Liz go back and forth between two laptops, hers and Archer's. The poor boy didn't even know I had taken his laptop from his room while he was sleeping.

"Because I need to go inside if I am to hack into their system and find the missing CCTV footage," Liz answered Barbara, her fingers flying busily across her laptop's keyboard. "Connie's family hired a night security guard when they found out about the deleted videos. Meg is coming with me so she can tell me if the security guard finishes his rounds faster than he should.

And Stefan will be watching outside by the door. Which leaves you at the car. We have at least an hour before the security guard gets back to the guard room."

"When does the security guard do his rounds?" I asked, deciding how Liz found out about the security guard was beside the point. There was one, that was what mattered.

"Every two hours, starting at eight in the evening. We have"—Liz checked her watch—"about five minutes before the next round starts. I'm done with this." Liz handed Archer's laptop back to me.

"What did you do?" I asked.

"Hacked into their CCTV and put it on a loop. My grandson showed me how, and we practiced all afternoon. It's not difficult. You want Archer to learn how?"

I rolled my eyes. Liz was not getting within ten feet of Archer with a laptop.

"For the next ninety minutes, the CCTV will record the same footage it's on now. It won't see us creeping into and out of the building," Liz said, "C'mon, let's go."

Liz, Stefan, and I got out of the car. We were all wearing dark clothes with gloves on our hands. Liz wanted to smear face paint on our faces. To conceal the shine, she said. I vetoed the idea, ignoring Stefan's pleas. But I did agree to wear scarves over our faces.

Barbara drove away. She would circle back every twenty minutes or so. Seeing the car go, leaving the three of us alone in a dark, lonely street, with a building full of meat saws looming before us, I questioned my sanity.

"Let's go, let's go."

I felt Liz pushing me forward. She must have sensed I was getting ready to bolt right then. Sometimes, having friends who knew you inside out wasn't very helpful. Thankfully, the parking lot wasn't fenced, and we walked right up to the main doors of the building. Liz went over to the keypad and, without hesitating, keyed in an eight-digit code. We heard the door unlock. Liz and I went in. Stefan stayed outside. I wondered where he was hiding while we were inside. Other than one lonely car, presumably the security guard's, the lot surrounding the building was empty, devoid of trees or even garbage cans. Liz moved through the building's hallways, taking each turn without hesitating.

"Did you bring your students here for a class trip?" I took a not-so-wild guess, following close on her heels.

Liz grinned at me over her shoulder. "When Connie was in my class. One of those show-and-tell classes we fall back on after any school break to settle the kids down."

"And the security code?"

"The security guard put Connie in the system as a treat, to show the class how it's done. Connie used her birthdate. She's much too lazy to remember any other code."

"And it's still there, years later? What kind of security is that?"

"The usual one. Most systems are not as secure as most people think. Human error and plain human inertia," Liz said. "What are you complaining about? It worked for us."

"Because that's probably how the killer knew the security code as well!"

"Believe me, I know," Liz muttered. "You want to bet Larry knows Connie's birthday? Here we are." Liz opened a door into a room full of monitors. Each screen showed a section of the building; some with split frames showing more than one section.

I found the monitors showing the entry door and the parking lot, but didn't see Stefan. Scanning the rest of the monitors, I looked for the security guard doing his rounds.

"The monitors are marked at the bottom left side with the location of the CCTV. If I'm right, the corridors leading to this room are these monitors marked S1, S2, and S3." Liz rested her gloved finger on a monitor with split frames and checked a piece of paper taped to the desk. "Yup, that's it. Keep an eye on these monitors. When you see the guard in the S3 frame, let me know right away. We have ten minutes to get out of here. Have you found him yet?" Liz put the laptop she was carrying on the desk and powered it up.

"The security guard? Or Stefan?" I said.

"The security guard. Don't worry about Stefan. He can take care of himself. And that screen showing the parking lot is on a loop, you're not going to see Stefan." Liz's fingers were already busy, going back and forth between the keyboard of her laptop and that of the security guard's computer.

"The security guard is right there on the monitor to your left, marked O5. Oh! He went through a door and disappeared from view. Wait, there he is again."

"Must have gone inside a bathroom to check if anyone's there. You can't put a CCTV inside a bathroom. Privacy laws and whatnot."

"I certainly hope not!" I said, stunned anyone would think of putting a CCTV in public restrooms. Sitting down in the chair beside Liz, I kept watch for the security guard while throwing quick glances at the monitors showing the entry door and the parking lot beyond it. If I hadn't seen Liz splice the loop in, I wouldn't have known the camera wasn't recording live.

Time passed.

I checked my watch and saw we had been in the room for less than fifteen minutes. How did people do this? My nerves were strung up so tight, it felt like ants were crawling up and down my body. Liz, on the other hand, was crooning and making happy noises to her computer.

"Did you find anything?" I asked.

"Oh yes, the files were in the trash. Amateurs! Don't they know they have to delete the trash as well?"

Who was complaining now?

"You have to see this." The barely hidden excitement in Liz's voice made me look at where she was pointing. On her laptop's screen was a shadowy figure. Black pants, black jacket, and a black stocking covering his face. Liz paused the video and resized the screen so we could see the black bag by the man's feet.

"Edna's cleared." I breathed out a sigh of relief. The figure was that of a man. Tall, broad-shouldered, there was no mistaking the profile. And, while I might not be as familiar with his physique as his late wife, this man was a ringer for Larry.

"You better believe it. Even that detective can't argue with this video."

"Why are you using your laptop? Isn't it easier to copy the files onto a thumb drive?"

"Some companies disable computer ports so no one can copy files off the network. I don't think that's the case here, but I didn't want to spend time trying to unlock a computer port so I can use a USB stick. Plus, it's not exactly easy to bypass that kind of security. It's easier if I use my laptop and take control of the security guard's computer. Come to mama," Liz hummed at her laptop.

A glance at the progress bar on the laptop's screen told me she was about sixty percent done with copying the files.

"I'm erasing us from the hallway monitor videos and putting those on a loop. My grandson showed me how. Give me a minute or two, and we'll be out of here," Liz said.

My stomach turned over when I realized how much we hadn't planned for, and it made me glad someone else was thinking of all the tiny details that hadn't even crossed my mind. A text came through on my phone. It was from Stefan.

"Liz, look"—I showed my phone to Liz—"Stefan says two guys are waiting for us by the entry door."

"Where's Stefan?"

"I don't know, but he must be around there somewhere. What do I say?"

"Tell him we got it. The security guard is"—Liz checked the monitors and found the man at O10—"finishing his check of the offices. He'll go to the plant floor next. And"—checking the progress bar—"we're done here."

Liz closed her laptop and tried to hand it to me, saying, "Here, use this on the men when we go out the door. A good whack at their heads should do it. I'll look for something else to hit them with."

I waved the laptop away. "Keep it. One year of kickboxing should be good for something."

We retraced our steps, back to where two unknown thugs waited for us. I wondered what worm had dug itself into our brains. We should be running away, not walking into what promised to give us more bruises on our battered, elderly bodies. Liz had her laptop up, holding it like a shield. Me? I was praying very hard my trainer was right, that I was ready for more than jabs and kicks at a bag that couldn't hit back or a sparring partner who wasn't out for my blood.

I saw the door at the end of the hallway. We reached it, and my hand rested lightly on the heavy door latch. I said a short prayer, met Liz's eyes, and turned the handle.

It happened so fast, I couldn't make out afterwards what happened when.

We must have stepped outside. The bully boys must have attacked us. Stefan must have jumped from somewhere and tried to defend us. We must have held our own. Because when my eyesight cleared and I could breathe easily again, we were back in Barbara's car.

Liz was cursing nonstop. I cringed at the words she was using. Stefan had his eyes closed, his head resting on the top of the seat. My hands were clutching the door tightly while my eyes checked every inch of my friends I could see.

We were okay. We were all okay. All four of us were here, alive and not too banged up and dinged.

I sent another prayer up.

"What happened?" I asked Stefan and Liz.

"That's what I want to know," Barbara grumbled.

"They got the laptop. After all that work!" Liz said, disgust clear in each word.

"Who were those men?" Barbara asked.

"I don't know," Stefan said, raising his head from where it was resting and arching his shoulders back.

I got the distinct feeling he was trying not to look at

me.

"Well, whoever they are, they're in for a shock. I didn't turn my laptop off. I just closed the lid down. If the laptop is not turned off properly in the next five minutes, it'll reformat itself. There'll be nothing on the laptop they can recover. My grandson deserves a medal. He insisted on putting a fail-safe on it."

"And the files?" Barbara asked.

"Gone," Liz said. "I decided to download the files onto my laptop instead of uploading them to the cloud. We didn't have the time."

Now, Stefan and Barbara were cursing while Liz nodded at each curse word.

The absurdity of it all hit me. I started laughing.

"OMG, Meg, you're hysterical." Liz nudged my shoulder. "Stop, honey. We're all good."

"No, no…Don't you see it? So what if we don't have the files? The cops, by now, must have the files. We can tell Fred what we saw, and he'll get Edna cleared. But those men, what do they have? After all their troubles, those men walked away with nothing but a wiped-out laptop. While we, the four of us, over-the-hill, past our sale date, senior citizens, golden agers, call us what you will, we managed to beat back two hulking bruisers, suffering nothing more than scraped knees." I looked at my friends with pride.

Slowly, one by one, their lips turned upward, their eyes unfocused, gazing inwardly, who knows where, before focusing back on each other.

Stefan and Liz high-fived and settled back into their seats, anger and disgust gone from their faces. Barbara kept driving, lips twitching upward before she'd wrestle them down again. In the utter silence of the car, we heard

Barbara say softly, "Old lady, my foot." It was good to hear the quiet confidence back in her voice.

I took my hand off the door. Something significant happened today. It was going to take time for us to absorb it all.

Chapter Twenty-Nine

Saturday, the day we go undercover. We all agreed we should still go ahead. The video was enough to clear Edna, but not enough to pin down Larry. And we wanted Larry.

I put on my diamond earrings, hoping to jazz up my boring black shirt and pants with some sparklies. Barbara was downstairs waiting, probably tapping her foot to a beat only she could hear. We had ten minutes left to get to Veronica's. Going downstairs, I heard voices. One was Fred's.

"I dropped by early to give you ladies an update. I will not be able to talk to you at the party. Not for long anyway." Fred's smile went all the way to his eyes.

It was hard to resist smiling back at him, but I managed. We hadn't told Fred about last night, and I was feeling guilty.

"What's happening? Can Edna go home?" Barbara asked.

"No, Edna is still a person of interest. But one of the sergeants did let out they're looking at Larry. Some bright soul managed to connect the dots between Larry, Brie, and Eleanor's deaths. And the cops should have the CCTV files this morning, but it's going to take some time before forensics recover the deleted videos."

Recovering those videos took Liz fifteen minutes. "That's what they said? Why so long? How about the blackmail?"

"I floated the idea of blackmail, but without any hard proof, they can't subpoena Larry's financial records to prove it. They tried with Brie, but there were no credit cards or bank accounts. The girl used cash. On everything. Again, not normal, but not something the cops can use."

"And before I forget, in case Edna calls and asks, there isn't a police report on Brie kicking anyone. Whether from a hospital, the girl, or any of those who saw the fight. So we can't track the girl that way. Tell Edna, I'm sorry." Fred grimaced.

"Where do we go from here then?" Barbara said.

"What we planned all along. You ladies get among Veronica's guests and listen. If you hear anything we can use, pass it to me and I'll feed it to whom I think best. You're not breaking any laws working as wait staff, and I'm certainly within my rights to attend as a guest. Miss Manners might think it's highly impolite to eavesdrop, but that's all it is. What you do with the gossip you hear is a different story. That's why you are to pass any information you get to me. I'll make sure it's handled correctly."

It was gently said, with soft eyes and a beguiling smile. It still stuck in my craw. Handle correctly? Did I start drooling in the twenty-four hours since he last saw me? Passing on what we found wasn't working with me. Or with Barbara, judging by the look on her face. Or with Liz and Stefan! We do the work; we get the credit. I was so not on board with Fred's I-will-take-care-of-everything attitude. We might be old, but we're not helpless, as those two men from last night had found out.

"I don't know what you're worrying about. If it were

only gossip we're hearing, there's no reason for us to tell you about it. You can't use gossip as evidence, right? And don't worry about us not knowing how to handle things. But if we do find out something we can't handle, we'll think about running to you for help. Otherwise, I think we'll go chugging along as we are doing now. Sounds good?" My voice had gotten sharper with each word.

Fred looked like he had bitten something very sour. "I probably could have said that better." He sighed as I continued to glare at him. "What I meant was…I don't want you…any of you…putting yourself in danger. If—"

"Fred, don't shovel the dirt out. You're digging yourself deeper," Barbara said.

"Deeper? When you ladies started throwing around the idea of going undercover, I didn't think anything of it. I mean, why would any of the bright stars of Sands Neck dirty their hands over Brie? She's a two-bit actor. Sands Neck is real money, not play money. This is different. If Larry had murdered Eleanor, you're placing yourself in danger tonight. Someone who has killed once will not think twice about killing again. Especially if it's to protect themselves from being caught for the first murder."

He made sense. Of course, he made sense. If he knew what we had seen in those security videos, he probably would have locked Barbara and me in Dora's house. But my nerves were stretched out tight, worrying over Edna, and now Archer. Plus, I had never in my life allowed a man to pat me over the head. The very idea!

"Thanks, Fred. You might have thought it was all fun and games. But we didn't. We've been serious about this murder investigation from day one. And we're not stopping now." Especially not now, when we knew who the murderer was. We just had to prove it without using those blasted videos.

I grabbed my bag off the sofa. "Let's go, Barbara." I marched out of the house and waited for the two to leave so I could lock up behind them.

The nerve of the man!

"You believe that?" I said to Barbara. "We're supposed to do all the work and then hand it over?"

"What did you expect we would do? Arrest Larry ourselves?" Barbara didn't look happy with me.

I started feeling uneasy. Fidgeting in my seat, I said, "No, of course not. But for Fred to say…imply…that we won't know what to do—"

"Do we?" Barbara cut me off. "We don't have any idea what we're doing. We're walking into a party knowing Larry would be there, and we think he killed Brie. If that's not scaring you, you're not thinking straight."

"Of course, I'm scared."

"Are you? Scared? I don't see it." Barbara hadn't looked over at me since we got in the car. "Your house was ransacked. You almost got killed. Last night, two men attacked you, Liz and Stefan. This is not some crime show. This is real life. We can get hurt. Die."

I chewed on my lips. "You didn't look any happier than me when Fred started throwing orders around. You even said—"

"—that he's digging himself deeper. Yes. That's because I saw the look on your face. When you get that look, nothing the other person says changes your mind. You burrow deeper, like a mole. He was better off saying nothing." Barbara turned into Veronica's driveway, parking beside Janet's two white vans with their black and gold lettering. "That's why I wasn't looking 'happy.' I knew you weren't going to listen to Fred. Come on, we need to get in there and start helping out. Veronica is spending a lot of money on this crazy idea of yours."

It was Liz's crazy idea, but I knew when to keep my mouth closed.

"What took you so long?" Liz called out to us as we walked in. She was covering the serving tables with linen.

Bar height tables were placed around the backyard. Stefan was walking around placing flower arrangements on top of the tables. Small mason jars with sprays of berries, twigs, and a flower or two. Daffodils and crocuses. Stefan moved this morning with a spring in his step. The only evidence of last night's fight was the eye patch he wore covering his left eye. A black, velveteen eye patch with Black Gloves written in silver glitter on it. He saw me staring in wonder at the eye patch, gave me a saucy grin, and kept moving.

The tent was up. Two men were stringing up white honeycomb balls from the tent's ceiling. Strings of rainbow-colored lights radiated from the tent's center peak while pastel colored pompoms were scattered here and there amongst the honeycomb balls.

Veronica had pulled all this together in three days? The woman was a marvel. Come to think of it, she probably made that eye patch for Stefan when he showed up with his bruised and battered black eye.

"Janet is inside." Liz tilted her head toward the house. "She's in the kitchen. Get over there, and she'll put you to work. It's late. Hurry up."

We walked into a scene of controlled chaos. Janet and a helper had taken over the kitchen. Kyle was filling up a rolling tray with boxes of booze. Another wait staff, a girl, was holding a tray in each hand, waiting for directions. Every kitchen surface was filled with trays and boxes.

"You're late." Janet pointed to the trays the girl was holding. "You, get those from her so she can go and get some more from the van." Turning to Barbara, she pointed at Kyle. "Help him finish stocking the bar. Go with him and help set up."

"How many did Veronica invite?" I hadn't realized how much work this party would take. I was expecting a simple backyard party, not this massive affair.

"The usual number. About a hundred. You invite the usual. Even if you only wanted to hold a small party."

"A hundred?" I asked in horror. "We're serving a hundred people?"

Janet looked at me, amused. "Relax. Only about fifty are coming. The rest said no when Veronica said it was an 'intimate party.' "

"Fifty is intimate?" Intimate to me meant immediate family and close friends. Twenty people, max. Who held an intimate party for fifty people? And at such short notice?

"You're not getting it. Intimate is Sands Neck's code word for 'you're invited, but feel free not to come.' Most took Veronica up on it. Get over here so I can put the food you're holding where it belongs."

It was too bad Janet wasn't in my kindergarten class. She had no lingering awe of me. I went to do as she said.

Hours later, the guests trickled in. Some dawdled at the driveway, while others strode ahead, homing in on the servers with drink trays in their hands. Kyle stood behind the bar underneath the tent. Scotch and whiskey bottles were lined up on a table behind him. Joined by gin, vodka, and a few bottles of red wine. Beer, white wine, and champagne were immersed in ice.

Stefan was walking among the guests, a tray of drinks balanced on his right hand. As was Barbara. I was bartending while Kyle went to get a particular bottle of scotch a guest had asked for, leaving the guest loitering by the bar.

Liz was coming out of the house with a tray of hors d'oeuvres, tiny portions of focaccia bread topped with slivers of thinly sliced sirloin tips, mustard drizzled on top. The girl who had been helping out before walked around with a half-empty tray of food. I couldn't see from where I was what was on the tray. Most of the guests were turning the food away, but not the drinks. It was an early afternoon party. Weren't they hungry? I was!

Looking at the food Janet made, I understood why her business was so successful. The food was presented invitingly. Small enough to hold in your hand and eat in a bite or two. Gone before the person you're with was finished with what they were saying. No mess. No fuss. I would have had a dozen before the server could have walked away with her tray to the next person.

Distracted, I didn't pay attention to the guests coming up for drinks. I poured whatever they wanted. Threw in ice when reminded. I also readied a tray of drinks for me to serve to the guests once Kyle returned.

Another joined the man who wanted the scotch. Talk of work and sports swirled about me, unnoticed until I heard a familiar name.

"So what was Larry up to last Friday night that he had to cancel?" one of the men asked.

I glanced their way and saw it was Kyle's scotch drinker asking about Larry.

"He never did say. Some personal emergency was all I got. You'd think for a man hard up for investors, he'd be more attentive to those with money to spare. One minute he's harassing me to meet with him, the next he's too busy."

This man was Martin? The one Connie said Larry had dinner with last Friday?

A beautiful middle-aged woman came up to the bar and asked for two glasses of white wine. I poured and handed them over, ticked off at how the men stopped talking to look her over from head to toe. The woman's dress clung to every curve she had, ending no more than three inches from her butt. I couldn't figure out if the dress was made of rayon or silk. I remembered where I was and decided it had to be silk. Her long strawberry blonde hair was half held up in a twist, with some strands escaping to flirt with her eyes and lips.

The woman took something from the tiny bag slung across her body, slit it open with her manicured nails, and poured the contents into a drink. She winked at the men and walked away with the glasses in her hand, the spiked drink in her right.

I stood stunned. Did she just do what I think she did? Was someone getting poisoned?

Stefan came rushing up to me and placed his tray of empty glasses on the bar next to mine. "What did Sonia get?"

"Who?" I jerked back, bewildered.

"That lady. What did you give her?"

We both looked at Sonia glide her way through the guests, smiling at everyone. "Did you see her spike that drink she's carrying on her right?"

"Never mind, I'll catch up with her." Stefan took the tray of drinks I had prepared and rushed to catch up with Sonia.

"Did I see Sonia getting drinks from you?" Kyle was back, the bottle of scotch in his hand. Opening the bottle, Kyle took a tumbler, filled it halfway with ice, and poured two fingers of scotch. At the other man's nod, he took another tumbler and did the same.

"Sonia asked for two glasses of white wine and spiked one." I could feel how wide my eyes were.

"It's probably an emetic," Kyle chuckled. "Sonia and Lauren have been feuding this spring. Something to do with Sonia stealing Lauren's hairstylist from her. They keep playing dirty tricks on each other. Janet told Mr. Papadopoulos to watch out for Sonia and Lauren. Don't worry, he'll get to her on time."

"Hair stylist?" I said weakly.

"Yeah. You see Sonia's hair? You think that's natural? Not that color. Sonia footed the bill when Lauren's hair stylist opened her salon. On the condition no one else gets that exact hair color. And the stylist stops working on Lauren."

"Why?"

"Because Lauren pirated Sonia's masseuse. She paid the man five times what Sonia was paying, so he'd switch his mornings over to Lauren. Now he goes to Sonia in the early afternoon. Sonia says it kills her social schedule."

"Why didn't Sonia pay the man more? Wouldn't that be cheaper?"

"I don't try to make sense of how these people live," Kyle said.

Stefan had caught up with Sonia by this time. He had ignored several requests for drinks. I thought the slighted guests would raise a fuss. Instead, when they saw who Stefan was following, they chuckled and turned to watch the two. When Stefan intercepted the drink, some of the watching guests clapped their hands while others, including the two men by the bar, called out, "Good try, Sonia."

Sonia turned to the watching guests and bowed a small curtsy, making her dress ride even further up. She didn't mind. A few male guests whistled. Sonia smiled even more.

"Are they out of their minds?" I asked Kyle.

He took the empty tray of drinks Stefan had ditched. Took clean wine glasses, poured, and placed them on the tray. "You better start serving drinks before Janet sees you."

I took the tray from him, intending to do just that. Then I stopped. "Kyle?"

"Yes, Mrs. B?"

"Was one of the men you served scotch to called Martin? The second man, not the first guy who asked you to get the bottle of scotch."

"Mr. Wehle? Yeah, his first name's Martin. Why do you ask?"

"Nothing," I said, moving away quickly in case Kyle wasn't satisfied with my answer.

Of course, Larry had lied about what he was doing Friday night. And we could prove it. Was this enough to pull Larry in for questioning?

Chapter Thirty

Connie was with Veronica, greeting everyone as if she were the one throwing the party. Veronica twiddled the stem of her wine glass. She saw me looking and went up to me.

"How are you holding up?" Veronica whispered.

"Veronica, dearest." A man joined her and took a drink from my tray. Gulped half of it down and leaned over to Veronica. "Why is my fifth-grade teacher walking around with a tray of hors d'oeuvres?" He glanced my way; an apologetic look on his face. Morphing to horror when he saw who I was. Ernest, Veronica's husband, was also in my kindergarten class years back, the same class Veronica was in. "Mrs. B! What are you doing with that tray of drinks? OMG, give it to me." He tried to take the tray out of my hands.

"Stop that." Veronica slapped his hands away. "You're giving them away. Act natural."

"Natural?" His voice squeaked. "What? Are they undercover or something?" He looked around at the other servers. "No. Please, no. Just no. Is that Principal Roker out there?"

I was having a hard time keeping a smile off my face. Veronica had bagged Ernest the day she showed up at school with a frog in her pocket. Hermit, Post Elementary School's mascot. At least until Barbara managed to convince the school's custodian to take

Hermit and release the frog in some pond somewhere. By then, it was too late for Ernest. The man was bowled over by Veronica's fearlessness, becoming her one-person groupie. Always there. Never left her side. Married her promptly after college graduation. And was blissfully happy with his wife and children, all of whom would do anything on a dare while he dithered around telling everyone to be careful.

"Veronica…sweetheart…why?" Ernest gave me a pained smile and tossed off the rest of his drink.

"I'll tell you later. There's Connie. Let's join her." Veronica took her and Ernest's empty glasses and put them on my tray. She grasped the hand her husband had out to take the empty glasses back from me and turned him around, but not before whispering "later" to me.

I checked on Barbara and saw her talking to guests who, if I wasn't mistaken, were former school board members. Liz was behind them, her arm slung over a guest. I looked for her tray and found it on top of a bar table. She saw me coming and took her arm off the guest. She took back her tray and offered it around. I was too far away to hear what was said, but the group took the remaining bites of food. Grabbing the hand of one of the group, Liz raised their clasped hands and took a bow, folding the tray to her waist and bending over it, to laughter and applause all around.

We were doing a great job going undercover. Fred need not have worried. Speaking of the man, where was he? My eyes scanned the yard for a medium-sized man with salt and pepper hair and a heart-tugging smile. There he was. The corner of my lips twitched upward. Then I saw who he was with. Larry. Of all people.

I walked over to where they were. "Wine?" I asked

the two, which showed how twitchy I was getting around Larry. The two men were holding tumblers of amber colored liquid.

"Mrs. B." Larry greeted me.

"Meg," Fred said.

"By the way, you were right." Larry swirled his drink around before taking a sip. "It was insanely difficult to get all of Cannoli's hair out of my car. My guy spent all day vacuuming."

If he were looking for an apology, he'd be disappointed. I did tell him. He insisted. I decided to move away from the man.

"How is your delightful pet?"

I jerked my head back. I wasn't sure if that was a smile or a sneer I saw on his face. "She's fine. Thanks for asking." And Cannoli was staying that way, I added under my breath, not wanting Fred to hear me. But then, something snapped inside me. I was done being threatened. My house was torn apart. I was almost killed. Bully boys had Liz's laptop with all the information on it lost. Now this man wanted to take away my Cannoli?

Enough!

I marched up to Larry. "Call your thugs off me and my friends. I know it's you, and if you're as smart as you say you are, you'll call them off." The words "or you're going to regret it" hung unspoken between us.

"I have no idea what you're talking about." Larry took a step back.

I saw the slight tremble in the hand holding his scotch, the liquid inside sloshing a bit before smoothing itself out. The man looked bewildered. Clueless. Fred winced and looked away. Did I get it wrong? I blinked, turned around, and headed for a clump of guests waving empty wine glasses at me.

The group of three ladies emptied my tray of drinks. I took their empty glasses and placed them carefully on the tray, listening as I worked.

"Connie looks fantastic today," said the skinny black-haired beauty.

"Hah! She's too busy with that friend of hers, she's not paying attention to Pip," retorted the heavy-chested blonde.

"Larry? Why wouldn't she? He's so much more amazing than Pip." The third woman twirled her auburn hair around her fingers and sent Larry smoldering looks. I swore she licked her lips when Larry raised his glass at her.

"Who cares about looks? He's skint," said Heavy Chested Blonde.

They were all in their late twenties. Were they second wives? Maybe third? Girlfriends?

Auburn Hair looked at Heavy Chested Blonde askance. "Skint? Where'd you hear that from? He's got all that lovely money from Eleanor."

"Big deal. He's throwing it after that sinking investment ship of his. Rupert said he should save it for a rainy day. When I asked him when he thought it would rain for Larry, he just laughed." Heavy Chested Blonde pouted.

I kept myself busy with the empty glasses.

"You can be so dim," said Skinny Beauty.

"Dim? I wanted him to laugh! Rupert likes to feel smart," Heavy Chested Blonde said. "It's not that hard to do. Pip, now. That's one smart man."

"You think Pip will share his money? He's so tight, his money squeaks before it gets out of his hands," said

Auburn Hair.

"That can't be right. The amount of money Connie throws around? I heard this was the fourth time she's redecorating. Barry won't even let me change the curtains," said Skinny Beauty.

"You've got a ring on your finger. Who cares about curtains?" Heavy Chested Blonde glared at the two "I don't think Rupert is ever setting a date. The divorce has been final for a month. And he hasn't said anything about getting married."

So Skinny Beauty was a wife, at least. I rearranged the glasses in my tray.

"I told you to make friends with his kids." Skinny Beauty lifted one bare shoulder. "Rupert is devoted to them. He's not doing anything to upset them even more."

"Kids." Heavy Chested Blonde huffed. "The oldest is ten years older than I. He wouldn't mind being friendly with me. But his daddy has all the money." She tugged her skirt down. "Did you hear what happened to Brie? She so got what she deserved. Imagine blackmailing us?"

"What us? You're just jealous Brie didn't try it on you," Auburn Hair said.

"What are you talking about? Why would I want to be blackmailed?"

"Because Brie only blackmailed the blue bloods around here. Didn't you know?" Auburn Hair shook her hair loose and fluttered her eyelashes at Larry, while the man kept stealing glances at her.

"You're wasting your time." Skinny Beauty lightly slapped Auburn Hair on the shoulder.

"The ladies turned the blackmail into a game," Skinny Beauty said to Heavy Chested Blonde.

"Everyone knew Brie was targeting only those stuck-ups—my word, not theirs—who had treated Brie and her family like dirt years back over some scandal. So if you were blackmailed, you had been around long enough. If you weren't, your money was so new, it still crackled or, worse, you were one of those panty-waisted liberals."

I hoisted the tray onto my hands and walked back to the bar to get a fresh batch. The more I found out about the lives people led in Sands Neck, the more I missed my two-story house in Whitman's Port. And to think Jim had lived in this swamp! I wanted to go back to my own side of the jungle.

The party had been in full swing for close to two hours, and my feet and back were aching. Everyone was mellowed out with enough alcohol and not enough food. Luckily for everyone, that was when Detective Storm came striding through the backyard. He headed straight for Larry, not waiting for the faithful sergeant following behind. Police forensics must have finally done their job and recovered the missing CCTV files.

I handed the tray of drinks I was passing around to the nearest person beside me and hurried to the two men, three if you counted Fred, still at Larry's side. I ignored the surprised yelp from the guest suddenly downgraded to server.

"Mr. Billings, I am surprised to see you having fun. Shouldn't you be meeting with your attorney?" The detective said out loud. Louder than he needed to.

"What are you on about?" Larry said, his voice tightly controlled.

"It has come to our attention Brie might have seen more than she cared to tell us about your wife's death." The man didn't bother to hide how self-satisfied he was feeling. His voice dripped with scorn and disdain.

"You know this, how? I doubt you spoke to the girl before she died. And you certainly didn't speak to her after."

I stopped a few feet away from the three. Heads and ears were turning toward the group. I saw Auburn Hair, eyes wide with horror, with her hand to her mouth, and beside her, smirking delightedly at her, were Skinny Beauty and Heavy Chested Blonde.

"But you don't deny Brie was your alibi for your wife's death," Detective Storm said, very pleased with himself.

A murmur went through the crowd. I heard Auburn Hair shout, "That's nonsense!"

Beside her, sounding amused, Skinny Beauty said, "So the rumors are true."

"He killed Eleanor?" Heavy Chested Blonde, on the other side of Auburn Hair, was stunned.

Everyone, including me, ignored the three women.

"So what? Brie is one of five witnesses. Four other guests saw the whole thing happen. They corroborated Brie's account," Larry said.

"Jonathan, this is a private party. You need to leave," Fred said. "Unless you're here to arrest Larry. Are you?"

"No, but we want Mr. Billings to come down with us to the station to answer questions. You do want to help out, don't you, Mr. Billings?"

Veronica and Ernest came bearing down on the men. Followed closely by Connie. Larry had locked gazes with the detective. I saw the slight smile on his face slip, then firm up again.

"Detective Storm," Ernest yelled out. "Can we help

you? Why don't we go inside the house? Leave the guests to enjoy the party?"

"Thank you, no. We're just leaving," Detective Storm said, his eyes not leaving Larry's.

Larry was the first to look away. He handed his drink to Fred and nodded to Jonathan and his sergeant. The three walked out with Ernest and Fred following. Connie and Veronica joined me.

"You okay?"

I nodded, my eyes narrowing. Larry had done a good job acting the part of the outraged innocent.

Chapter Thirty-One

The gym was exactly what I needed this Sunday morning. Stefan was still nursing a black eye, and I insisted he stay home and rest. Working at Veronica's party yesterday had tired all of us out.

I threw a punch and cursed under my breath. Fred had called very early this morning. Larry was home courtesy of his very expensive attorney. The videos were suggestive of Larry, but they did not provide definite proof. Neither was the canceled dinner appointment leaving Larry with no alibi. The cops were at the meat-packing plant yesterday and today, searching for DNA. Larry refused to give up a sample of his DNA for comparison on the advice of his attorney. To top it all off, the APB was still out for Edna. I knew I had to call her. I was stalling. Maybe something would come up, and I wouldn't have to admit to Edna how we had failed her.

I felt sorry Veronica had spent all that money. Sure, she had told us not to worry. She said she was due to hold a party, and she'd been dragging her feet. And the party had helped Janet, she said. With Brie gone, her old customers who were at Veronica's party had booked Janet for the rest of spring and even summer. Veronica felt her money had not been wasted. Meanwhile, Ernest had taken one look at us after the party and headed into the deepest part of the house. He told Veronica he didn't need to know. Didn't want to know.

I hit the punching bag with my right and danced away, moving my body, positioning it for the next hit. Craig watched from outside the mat, correcting me from time to time. Sweat poured from me. It was cleansing. I imagined all the seedy, tawdry secrets I'd learned sliding off me, and it felt good. How did Dora cope with the ugly side of life she dealt with every day in her work? Violence, neglect, illnesses, death.

"Let's mix it up." Craig turned to face me, holding partner pads. "Start with the punches. One, two, and two."

I jabbed at the pads, hitting across my trainer's face and in time to the beats he called out. Changing to kicks, then knee strikes, then back again to punches, stopping only when he called time. I grabbed the towel I had left hanging on the nearest gym equipment.

"Good workout," Craig said. "I'll see you and Tara in four days." He slapped my arm and left.

Toweling myself dry, I drank from the water bottle I'd brought with me. I was looking forward to another session with Tara. Taking a yoga mat, I dragged it to an open space and plopped myself down. Stretching my arms, clasping fingers around my toes, I arched my back, head down, shoulders hunched. At times, I didn't know which I liked better: the boxing session or the stretches that followed. I could feel the knots in my body loosening, my muscles unkinking. Finished with the last of my stretches, I sat on the mat, arms on my knees, head resting on my arms. I got up and tossed my towel over my shoulder. I looked over the treadmills, checking to see if one was free, as I wanted to go for a run. None were. I decided I'd go to Duck Harbor Park and run on the path. The view was better.

The parking lot was full when I got to Duck Harbor Park. I managed, however, to find a spot. Weaving my way through the crowd, I headed for the jogging path. Trees lined up by the edges of the park offered shelter from the heat of the day. I passed parents watching their kids swarm the playground, challenging themselves on the monkey bars, pushing the spinner while running to keep up, or jumping on it until it stopped. The kids went down the slides, the more adventurous headfirst, or sat on swings, straining their toes up in the air, then pulling them back, making the swings go higher and higher. And all around that bustle of humanity were the ducks Edna's mother loved to watch. Gray bodies, sandwiched between chocolate-colored breasts and black rumps, the ducks wriggled and waddled. They quacked incessantly, warning people to move out of their way.

I'd gone through the path twice, weaving to avoid the ones strolling, not running, lazily enjoying the breeze and late spring sun. Running freed my mind. I reviewed what we knew about Connie and Larry.

Everyone we spoke to said Brie kept asking about Connie. Why? What about Connie? In Europe for the weekend, Connie could not have been farther away from the crime scene. None of us could imagine Connie working with Larry to kill Brie. Not if Larry killed Connie's best friend, Eleanor. And speaking of Eleanor...

Lawrence Billings. The only one with a compelling motive to kill Brie the way she was killed and the nerve to do so. If he had pushed his wife off the cliff and slid himself off that same cliff, hoping he could hang onto the roots of a tree until rescue came, then his blood ran so cold, ice should be forming around his face. I could easily picture Brie with the blackmail, face alight with the power she thought she had over the man, Larry agreeing to pay, hiding his plans to kill Brie behind his urbane smile. But despite that video and the lack of an alibi, something was still missing in this story, and I wasn't as convinced as I had been on Friday. Not after seeing how shocked Larry was when I confronted him at the party.

Quacking and hissing nearby made me snap my head to the side. A mother duck was mantling her wings, the baby ducklings sheltering inside, whistling in alarm. The other ducks in the area had joined in the quacking, though they stayed away from the mother duck, whose head was bobbing back and forth, quacks and hisses streaming through its beak. A toddler a few feet away was crying, her head buried in her mother's skirt. The woman was moving her child to safety, one slow step at a time, while waving people away from the angry duck. "No, no, she's only protecting her ducklings. It's fine, leave her be. She's not attacking us, she's warning us." A few feet more, and the woman picked up her crying child, cradling the girl against her shoulder. The mother duck had retracted her wings, her beak touching each duckling. Counting and making sure they were all there. The woman turned her back on the ducks and walked off toward the playground.

I smiled, recognizing the mother instinct at work, protecting the young, then blinked several times. I remembered the girl Edna had been looking for. And what Kyle said about Brie and Rosita. I remembered where I had heard the name Leni before.

What if…

A few of the puzzle pieces rearranged themselves, sliding into their places. We were looking at this murder the wrong way.

I pulled my phone from my pocket, dialed a number I knew by heart. "Hey," I said when Liz picked up the phone. "Did you get a chance to find out who the girl was at the park? The one Edna was so worried about?"

Liz called back as I was pulling into Dora's driveway right beside the blue SUV parked on the right side. Dora was home.

I slipped the phone back into my bag and got out of the car. I was hoping Liz would prove me wrong. I didn't want it to be true. But everything fit. One foot on the door stoop, my phone pinged. Someone was texting me.

"You got that?" Dora had opened the door to the house. Cannoli ran out and jumped at me.

"It's from Archer," I said, bending to ruffle Cannoli's head. "Isn't he inside? Down, girl." Cannoli sat panting, her tongue out.

"No, Nico came over on his bike and they took off about an hour ago," Dora said as she leaned over my shoulder to look at the phone. "Why is he texting you?"

The text was brief, only one word. It said: Quiet. We exchanged glances. Cannoli gave little yips, wanting my attention.

The phone jangled, the sound grating on me. I swiped at my phone to see two faces come up. Two worried, pale faces. Archer and Nico. In a dimly lit room, barely visible to us. I heard Dora gasp, and I raised my hand abruptly, slashing at my mouth with my finger, motioning Dora to silence. Whatever the kids were up to, I wasn't taking chances. I put the phone on mute before answering the call.

Just in time since Cannoli was now barking furiously. "Hush, Cannoli. I need to hear Archer." She stopped barking and sat again, eyes trained on me.

Archer and Nico were frantically waving at their mouths, Archer with one finger in front of closed lips and Nico running two fingers across his mouth to pantomime zipping it shut. I set aside the panic I was starting to feel, straining to listen to the sounds coming from my phone.

A man was talking, his voice muffled, sounding as if he was outside the room the kids were in. I put my hand to my ear, hoping Archer would see and understand I couldn't hear very well. The phone went dark. The kids had moved it elsewhere. I heard the phone being placed on top of a surface, and a sliver of light could be seen at the edges. The man's voice sounded clearer to us.

"That's Larry!" Dora said, being more familiar with his voice than I was. "Don't fuss, you have the phone on mute. And that's Rosita"—when a woman answered Larry—"the kids must be at Larry's house. It has to be Larry's house. Rosita was supposed to come today, but she said Larry called her this morning. Asked her to clean his house. I thought that was odd. She cleaned it yesterday."

Cannoli yipped a few times, then stopped.

"Mr. Larry, I not know what you talking about," Rosita said. "You call me this morning. Ask me to come clean house today. That what I do. Clean your kitchen. You want me do something else?"

"Don't know?" Larry said. "The police dragged me to the station yesterday. Asked me all sorts of questions. Now, why would they do that?"

"I'm sorry, Mr. Larry. I not know what you mean."

"No?" We heard Larry say when Rosita had been

silent for a long time.

"No, Mr. Larry."

I imagined Rosita wringing her hands in her worry.

"It's just…I saw you and Mrs. Eleanor fighting that day."

"And you think what? Said what to the police? That I killed Eleanor? And Brie?"

We heard chairs being pushed aside. Cannoli's little yips had given way to growls. She was on all fours, eyes on the phone.

"Did you tell Detective Storm this fairy tale of yours?" Larry said.

"No, no, not the detective. He no come to my house."

"Who then?"

"The sergeant. The old cop. He come the other day. He ask. What do I see at party. I said I told them everything. But he says to think. Maybe I forgot something. Maybe I saw you and Brie—"

"Rosita, no!" I screamed at my phone, knowing Rosita would not hear me. "Quick, Dora, call the cops. Call Detective Storm and tell him to…" Cannoli's barking was making it hard for me to think. "Cannoli, shush!"

"What's happening? Are the kids in trouble?" Dora said, her voice frantic with worry.

"Go, go. Get Detective Storm on the phone and tell him to get to Larry's house as quickly as he can. Tell him Archer and Nico are locked in a room. No, a closet. The kids must be in the pantry if Rosita is in the kitchen. Tell him the kids are not safe if Larry finds out they're hiding in the pantry."

"Why would—"

We turned to the phone when we heard the creak of a door opening, and Archer cried out, "Stop!" Followed by Nico screaming, "Stop that, Mr. Billings! You're choking Rosita, she can't breathe!"

Cannoli gave a full-throated growl.

"Go!" I screamed, eyes wild with worry.

Dora fled.

Stumbling over Cannoli in my haste, I got back in my car, Cannoli right behind me. I gunned the car. Backed it out of the driveway. Fast. I turned toward Larry's house; my phone placed carefully on the passenger seat. I wasn't losing contact with the kids. In my mind, I kept screaming at them to get out and run.

Cannoli kept growling and barking. I wanted to growl along with her.

"Archer Brightbook. What are you doing hiding in my pantry?" Larry's voice came through the phone. "And who's that hiding behind you?"

"I'm not hiding behind him. Your kitchen is too small. There's no space here for me." A much younger voice, not Archer's, answered Larry.

"Not now," I whispered. "Not now, Nico." I put my foot firmly on the gas, and the car shot forward.

"You haven't answered my question, Archer. What are you doing hiding in my pantry?"

"Nothing, we weren't doing anything." Archer's voice trembled. "Rosita, you okay?"

"Never mind her," Larry said. "And put that pan down, Rosita. If you don't, I'll shoot you."

A gun. Larry was holding a gun on Rosita and Archer. "How much did you hear?" I heard Larry ask. "Nothing, tell him nothing," I urged the kids, even knowing they couldn't hear me, while maneuvering my car on the road, anxious to get there.

"Nothing," Nico said. "We heard nothing."

"Good boy," I whispered. "A few more minutes, give me a few more minutes."

"You came rushing out of the pantry because you heard nothing?"

"Mr. Larry," pleaded Rosita. "Let them go. They just kids."

"Unless someone tells me what these kids are doing in my house, hiding in my pantry, someone will get shot."

Chapter Thirty-Two

The house was up ahead, less than the length of two football fields. Jim could have run it in less than a minute.

A few seconds more, I begged. *Please, don't shoot.* I checked the rear-view mirror. No sign of cops. Where was Detective Storm? That man was never around when he was needed. A man with a badge and a gun, that was all I needed. *Someone* get here before anyone's hurt. I gritted my teeth.

"Kids stopped by to see me. I clean for Mrs. Dora. You know that. My car. He saw in driveway. That all, Mr. Larry. Nothing, they not know anything." Rosita was talking so fast; her words were tripping over each other.

"The pantry," Larry said.

"I think you get mad if you see kids in your house, so I said hide," Rosita said.

I wasn't hearing anything from Archer or Nico. I smashed my foot on the brake, the tires squealing as I stopped in front of Larry's house. My hand went out to grasp Cannoli's collar and held her tight, preventing her from hitting the windshield. My body pitched forward, slamming back when my seat belt tightened, drawing me back. Cannoli whined. We would hurt after. *If* there was an after. A shot sounded, jolting me. I let Cannoli go. Grasping the seatbelt, I threw it over my shoulder and jumped out of the car, phone in one hand. Cannoli scrambled after me. I bit my lip as my side twinged fiercely. Screams came through the phone, the sounds melding into one high-pitched tone scraping its fingers down my spine.

Reaching the front of the house, I yanked the door, thumbing the lock down and banging on the door when it wouldn't open, shouting "Let me in" over and over. When this didn't work, I turned and darted to the left, where I had seen a path laid out leading to the fence's gate. Listing sideways, I squeezed my right arm tight to my side. The fingers of my right hand were curled tight on my phone. I wasn't breaking my only link to my grandson. Cannoli was in a frenzy by my feet. She'd run ahead, doubling back to where I was when I couldn't keep up with her. I ran down the path. As best as I could. As fast as I could. Two bikes were on the ground right before the gate.

Through the bushes and windows, I saw cream-colored walls, a dining table that could easily seat twenty for dinner, a crystal chandelier, and an enormous flower arrangement. Next was a room lined with bookcases full of books and leather-covered chairs grouped around a fireplace. Each room empty. I was getting worried. The call was still live on my phone, but no sounds were coming through. What was happening inside?

I spied a pool on the far side of the yard, an expanse of green to its right, and beyond that green, a peek of Poet's Bay glinting in the sun through the leaves of the trees at the edge of the yard. Rounding the corner, I almost stumbled when the path ended, and my foot missed the stepping stones appearing about a foot apart from each other. I walked on, head scanning the yard in case Larry had taken the boys and Rosita out of the house. Step by step, I moved on, the slabs of stone leading me to the kitchen. The sliding doors to the kitchen were wide open, showing a tableau that stunned me.

Larry stood, hugging Archer to himself. His arm was pressed against the boy's neck. The smallest pressure of his arm guaranteed to choke the breath out of Archer. Archer stood still, his hands on Larry's arm. A gun was in Larry's other hand, the point leveled at Rosita. Behind Rosita was Nico. And beyond them were glass shards from the smashed light fixtures that used to hang over the kitchen island.

I stopped short and sucked air. Larry had fired a warning shot. No one was hurt. Yet. Where were the cops? I threw my shoulders back, prayed, and did a Hail Mary pass.

"Put that gun down, Lawrence Billings," I said, my voice firm with the unquestioned conviction that I would be obeyed. As countless children had obeyed me.

Larry jerked around. The four in the kitchen turned to stare at me, a kaleidoscope of feelings in each of their faces: amazement, then disbelief, then dismay.

But I wasn't Larry's kindergarten teacher. He had not played in the grounds of Post Elementary School. I was not the Voice of Authority to Larry. Capital V. Capital A. My Hail Mary pass fell short.

"Mrs. B." Larry paused when he heard an echo of his voice. I palmed my phone and slipped it into the pocket of my yoga pants, disconnecting it in the process. Larry didn't need to know Archer had called me.

"Come join us." He waved the gun at me, motioning me into the kitchen. "Over there, please." He moved to keep Rosita and me in sight, dragging Archer with him, backing step by step nearer to the glass-paned doors opening out to the yard. "Anyone else coming? It's getting crowded in here."

"Mr. Larry, let Archer go. Please. He only a boy. Take me instead—"

"Rosita!" I clutched the woman's arm. I was going to offer myself, but somehow it sounded worse coming from Rosita.

"It okay, Mrs. Meg." Rosita patted my hand. "Please, Mr. Larry. Not the boy. You no want to hurt the boy."

Archer whimpered; his terrified eyes met mine. I held one hand out to my grandson, ready to snatch him when Larry let go. Cannoli, at my feet, was growling again.

"No one's pinning Brie's murder on me. It wasn't me. Brie came to me asking for money. Said she saw me push Eleanor." Larry laughed, his voice coming out harsh and rough. All upper-class accent gone. "I agreed to meet her at the house. But when I came home, she was there, spread out on the kitchen floor." Larry used the gun to point to where Brie must have fallen.

I saw my chance. Then lost it. The moment went too fast. Larry's gun was back up, pointing at us. So I went ahead and asked the question that had been haunting me about this blackmail scenario. Maybe it would distract Larry. "Your wife died months back. Why blackmail you now? Why not then, when she gave you her alibi?"

"Who knows with that girl? I met her right after the police closed the case. Thought I'd find out if she wanted money. But nothing. Smiled and said it was her civic duty after all. Duty? That girl knows nothing about duty. All of a sudden, she's calling for money. Saying I took

Connie away from her. I left the house after her call. Went to ask Connie about Brie. But Connie had no idea what Brie was talking about. They barely talked since Brie came back. I went home, and that's when I saw Brie.

"Brie was dead. Dead, I tell you. I didn't lay a hand on her. I don't know what happened to her. Or who killed her. But it wasn't me. Brie wanted ten thousand dollars. Ten thousand? It was insulting. Ten thousand dollars was nothing. A pittance. Everyone she blackmailed said they paid once, and Brie never bothered them again. It was easier to give the money if it would make her go away. Why would I kill Brie?"

Larry turned to Rosita, the gun in his hand not wavering an inch. "Rosita, I knew you were here that Friday when Brie called. Here at my house, in this kitchen. You're the only one who knew she was coming over that day. And if I didn't kill Brie, then—"

Rosita said nothing.

"—I am not going down for something I didn't do. You guys stay back. Next time I shoot, it'll be at someone." Larry waved the gun at us once more, warning us to stay away. "I'm leaving, and I'm taking Archer with me. You're staying here and not doing anything, not calling anyone. If I get clean away, I'll let Archer go on some highway. I'm sure some Good Samaritan will stop and pick him up." Larry inched himself out of the kitchen. Archer moved with him, not struggling, his eyes fixed on me.

"Mr. Larry, please." Rosita took a step toward Larry, lifting my hand off from her and dropping it. "I no fight you. Please. Not Archer." Rosita put both hands up, palms out, surrendering to Larry. "You know cops not stop chasing if you have Archer. Me—" Rosita gave a bitter laugh. "—they not run hard to save me."

I opened my mouth to protest, but closed it at once, a lump in my throat.

Larry had been watching Rosita, taking his eyes off her only to glance over to me while ignoring Nico standing a few feet behind Rosita.

"Mr. Larry?" Rosita was within arm's reach of Larry. She reached out to Larry. "Please?"

I saw the moment Larry made up his mind. He threw Archer off him and reached for Rosita. I opened my arms, catching Archer as he ran to me. Turning sideways, I shielded my grandson even more from the man who had held him hostage. Nico crept up to us, and I pulled the boy into my arms as well. Cannoli went around sniffing the kids and me, her docked tail wagging.

A grunt from Rosita brought my focus back to the two by the door. Larry had twisted Rosita's arm behind her back and had the gun pressed against Rosita's temple. Cannoli went back to growling.

I put the boys behind me, holding them away from Larry and his gun. To Rosita, I said, "You sure?"

"I'm sure, Mrs. Meg," Rosita said. "Better this way."

I watched Larry drag Rosita away. He pulled on Rosita's arm, making her stand on her toes and stifle a shout of pain.

"Move, let's go," he said, keeping Rosita in front of him until they were far enough away from the kitchen. Then he moved her to stand in front of him and marched her toward the driveway.

"No, Archer." I caught Archer's wrist when he moved to go past me. "Rosita wanted you here." The boy shook his head, tears now streaming down his face. I took him back into my arms, holding on, afraid of what he would do if I let go.

Squealing brakes and sirens pierced the air.

Larry was backing away from the fence, Rosita in lock step with him, her hand still held up behind her back. A voice boomed out, the loudspeaker carrying the voice out past the yard and the house, into the bay and the neighbors' properties.

"Police. Come out with your hands up in the air."

Larry had stopped. There was no way out of his backyard except through the front. Unless he wanted to dive headfirst into the rocky beach behind his property. And I didn't think Larry was suicidal. He didn't claw his way out of his middle-class upbringing to stand, side by side, with the rest of Sands Neck high society, to throw in the towel now. He wasn't giving up without a fight.

"You're no good as a hostage." He pushed Rosita away. Stumbling, Rosita fell, her knees hitting the grassy ground hard. She crawled away on hands and knees, scrambling to get back on her feet.

"Boy, come here," shouted Larry.

"Mr. Billings." Jonathan had replaced the cop who had called out before. "This is Detective Storm. Come out before we come in shooting."

"Come here, I said!" Larry yelled at Archer, coming closer to where we stood. I put my hand out to keep Archer behind me.

"In a few minutes, our SWAT team will be here, and you won't like it when they do. Don't make this harder on yourself." Detective Storm's voice rang out from the loudspeaker.

Larry didn't move from where he stood, his head swiveling from side to side, scanning his neighbors' rooftops. He kept his gun pointed at us.

I measured the distance between myself and Larry. He was not putting his hands on Archer again. Not while I was alive. I saw Cannoli's ears go flat against her head. Lips pulled back. Teeth bared. She hadn't stopped growling.

"Mr. Billings, the SWAT team is in position now. We are not patient men, Mr. Billings. Let the women and children go."

Larry lunged toward me, his hand reaching for Archer. Cannoli launched herself through the air, teeth sinking into Larry's outstretched arm. My body flowed into the movement as it had done countless times this past twelve months. Muscle memory took over. I didn't have to think. Training took over, except I wasn't holding back. Not this time. My leg went up, my head went down, my foot snapped. I heard a thud, then something cracked. I hoped it wasn't my foot. I came back up, standing. Fists held by my chest, ignoring any pain, ready to lash out if needed. But there was no one standing in front of me. Larry was down on the ground. Out cold. Cannoli had let go of his arm. She stood over him, growling and barking at the man. I was amazed. It worked precisely as Craig said it would.

"Mr. Billings, we have you in our sights. Please put the gun down. You don't want my men to get confused." Detective Storm was still on the megaphone.

Cops dressed in bulletproof vests with helmets on their heads swarmed the backyard. They stopped short when they saw Larry on the ground, unconscious. One of them took over, motioning two to stand guard over Larry and another to go back outside. He lifted the helmet's visor and went over to us.

"Everyone okay here?"

I nodded, dragging Cannoli away from Larry, now regaining consciousness. Rosita was sprawled on the ground a few feet beyond us, having given up on the fight to get herself up. One hand clutched her right knee.

The cops standing guard hauled Larry up. The other wrestled his hands back and put cuffs on him. The cop who had checked on us snapped his visor back down and joined the two by Larry. They marched him out; their guns trained on the ground. Larry kept his gaze down and looked neither to the left nor the right.

It was done.

Or was it?

Chapter Thirty-Three

I sat with Rosita by the patio, watching Archer and Nico get in the way of the cops and marveling at the resilience of the young. Rosita gave a heavy sigh by my side. It was time to end this.

"Rosita?"

"Yes, Mrs. Meg."

"Why?"

Another sigh was my answer.

"How you know?" Rosita said.

"You nodded when Larry said he didn't kill Brie. And I know about Leni."

Rosita nodded slowly but said nothing. I felt her regret as she saw her future fly from her.

"Brie. She hurt my daughter. Bad."

I heard Rosita swallow. I saw the tears she blinked back from her eyes.

"Leonora…Leni…" Rosita moved her head from side to side, slow and labored. "My daughter, she a good girl. She not like what Brie did to Mrs. Gladys. She fight Brie. But Brie pushed her. And Leni fell."

"First, we think Leni good. Her stomach hurt. A few cuts. We think that's it. But evening come and Leni start bleeding. Bleeding bad. We take her to hospital. But too late."

"The baby"—Rosita stopped, covered her head with her hands—"my grandchild…mi hijo…" she mumbled,

242

looking at the ground.

I saw the tears fall. I looked up at the sky, searching for the sun behind the clouds, and kept my tears at bay.

"Leni lost baby. She not know she had baby. She and her husband been trying since wedding." Rosita put her hands down and clasped them. Her eyes, too, sought the sky, scanning the vastness of it. Was she thinking of what waited for her at today's end?

"They thought...Leni, she young. They get another chance. Another baby. But no, doctor said, no more babies. They take out. Do hysterectomy, they said. Because too much bleeding"—Rosita slowed down—"Leni almost died. Not her fault, her doctor said. But she not forgive herself. For not taking care of baby. You see, she no fight Brie if she knew she pregnant."

"My daughter not stop thinking of baby. And all the babies she not have any more. She keep crying for babies she not have...my daughter...her mind...it break."

I closed my eyes. Rosita's pain washed over me. I felt drenched. What would a mother do? What would a mother *not* do?

"We took her to doctors. Two weeks in hospital. They said maybe electric shock? To her head?" Rosita touched her temples. "But nothing work. My daughter, she stop talking. Just stare...at nothing. Day after day. We feed her, clean her. Her husband drink. Just drink. Not work. I work harder. So do Jose. And Maria help. Maria, our neighbor. We pay Maria to come and take care of Leni when we go work. But the money...it not enough. For doctors, medicines, and Maria. Not enough." Rosita deflated into herself.

"Connie always have money around. Just around." Rosita shrugged. "You know, on her dresser, on kitchen counter. In pockets of her clothes. I wash her clothes, you know."

"She tell me put money I find inside cookie jar. She never count her money. Never. Sometimes, cookie jar so full, I have to push money inside. Hard." Rosita pumped her fist down, showing me how she did it. "She not notice if money gone. So I take some. Not a lot. Enough to pay Maria."

"Brie"—Rosita sighed the name out—"that girl see me. At Connie's last party. I help clean up. The doctor's office. They call and want money. And money was on top of Connie's makeup table. First, that girl laughed. Told me it okay. Not to worry. I not trust the girl but Connie know me, I tell myself. She not believe this girl. Not over me. And how the girl prove it? So much money in the cookie jar, how tell some missing? I not worry."

"I go about my day. Cleaning. Helping. That girl, she serve food. Walk around. Smiling. I say to myself, all okay. But when day end, she come up to me. She call other server, a boy. They stand over me and no one see. The girl, she bring out her phone and play a video. I see me, taking money and putting in my pocket." Rosita ran her hand through her hair. "She tell me give them the money and to go to cookie jar, take more money and give to them too."

"I do as she say. She has her phone on me all the time. She leave laughing. The boy, he looked ashamed. Won't look at me."

Kyle, how could you stand by and do nothing?

"I think, okay, that it," Rosita said. "I go home. I take over Maria. My daughter, she not come out of bed now. Maria say she not eat. Not open her mouth. She getting worse. I curse girl who pushed Leni. Then I remember when the girl took money from me, the boy try to help. He said, Brie, no. I also remember friend of Leni said the girl who pushed my daughter was Brie. I thought maybe same girl? I ask Maria about this Brie. I ask, who is this Brie? How she look? Maria took Leni's yearbook and showed me."

Rosita, with these words, restored my faith in Kyle. But how terrible it must have been for Rosita to find out…

"Brie not only hurt Leni, she also take money I need for Leni," Rosita whispered. "Then, Friday when I clean house for Mr. Larry, phone rings. I answer, and I recognize her voice. She ask for Mr. Larry. I listen. Mr. Larry say to meet him here that night. When he hang up, I check phone. I take her number down."

"After Mr. Larry left house, I call her back. I tell her Mr. Larry told me to call her. I say Mr. Larry want her to come one hour earlier. She laugh. I thought she say no. But no, she say yes. Better, she say no," Rosita said.

"I finish cleaning. I go home. Maria said Leni still no eat. Leni only bones now. I pay Maria. I see no money left. Maybe tomorrow Maria not come. Then what happen to Leni?"

"I go back here, to Mr. Larry. Brie come." Rosita spat on the ground and cursed under her breath.

I flinched at the name Rosita used for Brie.

"She ask for Mr. Larry. I tell her Mr. Larry not here. She say why did I tell her to come. I ask for my money back. I tell her she hurt Leni very bad. I tell her we need money for Leni. For Maria to take care of Leni. She look at me. She laugh. She say, 'You the mother of the girl at the park? How funny.' She say, 'You take Connie away from me, I take your daughter away from you.' Who say that? I get mad. So mad."

Rosita was silent for a while. I waited for her.

"When I see again, I see blood. I see her on floor. Her head open. Blood. So much blood coming out. In my hand was a pan. The big, heavy black one Mrs. Eleanor like to use for pizza. Cast iron, Mrs. Eleanor said it was." Rosita turned pleading eyes on me. "I didn't mean to happen. It just happened. All I wanted was the money. But when she laugh…"

Birds flew by, settling on tree branches a few feet from us. Detective Storm walked in with Dora, who wasn't paying attention to him. Dora's head swiveled frantically, looking for Archer. I heard Archer cry out, "Mom." Saw him running to Dora. Saw Dora leave the detective behind and run to her son. Saw when they reached each other, their hands wrapping tightly against the other. Saw my neighbor walk into the yard, rushing to gather Nico into her arms. Both mothers were beaming, the simple happiness of seeing their children alive and well.

"They lucky," Rosita said. "What you think will happen to me?"

"I don't know." I took her hand in mine and squeezed hard.

Rosita nodded. We sat there for a while. Just watched the two mothers with their children.

Chapter Thirty-Four

Detective Storm and his men were processing Rosita's arrest while she and I sat waiting for them. At first, the detective refused to believe us. He thought Rosita was joking. Some joke, huh?

Rosita didn't back down. She had told her story to the detective. She wasn't repeating it. Once was enough.

I held her hand while we waited. Detective Storm kept talking about bringing me up on obstruction of justice. I didn't think he could. After all, I gave him Rosita. How was I obstructing justice? If anyone were to be arrested for obstruction of justice, it would be him. I smiled wryly at the idea of the detective arresting himself. If only that were possible.

After Dora had smothered Archer to the point the boy was fending her off, she looked around and saw us. Dragging Archer with her, she came up and gave me a fierce hug. "Thank you for saving Archer," she said, swallowing tears.

I hugged back, knowing how she felt. I felt the same for Rosita.

"And you are never scaring me that way again. I thought I had lost both of you, Mama Meg! And yes, I'm calling you Mama Meg. I don't care if you don't like it. I'm tired of calling you Meg."

I laughed, tears pooling in my eyes. I wasn't fumbling this chance I was gifted with. Mama Meg suited me fine. Dora and I turned to Archer, and together, gave him another big hug. The poor boy groaned this time.

Rosita hadn't moved all this time. She merely watched us with a sad smile.

One look at Rosita and Dora had known something was wrong. Dora hugged Archer closer to her. She asked me if she should take him home.

That was when the tears fell from Rosita's eyes. She spread her arms wide, inviting the boy she thought of as her own into her arms. I didn't begrudge her of it. Archer flew into her embrace, hugging her tightly around her waist. Rosita combed his hair out of his eyes, gave him a firm kiss on his forehead, and told him to be good. She sent him back to Dora, who took him back and led him away. Nico took his attention the rest of the way. Archer glanced back at us once and waved goodbye, out of Larry's house and out of Rosita's life.

But not mine. For which I thanked Rosita deeply.

The detective was on the phone. Arguing. We could hear him from where we sat.

"What did you say?" He said, annoyed.

It was impolite to eavesdrop. But as I learned at Veronica's party, there was so much you find out when you do.

"How do you know it's them?" He listened to the person on the phone. "Short, white hair, glasses, kind of dumpy looking? With another woman looking like her, except older?"

Was he talking about Edna and Gladys? I had forgotten about the APB.

"You were called out to a campsite to look for a missing old lady? Which one was missing? The older one. And you found her swimming in the lake? Naked?" Jonathan grabbed his hair. "They told you their names? Mrs. Edna Gomez and Mrs. Gladys Tolentino. And Mrs. Gomez showed you her driver's license? Well, okay. That's them."

OMG. They've arrested Edna and Gladys!

Wait…

They can't arrest Edna for Brie's murder. Rosita had already confessed to Brie's murder. I started to get up from the bench.

"Am I sure? What do you mean, am I sure?" He paused to listen to the caller. "Innocent? Everyone thinks they're innocent? How the hell do you know they're innocent?" Another pause. "Because they look like your grandmother? Don't you know ax murderers can look like your grandmother!" A very slight pause. "Name one? Are you out of your mind?"

I wanted to laugh out loud. I sat back down again.

Jonathan turned around and happened to look at us. His eyes locked onto Rosita. He took the phone away from his ear and looked at it, then back at Rosita. He cursed, repeatedly and savagely. The caller suddenly cut off whatever he was saying. Jonathan turned back to his phone. "Never mind that. Release them. I'm taking back the APB. They're no longer persons of interest. They can go. Anywhere. Wherever. I don't care where they go. What do you mean she wants to talk to me?"

"Yes, this is Detective Jonathan Storm." The man's voice changed, less harsh, more civilized. He fell silent for some minutes, head down, one foot kicking the grass.

Edna must be teaching the detective a few life lessons. I could almost hear her. Edna would be saying to Jonathan that she would never, ever, kill anyone. And scaring her so she had to run away with her mother was not acceptable. Did he know her mother was ninety years old? With dementia? The detective should learn how to do his job better so innocent people were not arrested. She and her mother were owed an apology. In her sweet third-grade school teacher's voice.

"I—" Jonathan swallowed. "I'm sorry, Mrs. Gomez. It was wrong of me to suspect you." Another deep breath. "Yes, of course, you can come home any time you want to. You have nothing to worry about."

I put my head down and hid my smile.

The detective shoved his phone into his pocket. Glared at us one more time and strode away.

I took in a lungful of fresh spring air. Edna was coming home.

After some time, the cops finished processing the arrest. Detective Storm's sergeant held onto Rosita's elbow, making sure she didn't stumble. Rosita walked slowly, her hands in front of her, in handcuffs. She walked almost as if she were dreaming. She hadn't paid attention to the sergeant as he droned on about her rights. Rosita had given up. Surrendered.

I was not having it. Fred. He'd know what to do. I called the man.

"Meagan?"

"Hi, are you free? I have a new client for you. It's Rosita Escobar, and they're taking her to the Fourth Precinct."

"On what charge?"

"Brie's murder."

"On what evidence?"

The poor man, he'll have to work hard on this one. "Rosita confessed. Just now. Right after they took Larry away in handcuffs, presumably for Eleanor's murder and assault on Archer, Nico, Rosita, and me. Oh! And some cop from New Jersey called and said they have Edna and Gladys in custody because of the APB. But they let them go. Detective Storm took back the APB."

"Whoa! Slow down. Run that by me again."

I told him everything that had happened. Including Friday night and everything else we found out. Leni. The miscarriage. Leni's illness. The sorry tale of a mother protecting her young.

From his silence, I knew he was not happy about the risks I took. But give the man credit. He was a fast learner. He didn't say anything at all. Not one word about keeping ourselves safe and out of danger.

Instead, he said, "I'm on my way. I'll take care of Rosita." He paused. "I don't want anything irreversible to happen to you…any of you."

"We don't want that either."

We left it at that.

I closed my phone, thinking of Rich while looking up at the clear blue sky. I thought of the countless blue skies and the even bluer seas we had enjoyed in our forty years together. Of the palm trees and white sands we had walked, the soaring towers and centuries-old art we had seen, the sauces dripping onto our plates we had savored, and the music we had fallen asleep to. It was a life I hadn't wanted to end. But Rich was gone. And here I was. Still wanting life. Was Fred my next chapter? But who was Fred to Edna? The girlfriend code was not one I would break. I smiled. Rich had given me a life I had only imagined when I was in my teens, dreaming of a white wedding gown. If not Fred, maybe someone else. Maybe no one.

I was content.

Chapter Thirty-Five

We had to fetch Edna and Gladys from the campsite. The cops taking her and her mother in were Edna's worst nightmare come true. After pouring her frustration over Detective Storm's head and realizing she was free of all charges, Edna simply fell apart. Tremors shook her body, and she couldn't stop crying. Even when she calmed down, the boys in blue deemed her unfit to drive. One of them—a young one, who kept calling her grandma and Gladys, great-grandma—drove Edna and Gladys back to the campsite. He took her phone and called us to let us know we needed to pick them up, please. Today, please, if you can. They shouldn't be left alone, he said. Such beautiful manners! I told Barbara on the way there we should send his mother a card congratulating her on raising such a nice boy. Barbara just threw a sour look at me. But that didn't matter to me. Edna was coming home.

The drive there took seven hours, with bathroom stops. It was late by the time we got there. We waited for an hour or two for Edna to finish packing and get their suitcases in the trunk before we started on our way back to New York. How did we do all that in our advanced age?

Fred took care of everything. He hired a car and a driver. A limousine big enough to seat all of us, and a muscular young man who looked like he could drive all of today and the next day as well. Of course, Stefan took the passenger seat. He said he could talk to us any day he wanted, but the driver was someone new, and it was only right for him to befriend our driver on this very long drive.

None of us was fooled.

Most of us slept on the way back, including Stefan. Not the driver, of course. We woke up when the limo glided into a parking lot. Dora had made us promise to take Gladys straight to the hospital. So there we went. After the hospital, the limo driver dropped each of us off at home. By then, everyone was so exhausted we were all looking for our beds.

Two days later, we were watching the doctor sign the discharge paperwork for Gladys. She had to stay in the hospital for exposure, exhaustion, and indigestion. Dora requested a bed for Gladys on a floor where Filipino nurses worked. Gladys got so comfortable, she almost refused to go home. Almost.

Edna was right beside me. She looked better. Her eyes were clear, and her face was not as haggard. But the constant smile on her lips was gone. She looked troubled, her eyes fixed on her mother, chatting happily with the doctor, making him and the nurses laugh. Her next words confirmed it.

"She was always like this. The life of the party. Made everyone laugh," Edna said. "My father was so in love with her. I was a poor substitute, you know. Didn't know how to do small talk, still don't. They should have had another child. Maybe they would have gotten one just like her."

"Of all the silly nonsense—" Barbara said, but I elbowed her hard, stopping whatever it was she wanted to add. Liz helped me out by shaking her head at Barbara, while Stefan just dropped his head into his hands.

Edna didn't bother looking at us; she kept on talking. "I took up teaching because children were easier to talk to. Show them love and they love you back. Then, when my husband and I weren't blessed with children, I decided to spend all my love on my students. It was the best thing I could have done. My students repaid my love with theirs, more than I could ever have dreamed."

Barbara opened her mouth to say something, only to close it when Liz mouthed "no" to her. I leaned over and whispered to Barbara to leave Edna alone. Our friend needed us to listen. We were going to listen.

"They say you get in life what you can handle, that making the most of what you have and being thankful for what is there is the best anyone can hope for. And I don't disagree."

The simple truths of Edna's words were choking me. I had forgotten to be thankful for what was left for me in life when Rich and Jim died.

"But knowing my mother is slowly slipping away is too much for me. There is no one to replace her. Certainly not me. I can never be her."

What do you say to that? I didn't know, so I kept quiet. We all watched the doctor shake hands with Gladys, waiting for Edna to continue. We heard her take a deep breath and let it out slowly.

"But running away taught me something. I don't have to be her. I don't want to be her. Yes, she's wonderful. Yes, everyone loves her. Yes, she always gets what she wants because everyone spoils her. But that woman has no idea how to survive on her own. I would rather be me, someone who can take care of herself, rather than some social butterfly you can't depend on in an emergency."

"Finally!" Barbara burst out, while the rest of us, including Edna, started laughing. "Edna, you are not, and never will be, the one who makes everyone laugh. But you don't have to be because you're the one who makes sure the party is a success. You organize everything, make sure there's enough food and drinks for everyone, and decorations to make the room look pretty. I'd rather have you by my side than Stefan, any day."

"Hey," Stefan objected, not meaning it.

"Thank you. But it doesn't erase the fact that my mother will forget who I am one day very soon. What do I do when I don't have her anymore?" Edna turned to me. "How do you do it? With Rich and Jim?"

"At first? I faked it," I said. "I wanted to die when it happened. But you guys wouldn't let me. So I faked it. Then somehow, one day, I was no longer faking it." I thought of how I felt when I almost died. When did I start wanting to live again?

"Fake it?" Edna turned back to her mother. "I suppose I can do that. She's going to need more care than I can give her very soon. The doctors say I can probably keep her at home for a few more months, but I need to start looking for a dementia facility. It wouldn't be safe for her to be alone. She'll wander like she did at the campsite."

"Are you going to look for one?" I made my voice as neutral as I could.

Edna gripped my hand. "Yes, I think it's time. That was another lesson running away taught me."

"Maybe you should send the detective a thank-you note," Liz suggested.

"Maybe not. You'd confuse the man," Barbara said.
We all laughed as we reached out to embrace Edna.

Chapter Thirty-Six

Saturday, and we were back at our usual table at Sweet Buns.

Dora and Archer were outside, standing in line for ice cream. Archer was busy talking to his mother, his hands waving around as he made his point. Dora was laughing at his antics. She had cut down on her hours at the hospital. She went to work later in the day and took care of Archer in the mornings, getting him on the school bus on time. I moved back home as soon as Jose finished fixing my house, and Archer went back to coming home to me after school. But Dora picked him up each night in time for dinner without fail, except this past Thursday when we three had dinner together. I cooked pot roast, and I managed to get it past the trash can and onto the dinner table. When they left, Dora kissed me on the cheek and said, "Let's do this again next week." The pain in my heart eased a bit.

The last person we had been waiting for walked in the door. Fred dragged out the chair we had left for him and sat down beside Edna. Veronica took off her apron when she saw him come in and joined us at the table.

"How did it go?" I said, anxious to hear.

"It went well, considering. Rosita agreed to change her plea to not guilty by reason of temporary insanity. We went to court yesterday, and she nodded when the judge called out her plea. I was afraid for a second she'd change her mind. It was tough getting her to agree. She thought it meant she would get stuck in a mental institution."

"Isn't she?" Edna asked.

"Yes, but only until doctors decide her sanity has been restored. Which it has, at this point. She'll go to jail, but it won't be for long. Then she'll be on probation. The prosecutor set bail, and Rosita is home now."

"Who came up with the bail?" Veronica said.

"A fund was set up for Rosita's legal expenses." I hadn't had a chance to tell them yet. Fred and Barbara knew, but no one else did. "Barbara went to see Selena."

"What?" Liz said, startled. "Why Selena?"

"Remember, she said, if we find out who killed Brie, to tell her so she can set up a fund to pay the killer's legal fees?" Barbara said.

"She can't be serious, it's her sister!" Stefan voiced the outrage I felt when I first heard about it.

"Her sister, who was blackmailing her husband over his cheating," Barbara retorted. "His cheating that would have given Selena the excuse she needed to divorce him and keep her money. Of course, Selena was serious. Especially when she heard what her sister had done and why she was killed. Selena wrote out a check for fifty thousand right away."

"Fifty thousand dollars?" Edna was amazed. "That's a lot of money."

"That was nothing. Selena started an online fundraising campaign immediately. Connie saw the post, put more money in it, and sent it on to her neighbors. She was horrified when she found out Larry used her meat processing plant," I said.

"Connie was spitting mad over everything," Liz

added. "She called me when she found out Larry confessed to Eleanor's murder. Said she suspected something when Eleanor died the way she did. But she convinced herself she was just getting paranoid. Then someone killed Brie. And Connie didn't want to say anything. She was so grateful to Larry, who she thought had tried so hard to save Eleanor, almost falling off the cliff himself when he dove after her. And it was all a lie." Liz continued, "I also found out why Brie was so obsessed with Connie. When Brie first came to town, she went to see Connie and, in a roundabout way, reminded Connie of a birthday party when the other kids were torturing Selena and Brie, freezing them out of all the games and taunting them about their dad. Connie had taken both girls under her wing and insisted her friends include them in everything. But it was such a small thing for Connie, a long-forgotten act of mercy. She didn't see how important it was to Brie and how disappointed Brie was when Connie couldn't even remember it."

"We think it must have made Brie mad when she saw how close Connie was to Eleanor. She didn't mind giving Larry an alibi, but she turned on Larry when Larry and Connie got close," Stefan said.

"And Connie was very close to Rosita," I said slowly, understanding why Brie had harassed Rosita over the petty amounts Rosita was stealing from Connie. "Rosita practically raised Connie. She told me she's the only one Connie allows to touch her clothes and cook her food. Do you think Brie knew Leni was Rosita's daughter?"

"Who knows?" Barbara murmured.

"How much is in the legal fund now?" I asked Fred.

"It was several hundred thousand yesterday and still

growing. Leni's story and Brie's blackmail went viral. The DA's office told me they will support Rosita's plea as long as I can get a doctor to testify for the defense. Leni's doctor had already told me to call on him. He is outraged over what happened to Leni."

Sounds of relief went around the table.

"That's good," Stefan said. "Better than we expected."

"Sounds like we all did a good job!" Liz said, leaning back in her chair. "Edna's back home. We found out who killed Brie. And as a bonus, we also solved Eleanor Billings's murder."

Liz was right. Justice was served. Even if it didn't turn out quite how I thought it would.

"What's happening with Larry? And why was Brie at their party?" I was so busy worrying about Rosita, I had forgotten about Larry until Liz brought him up.

"His attorney is negotiating a plea," Fred said. "One thing for sure, he's out of the investment firm he founded. He resigned this Friday. No one is really sure how Brie ended up working with Elegant Dining that night, but the caterer did tell the cops she put out a call for additional servers for that party."

"Brie could have heard it from someone then and grabbed the chance to stalk Eleanor." This was a guess at best, but I didn't think I was too far off the mark.

"There is one weird, open item left hanging." Fred turned to me. "You remember the guy they arrested for ransacking your house and pushing you to the street?"

I nodded.

"I stopped by the precinct yesterday to find out what else they had on the ransacking and attempted murder. No one had bothered to send me an update. First of all, both Larry and Rosita denied hiring the man. Rosita kept shaking her head when the detective asked her about it. Said she'd never hurt you. Or anyone else. And Brie...well, we all know that was completely different."

Nods and hums of agreement went around the table.

"Larry, when asked, got so furious. Said he wouldn't waste his time or money on killing little old ladies."

I didn't like where this was going.

"But Sunday morning, when the entire station was in chaos over the hostage situation with Larry, then Rosita's arrest, an attorney in a bespoke suit, costing way more than mine, turned up and bailed the guy out of jail. Do you know how much it takes to get an attorney to show up and work on a Sunday?" Fred said. "Then, get this, four days later, the perp turns up dead in his apartment."

"Who found him?" My heart started to pound.

"His downstairs neighbor called the cops. They noticed a terrible smell coming from the vents. The cops broke down the door and found his body. Toxicology said the man overdosed, an empty syringe was beside the body, and traces of fentanyl were found in the syringe. Post-mortem had his death happening sometime Sunday afternoon based on the decomposition."

"Isn't that the day he was released?" Stefan asked.

"Yes, and that's not the weirdest part. Saturday night, a drunk was pulled into the station. He had started a fight in Port Tavern." Fred named a popular bar on Main Street. "An off-duty cop was out with friends. He took the drunk to the station and told the desk cop to keep him till he sobered up in the morning. The desk cop threw the drunk into a cell. The holding pens only had those two men that night."

"The desk cop heard the drunk singing all night long. He couldn't make out the words. The drunk was slurring badly. Around midnight, the drunk stopped singing. When the desk cop checked on him, he was sleeping. Next morning, after the desk cop let the drunk out, he checked on the other guy. The desk cop said that guy was crying, sobbing his heart out, shoulders shaking. When asked if anything was wrong, the man waved the desk cop away and kept on crying. And when the attorney came, the guy wasn't exactly jumping for joy. The man looked like he was going to a hanging instead of being bailed out of jail."

"You think the drunk somehow persuaded the other man to kill himself?" Stefan's face showed how unbelievable he thought the whole thing was. "And who's the drunk? Did they ever find out?"

"The ID the desk cop got off the drunk turned out to be false. But even then, there is no reason to think the drunk had anything to do with the suicide. He was one cell over from the other man. How could he threaten the other man into suiciding? Both the off-duty cop and the desk cop swore they patted the drunk down. They didn't find a gun or a knife. Or anything else. Though off the record, the off-duty cop said he never saw someone trying so hard to get booked. At the end of the day, the perp injected himself with fentanyl. His arm showed repeated use."

Stefan cleared his throat. "I didn't want to say this before, but when we were at H Meat Processing…I heard the men talking. They kept saying 'he' would kill them if they came back without the laptop. But they never said who 'he' was. Meg, I don't think this is about Brie."

I felt chills creeping up my back. Stefan was right.

The ransacking of my house, pushing me into oncoming traffic, and stealing Liz's laptop; these had nothing to do with Brie. Those men were after the software Jim had put in Archer's laptop. But I didn't have the faintest idea why. Worse, what would they do when they find out they got the wrong laptop?

"I thought so as well," Liz said. "But don't worry about Archer. In case they're still looking for that CCTV program of Jim's, I deleted it from Archer's laptop. That's another reason why I wanted you to bring it. I did leave the icon for the app, so Archer thinks it's still there. Except it won't do anything, no matter how many times he clicks on it. He's safe from those goons."

I couldn't help myself; I burst out crying. We must have poked someone…something…something to do with Jim. And his cybersecurity firm. What had Jim gotten himself caught up in? Was this—whatever this was—why Rich and Jim died? It was horrifying. I wanted to throw up. My heart wanted to leap out of my chest. Barbara pushed a glass of water into my hands and told me to drink. Veronica got up and ran outside. That jolted me out of my fright. I dried the tears on my cheeks.

"We are not telling Dora," I insisted. "And we are certainly not telling Archer." Dora had only now gotten her feet back under her. She and Archer were spending time together—quality time. My friends nodded. They understood right away.

Fred looked at each of us and nodded as well.

Dora came running in. Archer right behind her.

"Are you okay? Veronica said you were having a heart attack?" Dora was looking at me intently. Not liking what she saw, she took my wrist and started counting my heartbeats. I willed my heart to stop pounding wildly. "Your heart rate is up. What happened?"

"We found out the guy who ransacked Meg's house and tried to kill her had committed suicide. It got Meg upset," Barbara said, straight-faced.

Veronica started to say something, then stopped, looking down at Liz in surprise. Dora, still fussing over me, didn't see how Liz had pinched and winked at Veronica. But when no one else said anything, Dora straightened up and stood there, arms crossed, waiting to hear more.

It was Edna who saved the day.

"Is it time now for my surprise?" Edna chattered into the silence. "I didn't know how to thank you for clearing me of murder. I thought—"

That did it. We all groaned, even Dora. Edna was famous for doing one thing when she didn't know how else to say thank you.

"Aren't they adorable?" Edna had pulled out a pink T-shirt from her bag. Bright pink. Edna loved pink. She showed it to us in all its glory. On the front of the shirt were the words, marching one after the other, down the length of the shirt...

Teachers
Out
On
The
Hunt

...in white letters, with the first letter in big bold caps.

My eyes widened. It took no time at all for my mind to read the acronym. It took more time for my ears to hear Edna's explanation.

Shaking her head at us with, nonetheless, a big smile on her face, Edna said, "I was so worried for all of you hunting the killer while my mother and I hid at the campsite. And all because of my mother's sweet tooth. If she hadn't wanted that ice cream, Brie wouldn't have given her a spiked drink, and I wouldn't have slapped Brie. Her sweet tooth had a lot to answer for. But when we came home, and I wanted to do something for all of you, I realized that my mother's sweet tooth meant something more. It stood for everything you did. So there you have it. You guys rule!" Edna turned the shirt and showed us the back.

It got worse.

On the back was a glitter-filled tiara crowning a tooth, a molar to be precise, and—if that wasn't bad enough—underneath the molar was the word "Rules."

Tooth Rules?

And I had to wear that?

Edna took out more shirts and handed them around. Even Veronica and Dora got one.

Veronica tried to stuff her giggles back into her mouth. Fred had his mouth covered with one hand. Except you could see the mad twinkle in his eyes. Liz's laughter burbled out until she was squeaking hysterically. Stefan followed shortly after. Barbara buried her face in her hands. Fred waved his hands, rejecting the pink shirt. Edna got mad at him. "Nanding, what kind of cousin are you?" Edna punched him lightly on the arm.

Cousin? They're cousins? Fred saw me looking at him. His face softened. I returned his smile. He winked.

"You support family. No matter what. Anyway, I didn't get you a pink shirt. Here." Edna handed Fred,

Stefan, and Archer blue shirts with glitter-filled crowns instead. Still with the molar underneath.

Fred promptly put it on and paraded around us women. Even Barbara was laughing now. Liz had put on her shirt and was trailing after Fred, who had moved on to the other tables. Stefan and Veronica were struggling to get into their shirts and join the parade.

I thought of everything else that had happened, the bad, and let's not forget, the good. How my house was destroyed and then rebuilt; how I almost died thinking it was my dearest wish only to find out life meant more to me than I thought it did; how Eleanor's death was unmasked for the murder it was and Larry brought to his just ends; how Rosita, who paid the price for defending her child, still managed to find the care Leni needed, and more importantly, how we found the first clue, the first lead, as to why Rich and Jim died.

Looking at the parade of four—excuse me, seven. Edna, Dora, and Archer had joined the fun—I knew we would solve the mystery of the deaths of my husband and son, as we had solved the murders of Brie and Eleanor and any other murder that might come our way.

Life was…not all good…but it wasn't all bad. I had Dora, Archer, and my friends.

I put my pink shirt over my head. "Come on, Barbara. Stop sitting there like a lump." I grabbed my best friend's hand and tugged her after the rest of our group.

A word about the author...

A former CPA and lawyer, GG Calpo now writes cozy mysteries and urban fantasies. She blends her experiences as a Filipino American immigrant with the everyday stories of life around her. She spends her time reading, crocheting blankets and sweaters for her five grandchildren, watching mystery TV shows and taking long walks in her neighborhood. She resides in Central New Jersey, with her husband and two corgis, Whiskey and Nugget. Visit her at www.ggcalpo.com.